Jo Baker

OFFCOMER

Jo Baker was born in Lancashire and educated at Oxford University and Queen's University Belfast. She is the author of *Longbourn*, *The Undertow*, and two earlier novels: *The Mermaid's Child* and *The Telling*. She lives in Lancaster, England.

www.jobakerwriter.com

Also by Jo Baker

OFFCOMER

OFFCOMER

Jo Baker

Vintage Books
A Division of Random House LLC
New York

FIRST VINTAGE BOOKS EDITION, DECEMBER 2014

Library of Congress Cataloging-in-Publication Data
Baker, Jo.
Offcomer / Jo Baker. — First Vintage Books edition.
pages cm
1. Young women—Fiction.   2. Self-mutilation—Fiction.
3. England—Fiction   4. Belfast (Northern Ireland)—Fiction.
5. Psychological fiction.   I. Title.
PR6102.A57O34 2014
823'.92—dc23   2014028960

Vintage Trade Paperback ISBN: 978-0-8041-7261-5
eBook ISBN: 978-0-8041-7262-2

Book design by Claudia Martinez

www.vintagebooks.com

Printed in the United States of America
10 9 8 7 6 5 4 3 2 1

For Daragh

OFFCOMER

Claire sat on the edge of the bath, her skirt hooked up around her thighs, her left foot balanced on her right knee, holding a razorblade between her thumb and forefinger. The bathroom door was locked. The house, all three floors of it, was empty. Beside her, balanced on the edge of the bath, were a box of tissues, an empty plastic bag, a sticking plaster, unwrapped but with its translucent backing still in place, and a thick fleecy roll of cotton wool, also unwrapped.

She let her hand drop down against her ankle, where the skin was pale and translucent, and began to cut. Her face, through the screen of mid-brown hair, was tight with concentration, but what she drew on the skin seemed unconsidered, undesigned, a doodle. A small, neat spiral, such as people draw on notepads while talking on the phone. Blood welled up, dripped round the ankle, onto the supporting knee, trickling down the leg.

When the spiral had twisted itself out to the size of her thumbnail, she lifted away the razor, and put it down on the side of the bath. Then she closed her eyes and took a couple of deep, shaky breaths, as if she had just surfaced.

She tore off a tuft of cotton wool and pressed it to the cut, then began mopping up the thinnish blood from her leg with a dampened tissue. She stuck a plaster down over the broken skin, stood up, shook down her skirt. She folded the used razorblade into its waxed-paper envelope and slotted it into the back of the box that the blades came in. She wrapped the bloody tissues and cotton wool in the plastic bag, crumpled it in her hand.

She stepped away, checking over the bath and cork tiles for splashes and drips, then unlocked the door and padded downstairs in her bare feet. In the back yard, she dropped her plastic bag into the wheelie bin, pushed back her hair and lifted her face to the sun.

ONE

∝

Claire Thomas walked down Stranmillis Road. It was a soft, sticky evening, the eighteenth of June, nine months since she had arrived in Belfast, and she was pacing out her route to work.

At the bottom of Stranmillis she turned onto University Road. The old lime trees were dropping a gentle drizzle of cool sap; she felt it freckle her face, felt the pavement sticky underfoot. She slipped through the gap between blistery, rusted wrought-iron gates and cut across Queen's front quad, onto University Square. Passers-by crowded her peripheral vision, indigo-denim-blue, files and folders clasped to their chests, bubbling with jittery half-heard phrases. It was exam time, Claire remembered.

And at any moment, Alan might appear. The door of the Philosophy Department might lurch open and Alan come stumbling out of the dark interior, a bundle of marking clutched to his chest, squinting in the bright sunlight. If he caught sight of her, he would stop dead. Unnoticed, a couple of essays would slither out of his grip. His mouth would fall slightly open. He would half turn to go back, then change his mind and hurry on, papers fluttering. He would pretend not to see her. While all the time she would walk on, head down, pretending not to have seen him. Looking down, she noticed that the paving stones were worn away in layers, like old leather soles. She watched her feet stepping over them, her slightly shiny suede shoes. She would get as far as the corner before looking up, she told herself, before taking another breath. Just in case he was there. Just in case he'd seen her.

On Botanic Avenue, chairs and tables had been set out in the sun outside the bars and cafés. They looked awkward and angular, like teenagers at their first party. A few seats were already occupied. As Claire passed Vincent's, a sunglassed young woman dressed in immaculate black stood to greet a friend with a kiss on both cheeks. Outside Maggie May's a pair of collies lay in the slatted shade of a table.

The railway station was closed. The tracks had been lifted; from the bridge a grey-blue line of slatey gravel stretched towards the City Hospital. Massive drills, stationary, higher than the buildings around them. She crossed Shaftesbury Square, a noisy muddle of junctions and traffic islands and dodging pedestrians, and overhead the giant telescreen played out a silent advert for Coca-Cola. Then the Stena HSS appeared, carving its way through pixelated waves, *the shortest, fastest crossing.* The temperature flashed across the screen. 24°. The traffic lights changed, cars slowed, halted, others slipped into gear and streamed away, out into the city haze.

The traffic fumes made the tip of Claire's tongue taste

metallic, like old coins. The cut was chafing slightly against the cuff of her shoe, and, although she tried to walk evenly, she still favoured her left leg. She felt hot. Her blouse was tight across her chest, the buttons gaping. Her trousers stuck to her as she walked. The rolled-up apron, clutched in her right hand, grew damp and limp with sweat.

She was heading for Conroys, down on the quay. There were probably shorter, faster routes to work, ones which would carry a smaller risk of meeting Alan, but Claire didn't know them. She was almost superstitiously cautious about straying off her beaten track. Outside her narrow familiar slice of Belfast, the city was hazy, indefinite. On her mental map there was a great deal of terra incognita, calligraphed with *here be dragons.*

Dublin Road was cooler: the breeze drifted in between the buttons of her shirt and touched her skin. It seemed like she was the only one heading into town. One-way traffic streamed towards her. A steady march of pedestrians passed by: suited office workers, jackets off and sleeves rolled, mothers pushing buggies, a solitary shambling bearded young man in dirty zipped-up parka and battered trainers, who wrapped his arms around himself and shivered.

A woman came towards her, smiling, bright lipstick.

"Excuse me—"

Claire slowed. The accent was foreign.

"Yes?"

"Can I interest you in coming to a Bible class?"

"No, thank you."

Claire walked past her. The woman stepped back, smiling.

"We meet every Friday night: it's great fun; there's singing—"

"No, really, thank you. I'm in a bit of a hurry."

Claire made to slip past her again; the woman stepped into her way.

"If you'd just give me your phone number, I'll call you: we can meet up and talk when it's more convenient."

"No. Really. Thank you. Actually, I'm Jewish."

The woman hesitated. Claire managed to duck past her, heart pounding.

"Hear the word of the Lord when He cries out to you in your darkness."

Claire, breathless and trying not to hear, walked uncomfortably on, shifted her crumpled apron to her other hand. There must be something odd about her face, she thought, something different, some reason why they always seemed to home in on her. And, every time, she let herself be stopped, and smiled politely, and still expected to be asked directions.

Bedford Street was cold. There was always a gale blowing down there, even when the rest of Belfast was without a breath of air. At the end of the street, the City Hall stood, all acanthus leaves and pillars and green copper domes, lavish as a wedding cake. A right turn, and now only a couple of cars, a couple of stragglers late from the office. Everyone else had got where they were going.

She turned up towards the Waterfront Hall. The glass front reflected the young trees, the chalky limestone paving. The open sky surrounding it was blurred with traffic fumes, the sun was low. Claire saw a tiny distant silhouette walk the length of the upper balcony, turn and disappear into the cool dark interior. The hall still looked impermanent, as if it had just landed. As she got nearer, the yellowbrick towers of the Hilton and the multi-storey carpark loomed into sight, overshadowing the low smooth dome.

She turned the corner, and she was at work. From the moment she could see the bouncers outside Conroys, everything felt green and dark and slightly slimy, as if she had taken a wrong step and tumbled foolishly off the quayside, and was stumbling through old riverwater instead of air.

There were two of them, bulky and vivid in their purple shirts. They stood with their hands clasped in front of them like nuns, shifting from foot to foot, the sunlight reflecting off their shaven heads.

"How's about ye?" said Dave. He pushed the heavy door open for her, held it as she passed. Claire smelt something sweet on his breath, like peardrops.

"I'm fine," Claire said, awkwardly, half inside, half out, never quite knowing how to answer this. "How are you?"

"Grand." But she was still moving past him, into the noisy bar, blinking in the dark. She smiled back at him unevenly, over her shoulder, but couldn't quite be sure if he had noticed.

Inside, the noise was deafening. Loud music, loud voices. As she walked down the long high room Claire unrolled her apron, reaching back to pass the strings round her waist, tying them at the front. Her eyes readjusted as she went; she began to pick out figures, people.

Gareth was turning from the optics with a glass in one hand and a Club bottle in the other. She smiled awkwardly at him. Dermot was sitting at the bar. He glanced round, gave her a grin, lifted a hand. Next to him, straight from work, in his three-piece suit, pushing his glasses back up his nose, was Paul.

She shoved through the double doors, into the kitchen.

Jim, the Scottish chef, shaved head, goatee beard, was standing in his black-and-white checked trousers, jacket sleeves rolled up to the elbow. His tattoos looked as if they had smudged in the heat. He was in one of his creative furies.

"Where the fuck have you been?"

"I'm not due in till seven."

"These are stone cold now." He was pouting, one hand flung out towards the platters on the counter. Claire lifted a teacloth, spread it over her forearm, picked up a tray of pizza slices.

"They look fine to me. I'll get them out now."

The edge of the metal platter cut into her arm. Whatever way she held them, she would never get the trays to sit comfortably. They were just too big for her. At least this one was cool. When they were hot, they left tender little pink burns on her inner arm. And the taint of this food, bloodwarm and tucked in close and hip-high, would be on her skin when she woke up in the morning, and stay with her all day.

Conroys was split level. As Claire moved around the bar, abbreviated flights of stripped pine steps took her up a few feet, down a few feet. The highest section, at the back, was stone-clad and set out with long wooden tables and benches, like a medieval banqueting hall. It was balustraded along its length with wrought-iron rails, twisted and contorted like candlewax. When the place was full, customers leaned along the whole length of the rail, looking out over the heaving mass of bodies on the level below.

When the middle section was empty, Claire thought, it looked like a ballroom. The scuffed wooden floor stretched for what seemed like acres, lit by wrought-iron chandeliers. You could fit two hundred drinkers in there, no bother. No chairs or tables to get in the way.

The lowest level, at the front, looked out onto the street

through frosted glass. Three steps down from the middle bar. Claire made her way down them sideways, platter cantilevered out from her hip, watching her feet as she descended. The room was low, dark and smoky, with sour-smelling deep leather benches, padded stools and a snug at one end. There were old murky photographs on the walls. Conroys. Generation after generation, muttonchopped, moustached and aproned, hands on hips, squinting in the daylight outside their bar. When one retired, the next one took over with no perceptible difference, except in the quality of the photograph. Glancing up at the fading images as she passed, she remembered asking who the bar was named after. If it was the original Conroy, or a partnership of several Conroys, or all the generations of Conroys that had ever owned it. Where, in fact, the apostrophe should go. Gareth had laughed. He didn't know. Gareth's daddy was a McIlhenney. He had made his money in haulage. He had bought the bar years ago from an ageing Conroy junior, and later bought the failed chandler's next door, and then the clothier's on the other side, and then the bank on the corner, when it closed down. Then he ripped through and up and back. The front bar was all that was originally Conroys. And there had never, as far as Gareth knew, been an apostrophe at all.

The food had been Gareth's idea. On Fridays the bar was always heaving early on, from five or so. It was down near the law courts, the offices, the businesses on the quayside, so it filled with people straight from work, still in their suits, still clutching briefcases. By eight, things had tended to flag as, already drunk, the professionals dragged themselves off home for their tea. The younger, later crowd arrived from around half nine. Gareth fed the early drinkers in the pub, so they wouldn't get hungry and leave. Pizza slices sopped up the beer, made the customers feel loved, and notched up the profit. If Gareth hadn't had that idea nine months ago, Claire wouldn't have had a job. She wasn't barstaff, she wasn't really a waitress. It didn't even have a name, what she did.

It was quieter down there: just the background buzz from the main bar. A couple at a table and an old man at the counter, his papery hand curled around a pint glass. His name, she thought, was Tommy. She held her tray out towards him. He lifted off a pizza slice, laid it down on the scarred bartop like a dead fish, began to pick at it with his fingernails, didn't say a word.

There was a shout of laughter from the snug. Through the frosted glass panels she could see shadows, movement. A rising wave of talk: English, northern accents, she noticed, and tried to make out what they were saying. The heavy vowel sounds suggested something further south than home, but then she had never been good at placing accents. She turned towards the couple at the table.

The woman was bronze-haired, a cigarette held to her lips, her red top pulled firmly down over a round belly. The man pressed his cigarette down into the notch in the ashtray, his belly bulging against the buttons of his shirt. They sat side by side, a half in front of her, a pint in front of him, looking straight ahead. Claire held out the platter, smiling for them.

"You're a wee honey." The woman blew smoke out through pursed lipsticked lips, balanced her cigarette on the edge of the ashtray, took a piece. "You're a lifesaver."

The man reached out, peeled away a slice, said, "That's enough, Joyce." She pulled a face. Claire smiled back at her, turned away.

Tray balanced awkwardly on her left arm, she pulled open the snug door, propped it with her right hip. The tiny space was packed full, shoulder to shoulder.

She remembered afterwards the open pores of a sweaty nose, thick squarish reflecting glasses, neat clean close-clipped fingernails, the reddened curl of an ear. There were smeary fingerprinted glasses cluttering the table, an overflowing ashtray. She remembered later the weight of a hand on her hip, her waist. She never got a clear idea how many of them there were.

They stopped talking. They stared at her.

She felt her face go tight and numb. She felt her eyes go out of focus. She held out the tray. Nothing happened.

"Compliments of the management," she said.

"Now that's nice," someone said. "That's a nice touch."

"Irish hospitality, you know." Another voice. Yorkshire, Claire thought. "They're famous for it."

"And a what do you call 'em, an Irish Colleen."

"They're famous for that too."

A hand descended on her waist. She shifted slightly, uneasily.

"What's your name, then, love?"

She looked round at him. Squarish glasses, wet lips. One hand resting on the table, a cigarette crumbling between mauve fingers, the other hand resting on her. She felt its weight begin to slide down, following the curve of her hip. Behind the glasses, the eyes narrowed.

"C'mon now, don't be shy."

Claire, burdened by the platter, wedged between the door and the table, felt helpless, felt her chest cramp up, her face burn. She looked up, looked round the snug. Smiling, most of them. One lifting a pint glass to his lips. Watching her over the rim. The hand slid down still further.

"No—"

She jerked away, her tray crashing down onto the table, sending glasses skidding off the edge. The ashtray, shunted, coughed up a sputter of fagash. She stumbled out of the snug, she heard the door slam shut behind her. A moment's silence. Then—inevitably, she thought—laughter. Walking unevenly down the bar, she felt the regulars staring, the teatowel hanging over her wrist, her hip burning as if branded. She felt hot. She didn't know what to do with her hands.

Because it was nothing, she thought, nothing really. Not as if a glimpse of washed-grey BHS bra through the gaps between her buttons had driven them wild with lust. Not as if she was in danger of her life. Just a touch. The slightest of invasions. A couple of words would have sorted it out. An eyebrow, properly raised, could have defused the whole situation. Arsehole. Stupid arsehole. She caught up the teatowel, folded it, unfolded it. Jennifer would never have lost it like that. Jennifer, with a slight twist of her lips, with half a dozen words at most, would have cleared the air completely. Like opening a window. Claire could almost see her there, at the bar, perched on a stool, sleek and glossy and completely at her ease. She would be shaking slightly, perhaps; she would be trying not to laugh.

"Fucked that up, didn't I?" Claire said inwardly.

"Too right you did." Jennifer would shake her head in mock despair.

"Well what would you have done if you're so bloody smart?"

"I wouldn't be working in this fucking hole in the first place. You've got no class, Thomas. That's your problem."

Claire was still nodding slightly to herself as she climbed

the steps, turned the corner into the main bar. You work in a pub, she thought, you serve wankers. You deal with it. And while they were laughing at her, they couldn't be too pissed off. So no big deal, no real harm done. But her hands, as they folded and refolded the cloth, were shaking.

Paul was still at the bar. He leant one elbow on the counter, one hand on his thigh. He was listening to Dermot. Two pints, half-drunk, the glasses ringed round with foam, stood on the bar. Dermot was talking, glancing at Paul, then back at his hands as he shredded a beermat, peeling away little flecks of cardboard and dropping them into an ashtray.

That was it. That was exactly what it did to her. Talking to Paul always left her stammering, fidgeting like that. Paul never fiddled with anything, never played with a beermat or a cigarette. When he smoked, you knew it wasn't nerves. It was with some people: not with him. With him it was a ritual; deliberate, neatly done. He never tapped off the ash too soon, never sucked too frequently on his cigarette. He was monumentally still. And that just made you fidget.

And he made you talk, Claire thought. He forced you to, just as much as if he twisted your arm up your back and growled threats in your ear. He always seemed sympathetic, but he never gave the impression of registering much of what you said, so you kept on talking to him until you knew you had said too much, but still you blundered on, giving yourself away. Trying to make an impression. You always ended up saying something unforgettably stupid. And you could never tell if he'd even noticed. Nothing, Claire thought, ever bothered Paul.

That Thursday night back in October. Bar Twelve. Two steps behind Alan, Claire had gazed round the bright bustling room looking for she didn't know who, cheeks glazed from the cold driven rain, hair dripping. Paul was dirty-fair, wore glasses, was an architecture student, Alan had said. So Claire had imagined another Alan, abstracted and dishevelled, blinking out at the world through smeary lenses.

Alan had set off across the room, towards the bar, and she had followed. They had got there first, she decided, before the others. Then she saw the suited slight young man with honey-coloured hair, and next to him a slim dark-clothed woman. He reached out and grabbed Alan's hand and for a minute there was noisy good-willed confusion.

"Alan, how you doing?"

"Paul."

So this was Paul. His hand, when she shook it, was dry; not too soft. It made her own feel damp and grubby. And this was Grainne. Slender, smooth-skinned, she took Claire's arm and began to talk. Kind, quick-fire questions that she never got the chance to answer. Paul bought a round of drinks, and they sat down.

"So, you're back," Paul said. He settled himself, glass in hand.

"I'm back," said Alan.

Throughout the evening, with Alan's arm clamped around her shoulder, faced with Paul's cool smile and Grainne's kind questions, Claire rolled up the till receipts from the bar, pulled her rings round and round on her fingers, twisted her hair into tangles. She tensed every time she felt Alan's ribcage and diaphragm swell as he prepared to speak. For some reason he was telling them everything, every little thing he knew about her.

Her family, her home, her Jewishness; *Jewishness,* she thought, but didn't speak. And all the time they were talking, she just wanted to lean across the table towards Paul and tell him, *this is not me.* She thought that he might understand.

Now, she met him most nights on the stairs from the bathroom, or in the kitchen at weekends when he made the morning coffee. His neat body in Grainne's green towelling dressing-gown, his specs upstairs on her bedside table. His hair sticking up in odd tufts, the warm skin of his throat. Claire slipping anxiously from Grainne's spare room, parched and headachy from another night's insomnia, guiltily conscious of the memory of listening last night to what she should have tried to ignore.

Paul ran a finger over his collarbone. He looked up, saw Claire, smiled. "How you doing?"

"Fine." She wound the teacloth round her hand, unwound it. "Is Grainne coming out later?"

"She's gone home for the weekend. You'll have the place to yourself."

"Oh."

That meant an empty house all day Saturday, all day Sunday. An empty house tonight when she got in. Not even the dubious comfort of a stranger passed out in the front room. Anyone who needed a bed for the night seemed to end up on Grainne's sofa. Friends of friends, little brothers, anyone who got stuck without the cab fare home. Claire kept stumbling in on them after work, switching on the light to find the room a stinking haze of smoke and alcohol and sweat and dirty carpet, and an unconscious drooling body lying on the couch. Grainne picked up strays like other people picked up colds.

Paul was still looking at her. She could feel him looking at her. Was her make-up smudged, could he see up her nose? She held a hand up to her face, touched her upper lip which felt damp. "Dermot, if it's no bother," she said, "would you tell Gareth, when he gets back, if you see him, will you tell him there's some guys in the front bar—" She felt the sentence bloat and twist and fall out of shape, but lumbered on, blushing. "It's no big deal, I mean, they were just being a bit—you know—"

"What?" Dermot said.

"Just, well, just blokes in the snug, a bit drunk, a bit hassly. I don't know, a stag party or tourists or something. No big deal."

"What happened?" Paul asked.

"Nothing, really. Nothing." She paused, glanced at him, embarrassed. "Just thought Gareth ought to know. Just in case."

"Should I get Dave?"

"No. Really, it's no big deal. It's just it's early days yet. There'll be a lot more drink drunk before the night's out."

"Aye, well," Paul said, drawing himself up, puffing out his chest. "If you get any more trouble from them, you let me know."

"Right," she said. She smiled at him.

Music so loud that you had to shout to make yourself heard, shout louder to be heard over the shouting. The late custom swarming in. Young women in tight man-made fibres and unstable shoes, suntanned flesh and glossy hair. Claire, collecting glasses, rubbed a grubby hand through her own crop, thought she shouldn't have cut it, realised it didn't matter. As she slid between the close-packed bodies, drifted from table to table, lifted greasy empties and stacked them one inside the other in a Lego-like tower, leaning up her chest and against her shoulder, she knew that she was invisible. It was as if the glasses gathered themselves. She was more transparent than they were, only noticed when she lifted a glass with a breath of drink still in it, and the owner protested and clutched at it as it floated away.

In the bottom bar, with its dark wood and its drink-tanned regulars, the spaces had been filled up by the younger crowd. Tommy still silent at the counter, Joyce and her husband's still stares still parallel, the other tables full of the chattering slabbering blethering night-crowd, glad of a seat and the chance to talk over each other without straining their voices. One hand clutching the stacked glasses, the other reaching out for empties, Claire slid between the tables, slotting each glass into the one before. The barstaff were supposed to clear the bar, but she reached out to pick a glass, in passing, off the counter, and her hand was caught.

The touch materialised her. She was suddenly horribly conscious of her body; vividly aware of the stickiness under her arms, the warm greasiness of the glass in her hand, the raw cut on her ankle.

The hand that held hers was hairy. The nails were neatly cut. She looked up from it. Squarish specs gleamed back at her.

"Pint of Carlsberg," he said.

She wondered, briefly, if this was the same hand that had touched her before, if this was the same man, or whether some composite had pulled itself together from the soup of limbs and features she'd seen in the snug. He was smiling. The teeth were uneven, tea-stained.

"I'm sorry," she said. "I don't work the bar. You'll have to ask one of the barstaff."

"I'm asking you. You spilt my last one. In fact, you spilt everyone's. So you'd better get a round in."

She tried to tug her hand away; he held on tighter.

"D'you want me to call the manager? Because I will." He leaned forward over the counter, still holding her by the wrist, and stared impatiently down the bar, towards where Gareth stood, angling a glass under a tap, watching it fill. Claire twisted her hand round in the man's grip. It hurt, reminding her suddenly of school, and the slow sting of Chinese burns. The columned glasses shifted in her grip, teetered. She felt hot; it was becoming difficult to breathe.

"Excuse me," the man called, and Claire saw Gareth turn towards them.

She wrenched her hand out through the man's fingers, lost her balance, stumbled. The glasses slithered out of her grip and fell. They hit the boards, smashed. Glittering splinters skidded out across the dark floor. The bar fell silent. Eyes turned on Claire. Somewhere someone laughed. Claire cupped her hand round her sore wrist, glanced back up at the man, and felt a sudden stupid urge to cry.

The man grinned at her, shook his head a little, held his hands up as if capitulating. He turned and walked away.

"What's going on?" Gareth was behind the bar.

"Sorry."

He looked at her a moment, then leaned over the counter to glance down at the floor. Raised an eyebrow.

"You causing trouble again, Thomas?"

"Sorry."

"Here."

He passed her a dustpan and brush over the counter. Her hand, as she reached out and took it, looked shaky.

"You okay?" he asked.

"I'm okay."

"Are you sure? What happened?"

"Nothing. Nothing. Just me being a dick."

And she bent to sweep up the broken glass, crawled among the feet and handbags and chairlegs, breathless, her face burning, her hands sticky and hot.

The kitchen was empty. Jim stood just outside the back door, in the alleyway, smoking. Unnoticed, Claire lifted down the first-aid kit from the shelf and walked through to the back of the kitchen. She slipped into the store cupboard, sat down at the back on the floor amongst the five-litre tubs of barbecue sauce and giant jars of mayonnaise and pulled off her shoe. The plaster had got rolled up and rubbed off, that side of her foot was tacky with old blood, but the cut had stopped bleeding. The blood was congealing, a scab was beginning to form. She touched it gingerly, with a fingertip. It stung. It always puzzled her, every time, that something that had hurt so little while she did it should hurt so much later, while it healed. She rummaged in the first-aid box: safety pins, antiseptic cream, a bandage and bright blue caterers' plasters. She stuck one on, pulled on her shoe, tied the laces. The edges of the plaster stuck up above the cuff, conspicuous, but there was nothing she could really do about that.

Faces blurred now, voices loud and thick. The crowds swayed and stumbled in the viscous, heavy air. Sober, Claire felt as if she was walking through a different dimension, in which she alone was agile, alien. She was emptying ashtrays.

The wooden floor had grown sticky. Spilt drink and ash and spit and dirt off the street churned together by hundreds of feet into a black tarry glue. Down below, in the main bar, the crowds were jostling, packed shoulder to shoulder, jaw to jaw. Narrow streams of movement wove between the bodies, to the bar, down towards the toilets, to and from the exit, searching out the line of least resistance, like water. Up on the higher level, Claire threaded her way among the tables, sliding between the close-packed elbows, stacking up dirty ashtrays to take out for washing, putting down clean ones in their place. There were streaks of fagash down her front, her nails were edged with grey. Leaning over unnoticed between two seated backs, she laid her last clean ashtray down on the end of a table, turned to descend the slippery blackened steps and go to the kitchen with the dirties.

She didn't see how the fight broke out. She was shunted sideways as the crowd swayed, broke, and someone fell. A young man in dark clothes. He pulled himself up, disappeared back between the moving bodies.

The crowd swayed again, pushing against her. Her feet were trodden on, her shins scuffed. She was forced back towards the steps. A woman was shrieking, the sound thin and high over the dark rattle of men's voices. Claire caught hold of the railings, was pressed back against them. A damp checked-cotton back squashed her cheek, pressed her nose askew. She smelt washing powder. A heavy foot crushed her toes. Her shirt stuck to her belly. Something had been spilt down it. She had lost her ashtrays.

Suddenly, it was over. The pressure against her lessened.

The floor began to clear, the bar was emptying. Through the thinning crowd she could see the last of the brawlers being chucked out. They buckled and writhed, their arms were twisted and held up their backs as they were steered towards the door. The place had fallen strangely quiet. She could hear the close-by throb of police sirens. Gareth had switched off the music. He was behind the bar, speaking into his mobile phone. Dermot was standing nearby, awkward. Leaning on the counter, hand to his head, was Paul. He was bleeding.

"Cab's on its way," Gareth was saying.

"I'm alright," said Paul.

"What happened?" Claire was breathless. Her ribs ached.

Paul's collar was open, his tie loosened. There was blood on his shirt, blood trickling down his cheek. She reached into her pocket and pulled out a clean tissue. She handed it to him, nervous of touching. He took it from her, folded it and held it to his cheek.

"You should see the other guy," he said, and smiled.

"Girl, you mean," Dermot said. Gareth cuffed him lightly round the head.

"Didn't see you tackling her."

"Fuck no. See what she did to Paul's pretty face."

"Are you going to the hospital?" Claire asked.

"No. I'm alright. I'll just go home." He lifted a hand to his forehead, closed his eyes. "Fuck, my head hurts."

A pause. Gareth glanced around the bar.

"Claire, you go with him," he said. He pulled his wallet out, held out a fiver. "Take that for the cab."

"But, my shift—"

"Never worry. Just get him home and keep an eye on him. He hit his head. I don't know if he's concussed or what but he won't go to casualty. You could clean him up a bit, anyway. Put some Savlon or something on that scratch."

She took the money. Gareth stuffed his wallet into his back pocket.

"Just you sort him out. We'll take care of things this end."

Claire sat silently beside Paul. Eighteen inches of skin-like velour separated them. She had followed him to the taxi, anxious, hands stretched out in case he fell, wanting to ease him down from step to step and out of the back door of Conroys, curl him gently onto the seat, strap him in like a baby. It made her panic, almost, to see Paul so unsettled, so altered. He reminded her of her father.

The car sped them through the empty, orange-lit streets. Past a derelict church, shuttered shops, darkened offices. They crossed the river. A wide dark expanse of park opened out to the left, a row of gothic Victorian buildings rose along the right. Nothing was familiar. She was out far beyond her knowledge of Belfast.

"Is it far now?" she asked, quietly.

"Not far."

She waited awkwardly at his elbow, watching him fumble the key into the lock. He pushed the door open, found the light switch, flicked it on. An unshaded bulb hung from the ceiling. Uncarpeted stair-treads led up to the first floor, edged with old white gloss paint. A telephone on an upturned box. He walked past it, up the stairs. Claire followed him up to the landing.

He tugged on the lightcord. Clean white ceramic glittered in the sudden light. He leant on the basin, looking in the mirror for a moment, then turned on the hot tap, rolling his sleeves up to the elbow. His skin was brown against the white shirt.

Claire felt useless, helpless, out-of-place. Grainne, she thought, regularly woke up in his bed, showered in his shower, dried herself on his towels. She probably got splinters off the stairs. She would know what to do with Paul, what to say, where to find cotton wool, lint, plasters. All this would be familiar to Grainne, almost home. Claire leant awkwardly in the doorway, asked again, "What happened?"

"That bunch of English fellas. Spoiling for a fight. I just got in the way. Fucking typical really. I don't even know how it started." He bent down, scooped the water up to his face, rubbed his eyes, looked back in the mirror.

"D'you feel dizzy?" Claire asked.

"No more than usual." His reflection smiled at her. "But my head hurts." He reached out for a towel, dabbed his face dry. "There's some stuff in that basket over there." Paul gestured to the corner of the room. Claire turned to fetch it for him.

He sat down stiffly on the edge of the bath. She unrolled a wad of cotton wool, ran water onto it, splashed on some TCP. She looked down at him looking up. His eyes were slatey blue, long-lashed, clear. She could smell the warm sweet scent of malt on his breath, see the curve and dip of his collarbone through his open shirt collar. She wanted to reach down and cup his cheek in her hand, turn his face towards her and kiss his eyelids, his cheekbone, his throat, to taste whatever it was that his skin tasted of. Grimly, she dabbed his scratch with antiseptic. He winced.

"Sorry," she said.

She dabbed again, lightly. He looked gravely up at her.

"Your eyes look fine," she said. "I don't think you're con-cussed."

Then he reached up and took her hand. His fingertips were cool which made her notice again how hot and sticky her hands were. She should have washed them before she started. She should have scrubbed her nails. He turned her hand palm up. The cotton wool was wet and pink with blood. She pulled gently away, turned to drop it into the bin.

"So, I'll head on then, if you're okay." She wiped her hands down the front of her trousers. He didn't reply.

"Grainne won't let you out on your own again in a hurry, you know."

He gave a short, dry, startling laugh.

"Can I use your phone? I'll just call myself a cab, if that's okay."

She turned towards the door. He reached out and put his hand on her hip, where another hand had touched her ear-lier, where the bone pressed out against the thin cotton of her trousers.

"Stay," he said.

TWO

⚭

Alan's long-standing fascination with phenomenology had turned his eyes inward. Things did not exist, for Alan, except in the conscious puzzle of his experience of them. Which was why, when he first noticed Claire, it seemed like a triumph of perception, a work of art. He felt that by perceiving her he had called her into existence. It seemed appropriate to Alan that this should have occurred in life-drawing class.

He went every week to the class, had been going every week for three years. Every Thursday night at seven he would arrive at the Oxford College of Further Education and for the following two hours of the class he would be lost in intense concentration. The act of drawing pleased him, puzzled him. It seemed unaccountable, almost mystical. Curves and creases became scratchy black lines on his A3 sheet. His charcoal snapped in his fingers, his fists rubbed and smudged the paper. Mrs. Blundell could teach him nothing: she had given up trying to.

Then, one winter evening, the second Thursday of the Michaelmas term, he noticed her. She was leaning down to dip her pen into the inkpot by her feet. Her drawing board started to slip, and she clutched at it. Alan watched, expecting to see her drop the board, but she straightened up, righted it, settled back on her stool. Solemn, she glanced up at the model, back down at her picture, drew her lips in against her teeth.

Alan glanced at his watch. It was a quarter to eight. The curtains were drawn against the November night. They were of a thick, man-made material, with a texture like Shreddies and a geometric design in red and brown and yellow. An electric heater blew warm air at the model, Mrs. Peters, who was reading a paperback. She turned a page, sighed, shifted on the upright wooden chair. The rolls of her flesh settled back, not quite as they had been.

Alan noticed all this, his eyes fixed on the young woman. He couldn't look away. She was so utterly absorbed, so caught up in the act of perception that she seemed to have lost all sense of her physical self. She bent over her drawing board, hunched up so that her forehead nearly touched her paper. Her legs were crossed, drawn up, supporting the board, her whole body a rictus of concentration. Her eyes flickered continuously from the model to the page. Each time she leant down to dip her pen, she teetered on the brink of disaster, her drawing board and paper slithering out of her grip. Each time she managed to shift her balance just before she fell. Her pen seemed to need constant dipping.

Mrs. Blundell, dusty and nicotine-stained, passed behind

the students, stopping to comment and encourage. She came to the young woman, stood at her shoulder. Alan watched. The older woman's expression seemed appraising, grim. She leant down to the young woman, spoke to her. With permission, she took the pen from her hand and made a few quick sure strokes across the paper. The young woman watched, frowning, concentrating, nodding. Mrs. Blundell handed back the pen with a smile, then a pat on the shoulder. She stood and looked at the picture a moment longer, moved on.

The young woman stared at her drawing. She looked up at the model. She held the barrel of her pen to her lips, folded her lips in against her teeth. She tapped gently several times. She drew nothing more.

"Coffee break," announced Mrs. Blundell, reaching into her handbag for cigarettes. "Mrs. Peters must be getting stiff."

Alan tended to be brisk in the matter of the coffee break. He liked to be first at the confectionery machine so that he could be sure of getting his usual three-biscuit pack of chocolate digestives. He kept these in his pocket as he dropped the right money into the drinks machine and selected number 26: sweet milky coffee. Then he sat down at the table near the window, to keep away from the others' smoke. He still found it uncomfortable that Mrs. Blundell, a teacher, smoked in front of the class.

But somehow the coffee break didn't have its usual urgency for him that night. Instead of bolting for the door as he rummaged around in his pockets for change, he walked calmly over to the sink and began rinsing his sooty hands under the tap. He could hear the usual friendly clamour of the group as they funnelled out, the scratch of Mrs. Blundell's match as she lit up even before she left the room. And as he stood at

the sink, from the corner of his eye, he could see the young
woman still sitting, pen on lips, looking at her picture. Mrs.
Peters buttoned her dressing-gown, stuffed her feet into her
furry slippers, followed the class out the door. Alan, wiping
his hands on the seat of his jeans, turned and sauntered over to
the young woman, preparing a smile.

"Hello," he said.

Her head jerked up. He had startled her. Brown eyes
looked up at him, edgily. She took the pen away from her
mouth, tucked a loose strand of hair behind her ear.

"Hi."

"You having problems?" His tone was friendly; helpful,
he thought.

"You could say that."

"This your first class?"

She nodded, drawing in her lips again. A nervous tic.

"Maybe I could give you a few pointers." Alan drew himself up, rolled back on his heels. His grey cable-knit sweater
rose up slightly and he tugged it back down into place.

"I need all the help I can get."

He made to walk round her, to look over her shoulder at
the picture. With one quick threatened movement she tore
away the page and crumpled it in both hands.

"No. Not this one. It's crap."

"Well," said Alan, eyebrows raised, "would you like a coffee?"

He walked down the stairs behind her, not watching the
inky hand that ran down the black plastic banister, watching
instead her backside as it moved in her faded soft jeans, as she
stepped down each tread of the stairs.

She bought her own coffee: black, thin. She sat down on the
empty chair at Alan's table. She accepted one of his biscuits.

Her face, apart from the big inky eyes, was not beautiful. Not even, thought Alan, really pretty. Her nose was just too straight and there was a quality about her skin he didn't quite like. It was pale, but that wasn't the problem. It seemed to be too thin. It wasn't quite transparent, because you couldn't actually see the blood vessels and lymph nodes and sinews through it. It was translucent, Alan decided. Like greaseproof paper.

He was still trying to work out if she was his type. He wasn't really sure what his type was anymore. He hadn't had much luck since he came to Oxford. He blamed the fact that there were so few female postgrads, women of a similar age and understanding. The undergraduates were only interested in one thing—celebrity. In that small pond if you weren't President of the Union or taking time off to direct your first feature film or in possession of a Blue you didn't have, Alan had decided, a hope in hell of getting laid. And Alan had none of these attractions. After one desperate term of sharking in college bars and discos he had settled down to three years' (one year B.Phil., two years of a Ph.D.) masturbation and the occasional guilty visit to Northgate Hall of a weekend. He never picked up the same boy twice. He never took them back to his rooms. He never analysed his hostile and boorish post-coital behaviour towards these smooth young men. He only ever thought about them again while he masturbated, guilt-ily, into one of yesterday's socks.

So he had little context in which to fit this young woman. She wasn't of a type with the other female undergraduates he had tried to chat up; polished, hard, dismissive. Nor was she like the ones he hadn't bothered to talk to, the unformed, muddy-looking girls who seemed never to have cut their hair. She wasn't like the young women back home who had gobs on them that could kill from fifty paces and who seemed only to come in bunches of three or more. She didn't fit into any of his categories. She was polite, he noticed, deferential. Not unattractive. And she seemed to be impressed.

"So you're Irish," she asked. Alan nodded. The ghost of his Orange grandfather growled at him, but was ignored. This was too good a start, he thought, to be missed, if he decided he fancied her after all. English women, he'd been told by a Ph.D. student from Offaly, just could not resist the Irish thing. The poetry, peat and Celtic mist sob-stuff. He should have tried this before. And being from the north, of course, the glamour of violence. Irresistible. They'd lap it up.

"Where're you from?"

"Belfast," he said, accenting the word harshly, deliberately.

"Ah. What's it like these days?" She smiled at him.

"Depends where you live." He frowned, gave her a troubled look. "I had to get away. Nothing for me there." He paused a moment, then added, his accent shifting towards the authoritative tone he would soon, he thought, assume with his students: "You know, in German, the verb 'to be' is very similar to the verb 'to dwell.' It comes from the same root. So, 'to be' is literally 'to be in a place.' Heidegger called it 'being-in-the-world.' To be a human being is to be a human being somewhere. So it really matters, the place where you choose to be. It makes you what you are. That's why I left."

She looked up from her coffee, looked at him, eyes wide with interest. In her eyes Alan saw himself, magnified, and fell in love.

The other students were stubbing out cigarettes, scraping back chairs, standing up and making their way back to class.

"I guess we'd better go," Alan said. She drained her plastic coffee cup. He twisted the biscuit wrapper into a knot, then followed her up the stairs.

For the next half hour the young woman stared at Mrs. Peters. She didn't once lean down to dip her pen into the ink, didn't make a single mark on her paper. Whenever Alan glanced up from his own murky sheet, he saw her sitting, pen on lips, lips folded in against her teeth.

Mrs. Blundell pulled a stool up next to her, sat down, began talking. The young woman listened carefully, mutely, pen on lips. Once or twice she lifted the pen to reply to the teacher's comments. Then she folded her lips in again, put the pen back. She sat like that until the class ended.

While the other students were shuffling on their coats, Mrs. Blundell went to talk to her again, a cigarette dangling from her hand. Alan slowly coiled his scarf round his neck, listening.

"I hope I haven't put you off . . ."

"No, no, no . . ." The young woman was dragging on her heavy overcoat. "It's just it's hard . . ." Mrs. Blundell nodded eagerly, agreeing.

"Oh, I know . . ."

Alan dropped his stubby bit of charcoal into its box, rubbed his hands together. He clamped his drawing board underneath his arm and waited, proprietorially, for their conversation to finish. Mrs. Blundell began gathering her things, setting the room to rights. The young woman pulled on a pair of grey gloves and picked up her board.

"Goodnight," she said.

"See you next week."

Alan fell in beside her as she trudged down the stairs.

"You should try a different medium," he said generously. "You should try charcoal."

"I'm useless with charcoal. I just make a mess."

They reached the bottom of the stairs. Alan regarded himself a moment in the glass-panelled door before opening it. He stepped out into the carpark. She followed and the door slammed shut behind them. Their breath disappeared in the mist. She held her drawing board between her feet as she buttoned up her overcoat. He wondered briefly what her breasts were like. They walked across the carpark together, and Alan became aware of a strange warmth spreading out through his chest, like when he drank his tea too hot. He found himself blinking away tears, sniffing in the cold. This little frail being walking along beside him had listened to him. For the first time since he had come to Oxford, he had met a woman who looked at him while he was speaking, who didn't stare over his shoulder, glaze over, or just wander off to talk to someone else. And she was even quite good-looking. If he could just persuade her to get some decent clothes, make her realise how unattractive it was when she folded in her lips, he was flying.

"Are you coming back next week?"

"I'm not sure."

"Well, we should meet up sometime."

"I'm at Somerville. You could drop me a note. Claire Thomas."

She shifted the board under her arm, settling it as comfortably as possible for the walk back to college.

"Goodnight." She headed off into the dark, up towards Hythe Bridge Street. Alan was vaguely disappointed. If she had been going his way, he would have walked her home.

It was the place, she thought. It was the weather and the geography and the architecture all working together. A mist-filled airless swampy lowland ringed round by hills. Filled with walled-in spaces. Walls that guarded libraries, lawns and cloisters like children shielding their answers with an arm. Great wooden doors, studded and barred, that creaked open for you if you knew the code, if you had the key. Bolted side doors, back gates, barbed wire and blackened sandstone. Men in bowler hats patrolling the street in front. She tried to look confident, to look like she belonged, but she knew that it was only a matter of time before she got caught out.

She kept every letter sent to her by the college or the university. Anything with a crest or a letterhead or an official stamp. She laid down each sheet of paper in her desk drawer, filling it eventually so full that she could hardly shuffle it shut. She was never quite sure whether the papers were souvenirs, an archive or evidence.

There was a code, Latinate, ecclesiastical, abrupt. She learned it, but it never seemed quite natural. The sounds did not attach themselves to the world around her. There seemed to be fewer articles and more capitals than in the language she was used to. Schools was just one building, many-roomed, draughty, where they had exams and Freshers' Fair. Sub fusc were the clothes you wore underneath your gown. Halls were where you lived, Hall was where you ate, Front Hall was where the notice boards were. St. Cross was a college just down St. Giles, but it was also the name of the Faculty building.

It had taken her a whole term to learn her way around the college, the university, the city. When she tried to cycle to St. Cross for her first lecture she got swept up by the traffic, unable to pull over, looking desperately around her for the turning, the right way. She was deposited, like jetsam, halfway up the Banbury Road. By the end of the year she still had not found an easy way to get from College to Faculty and back. Each time her journey was nervous, faltering. She dodged down the Lamb and Flag Passage, careered across St. Giles, dismounted to push the bike through the churchyard.

Her room was draughty. When someone left the hall door open, wind rushed in under her door where the floor was worn away with age. The warp and weft showed through the carpet, which didn't reach the walls. Her desk was too small. It wasn't a desk at all really, but a narrow fragile hall table, an occasional table. She couldn't cross her legs underneath it, but sat sideways, twisted round, to lean over her work. She didn't think to ask for a different desk. It didn't occur to her that it mattered.

Brown mineral scum floated on the surface of tea and coffee. When she washed her hair, the hard water left it dull and rough. She got used to the metallic taste in her mouth, but found herself daydreaming of soft clean water from off the fells, tasting of geraniums and grass.

She got used to feeling hungry. There was nowhere to keep food fresh, nowhere to cook but a baby gas-ring in a cramped, overpopulated pantry, up two flights of stairs. There was never enough money to eat out. When she ate in Hall, the food was pale and flaccid, cooked almost beyond recognition. And she quailed at the communal joviality that the awful meals generated, the girls' school laughter. She ate only when it became necessary, when hunger threatened her concentration. She ate furtively, in her room, bread and peanut butter and apples that she kept in her bottom drawer. If anyone knocked while she was eating, she froze, apple juice gathering and running down her chin, until the caller walked away.

Her bed was metal, narrow, and creaked when she turned.

Sometimes, at night, under the parchment-shaded lamp, when she should have been working, she drew. Pictures in ink, moments in ink. Ink that should have been words pacing out an essay, laying down arguments in straight lines. Her old ink pen. She drew Jennifer's face, the patterns of her body. Turning, smiling, laughing, always moving, hair swinging round her face, eyes looking sideways out of the picture. Patterns of home: carious drystone walls, soft mulchy curves of moorland, massing windblown clouds.

Cycling back to College from Schools on the first day of exams, her gown fluttering like a bat in daylight, she noticed metal mesh barriers sealing off the sidestreets, holding back massing onlookers as if there were a parade or a carnival or a celebrity about to arrive. Thinking she was out-of-bounds, expecting to be challenged, she pulled over to ask someone in a bowler hat,

"It's okay to cycle up here?"

He frowned at her.

"Of course."

"But isn't it sealed off?"

"Yes." He said it slowly, drew out the vowel sound, as if he were talking to a child.

"So how come I'm allowed up here?"

"It's sealed off for you," he said, exasperated. "So you can all get back to your colleges for lunch, and then back to afternoon exams. So none of you get hassled by the tourists or run over."

"Just to make it a bit easier for us, they've sealed off the whole area?"

"That's right."

She slid back onto her saddle, cycled on, trying not to look at the clustering sightseers. Put up a barrier, she thought, and people gather.

The June sun glared outside. She lifted the fork to her mouth, felt the mushy food spread out across her tongue.

"This stuff is disgusting." Emma dropped her tray down opposite Claire, dropped herself down into the loose-jointed wooden chair. Over Emma's shoulder, through the crossed bars of the windows, Claire could see the heavy-leafed tree, the thick grass of the quad. "You can smell it from Front Hall," Emma went on. "It even gets into my room. It stinks the whole place out. By lunchtime, you've got no appetite left. It's revolting." She prodded the stew with a fork. "I think that's one of the cats."

Claire looked down at her plate, placed her fork down on the table. Emma was right. It just hadn't occurred to her that it mattered.

"So how did it go?" Emma asked, reaching forward to fill her waterglass from the earthenware jug.

"I don't know." Claire's head had been full of dancing letters, morphemes, words. Prefixes and suffixes, the elegant declining of a noun, a conjugating verb. They had stepped and slid about in a formal dance, taking partners, spinning away. Two and a half hours had passed in a loop. She had looked up from her finished translations to find the time was up. Lost inside her concentration, she had inadvertently taken a shortcut, while the world had gone the long way round.

"Did you get the pieces you wanted? I did. More or less.

The bits I'd memorised. Bluffed the rest." She stuck her fork into her mashed potato. "Stew on a day like today! What about this afternoon? I'm crapping myself."

"The poetry paper? That's okay. I like the words. I like the compounds. Lœnfeat for lamp. Dægred for dawn. That kind of stuff. Light-vessel and day-red. Like we have railway or greenhouse. It makes you think." Claire grew self-conscious, her voice faded out. She lifted her waterglass, sipped. She had said too much. Emma would start to take the piss.

"When you put it like that it sounds almost interesting. But all that endless whining about being lost on the freezing, benighted whaleway. I wish they'd just bloody stayed at home and not bothered with their miserable pilgrimages. Or I wish I'd done PPE." She lifted her spoon, let the lukewarm custard trickle back into the bowl. "Guess this counts as revision, though. For Virginia Woolf. *Room of One's Own.*"

Claire padded up the footpath, past the library and round the side of the quad. It was a threatening evening, heavy and hot. The bar windows were open onto the quad, people were sitting out on the lawn with their drinks. Crushed plastic glasses flattened in the grass. Smooth round vowel sounds rolling over her like water. She rounded the corner and heard a rippling high laugh; Emma's. She stopped between the windows, took a packet of cigarettes from her pocket.

She could walk into the room and straight to the bar and get herself a drink. Then she would have something to hold, some time to adjust to the room, to the push and din and swelter. She took a cigarette from the packet, tucked it between her lips, lit it. She inhaled and the smoke made her shiver. As she walked in her expression would stutter and shift, her smile would suddenly feel hard and uncomfortable. Her shoulders would stiffen and she would force her hands deep into her jeans pockets, shoulders arched high and awkward. Her smoking would look like exactly what it was. An affectation. Something to do with her hands.

Claire knew she was a freak. She'd been born and grown up and lived her life so far without a skin. There didn't seem to be a line where she stopped and everything else began. Her surface was smudged and pulpy, too permeable. And there she was, standing, smarting, on the edge of the sea, and was expected to leap in and swim and splash about in the salt water, happily, like everyone else. She drew on the cigarette again. The noise ebbed. One voice rose clearly above the rest, Emma's actress tones:

"Claire is so—"

But the voice dropped, and the noise swelled, and she never heard what she was.

It wasn't raining. Damp hung in the dark air, did not fall. It condensed on her eyelashes, her cheeks, on the fuzz on her upper lip. It seeped through her clothes, through layers of wool-acrylic mix and cotton, making her skin cold and clammy, despite the inner flush of exercise. It left her feeling shivery, feverish.

Feverish was a good word for it, for the way she was feeling. A kind of nauseous hunger, a chill heat. The exhilaration of having made a decision and being about to go through with it, like the moment before jumping.

She freewheeled down Longwall Street. Her vague

dynamo-powered bicycle light followed the tortuous descent of the double yellow lines. She felt as if she was slipping down them like a counter down a snake. The headlights of a passing car, grinding round the cold steep bends, made the fog glare back at her, for a moment appearing as solid and impenetrable as a wall, then it passed, and the air glowed red with the tail lights. Where the street opened out at the bottom, spilled itself into the High, she pulled over to the steep kerb, slid off the saddle. Another car passed, crawling round the final bend, growling past her too close as she stood on the edge of the pavement, waiting to cross.

She had just come from the library, a heavy bag of books strapped to her back, the straps cutting into her shoulders. Her eyes, dry from long hours' reading in white artificial light, were softened by the fog. Her eyelids felt damp and heavy.

Above her, in the dark, yellow lights glowed. Windows, curtained and uncurtained, illuminated the wet night air. She crossed the street at a half run, pulling the bike along beside her, bumping it up onto the far pavement. She leaned the bike on its elbow against the wall, beneath a dark-paned window, and bent to shuffle the chainlock through its spokes. There was a keypad beside the high dark wooden door. She pulled out and unrolled a softened, smudgy scrap of paper, made out the numbers in the half-light. She looked up at the keypad, pressed the cold metal buttons with a fingertip. The door clicked. She pushed it open, slid through.

When Alan had first walked into his rooms (he had two) he had been delighted with their spare shabby grandeur, the scarred boards, the chipped marble fireplaces, the empty shelves begging to be filled and furnished with his books. He folded his two jumpers and placed them in his deep, papered bedroom drawers, he pushed his boots under the bed. He flumped down on the faded grosgrain armchair, balanced his feet briefly on the sofa. He found the kitchen, one flight down and quite bare, and decided to keep his kettle in his room and his milk on the windowsill. His study window looked out across High Street, his bedroom window peered over the college wall, giving a glimpse of lawn, metal fence, and the edge of the deerpark.

At home, Alan couldn't cross his legs without knocking over a china figurine or displacing half a dozen cushions. His mother, never having had a daughter to dress up, dressed up her home instead, filling their pebble-dashed detached villa with frills and lace and flounces. And when Alan caught a glimpse of the outside world through the pattern of the net curtains, all he could see was another grey house staring back at him from across the street. Here, in his new rooms, Alan felt himself expand in the unforeseen space, shake off the suffocating air-freshener atmosphere of home.

That was before he had seen the other college accommodation. That Ph.D. student from Offaly had invited him round for coffee once, in first week, to a set on stair six. Alan had shrivelled with envy. The rooms were beautiful. The walls were panelled in dark wood, the ceiling vaulted. In the study, a fireplace set with intense blue art deco tiles cupped a real, flickering fire. Mullioned windows overlooked the bare rose garden.

And it wasn't just the postgraduates. Even the freshers seemed to have better rooms than Alan's. In the Georgian New

Buildings, where they were mostly housed, the rooms were bright, high-windowed, the walls chalk-white and smooth, patterned with reflected light from the river. You could hear the dip and splash of punts going by.

He came to resent his rooms, the other students' good fortune, and to feel he was being deliberately excluded. He applied assiduously and unsuccessfully for the better sets in College. He suspected everyone from the Dean to the cleaning staff of conspiring to keep him out. There was one consolation, however. The building opposite his, on the far side of the High, was a Rhodes House. He saw strong, brown, athletic-looking women with unfamiliar university sweatshirts and bouncing ponytails streaming in and out during the day. In the evening, some of them left their curtains open. At the end of three years, Alan was still bitter about his accommodation, but would have been unwilling to move.

That day he had bought candles and set them on the mantel-piece, on either side of his graduation photo. He had bought a bottle of wine. Then he remembered that he had nothing but a Smarties mug to pour it into, and had to walk all the way back up to Spoils to buy wineglasses. In a flash of inspiration, he had picked up a corkscrew and paid for it with the wine-glasses. He had set this equipment out on his desk, beside his computer, and totted up the money in his head. If he'd asked her out for dinner, it would have almost certainly cost more, even if she'd paid for her own.

Hands stuffed into jeans pockets, he rocked quietly back on his heels, looking out across the dark at a blonde woman bent at her desk, hair shining in the light from her anglepoise.

He heard a creak in the hallway as a floorboard moved, then a tap on his door. Alan pulled the curtain across the window, turned to open the door.

"So that's how I see it. That's the plan," he concluded. Claire watched him as he leaned back into the dusty sofa, swirling the dark wine round in his glass. "One more year, eighteen months tops, and I'll have the thesis cracked. I've a couple of essays ready for publication, and it won't take long to turn the Ph.D. into my first book. It's a tough business, these days, but I stand as good a chance as anyone." He smiled. "Who knows. Mightn't be that long before I get my professorship."

"So would you want to go home? Is there a university in Belfast?"

"Yes," he said, briskly. "Two, in fact. UU and Queen's. I did my BA at Queen's." He gestured up to the mantelpiece and Claire rose and padded across the room, stepped up onto the empty hearth to look at the picture. She had taken off her shoes.

On the mantelpiece the steady candlelight illuminated the unframed, brown-cardboard backed picture of Alan. In the photograph he was solemn, gowned, squinting in bright sunshine, clutching a blue folder. Behind him was a fuzzy, unfocused redbrick gothic building.

"It looks a bit like Somerville."

"It has a very good reputation."

She nodded, stood looking at the picture a moment longer, then came back across the bare boards. She sat down, picked up her glass. The sharp, dark wine had taken away the shivers, left her feeling warm and hazy. She remembered she had not eaten since her early, starchy college breakfast. She sipped again, felt the wine coat her tongue, dust the roof of her mouth. She felt, for the first time in she didn't know how long, relaxed. The decision to come here had been hers, and she felt that she had done her bit. Whatever followed, followed, and was up to him.

"You haven't been back to class." Alan reached out with the bottle, sloshed some more wine into her glass.

"No. I've been busy. Essays." She smiled at him. Her lips felt dry from the wine. Her teeth were probably stained too. She licked her lips. They tasted sour. "How have you been getting on?"

He grinned. "I'm doing grand," he said. "I think I'm really breaking through, you know."

"That's great," she said.

"It's very frustrating, though." He put the bottle down on the coffee table, continued looking at it.

"I know," she said eagerly, leaning forward. "I can never make anything as good as I want it to be. I'm always trying and trying and doing more and more until I completely bugger it up. Until it's irreparable. Either that or I just can't get started."

"No," he said, "I don't mean that." He glanced away from the bottle, looked up at her quickly, laughed. "No, no problems there. It's the models I mean. That's what I find annoying. I just get fed up drawing Mrs. Peters or yer man Steven week after week."

"Oh."

"I mean, it's their bodies. They're ugly. There's no satisfaction in drawing well if what you're drawing is ugly."

"Do you think?"

He nodded gravely, ponderously, swallowed. "So," he said. "I was wondering if you'd like to sit for me."

His eyes, behind their thick lenses, dropped downwards, watching his glass as he raised it uneasily to his lips. And in this momentary awkwardness, in the clumsiness of his request, Claire suddenly realised that he was real; that he was, indisputably, there; and the shock of seeing this was so strong that it almost choked her. She had stopped believing in other people. Somehow, everything had shrunk down to this: one tiny wizened self staring out upon unknowable strangers. And she could not go on like that, she thought. That was no way to be.

His eyes climbed back to meet hers. He looked anxious. She smiled.

"Okay," she said.

She stood in the unlit bedroom, caught between the closed door and the uncurtained window. A single bed lay beneath the window. The duvet was twisted and tangled like a crisp packet, the bottom sheet creased and loose. Outside, the mist had condensed into fine steady rain, beading the window, refracting stray light from the streetlamps. From up here, she could see into the college. Yellow lights in high up rooms, an edge of the floodlit tower, a corner of the chapel.

She climbed up onto the bed, knelt, pressing her cheek against the cold glass. Looking out across the parkland behind the college, she could see wet dark grass and thick deep trees. Near the boundary fence, in the shadow of a heavy dripping tree, a paler shadow moved. Claire pulled up the sash, leaned out into the wet night.

A deer. Picking its way delicately through long grass and fallen branches, sheltering from the rain. It seemed strange that it should be alone, that it should have drifted off from the rest of the herd. It dipped its head and began to graze. The rain settled on Claire's hair, spangled her face. She leaned out further, staring into the dark. The deer's head went up. In one long sinuous movement it turned and fled, skimming the grass like a ghost. She couldn't see what had startled it. She watched its white, heart-shaped rump as it bounded away.

She sat back on her heels. The bed creaked.

"Ready?" Alan called.

"Not yet."

Claire reached up and began unbuttoning her blouse.

THREE

Claire gently pulled the door to behind her, heard the Yale lock slide into place with a click. She turned, hesitated on the doorstep. She would have to go back to Grainne's house now. She felt stomach acid rise at the back of her throat, swallowed it down.

Fuck.

She looked up and down the street. Dark windows, neat gardens, cars tucked into the kerb. This could be anywhere in Belfast. This could be any street in any city. Even if she wanted to get to Grainne's, she had no idea which way to go.

For a moment she saw herself turning back, trying the door. It would open smoothly and she would slip past it, back into the dark hallway. She would silently climb the stairs to the bedroom, step out of her clothes and slide into bed, curling up against Paul's warm back, pulling the downy duvet over her and sinking into the soft mattress. Shutting her eyes and drifting away from herself. And, all night, her sleeping body would lie beside his, as if it belonged there.

But the door was locked behind her. She had heard the lock click into place. Going back was not an option.

She paused again at the garden gate, hand already on the latch. The metal was cold and dewy. She glanced up and back at the bedroom window. Unlit. All she could see was the pale lining of his curtains. She slipped out through the gate.

She would go back to Conroys. If she walked back the way they'd come in the cab, she would get there eventually. It would be the last time she could walk into the bar and find everything the same.

Claire turned down the street. She walked quickly, unevenly. The cut on her foot was hurting her. It was weeping again; she felt the lymph sticky against her shoe. She stroked her thumbs absently across her fingertips, became gradually conscious of their texture, aware of the tiny rub of their print-patterns, their tenderness. The tip of her tongue was pressing against the smooth back of her teeth, moulding itself into the sensitive silk of her hard palate. She became aware of her hair brushing against the tips of her ears, of the still-wet softness between her legs.

She was going downhill. Conroys was on the docks, and the docks were by the lough, and that was almost sea, so downhill was the way to go. She passed shut and shuttered shops, bright-lit phone booths, overfull rubbish bins. She smelt the scent of freshly baked bread in the air and water rose in her mouth.

The road was deserted. No passers-by at all. Not a cab, not even the occasional solitary staggering drunk. It was late, she realised suddenly, uneasily. It was very late. She stopped dead. She cast around her. The sky was deep blue, scattered with orange-reflecting clouds. There was a dark, leafy park on the right. She turned round, glanced back up the hill. A clock hung high up on the building behind her. The hands pointed to half-past two. Conroys would be shut. Tired and sore, she would turn the last corner to find the bar in darkness, the shutters padlocked into place. She would stand there, at the bolted doors, frozen by the knowledge that there was nowhere else to go. By half-past two the place would be empty and Gareth would be at home showering, or asleep, Dermot's head cradled in the crook of his arm. But perhaps the clock didn't work. Perhaps that was half-past two on a sunny afternoon in nineteen-fifty-three when the clock had seized up, stopped for good, and no one had glanced up there for years to tell the time. Perhaps it was half-past two on an entirely different night, years ago, in winter, when the frost had bitten into its workings and frozen the hands in place. Claire glanced around her, shivered.

She couldn't go to Conroys. Not now.

A side street opened off to the left. She turned down it.

The street was darker than the main road. It was lined with thick-trunked lime trees. She got a vague impression of red brick, bay windows, hedges. The street ended, and without much consideration, she turned left.

Side streets opened off the new road. She glanced down them vaguely as she passed. A sense of exhaustion came down over her, overwhelming her. The night's long work, the din and press of the bar. By now it all seemed like weeks ago, because of afterwards. She paused at a junction. Neat little Victorian terraces snaking downhill. Downhill, towards the river. They had crossed the river earlier, in the taxi. She had seen the water rippling underneath the bridge, reflecting back the city lights. Stranmillis, and Grainne's house, were on the far bank. She had her door key in her pocket. If she got back to Grainne's house, at least she could take off her shoes, bathe her cut, go to bed. Grainne would not be back till Sunday. Breathing space, at least. She could at least lie down and close her eyes. She turned down the narrower street.

It sloped gently downhill. The houses clung to the pavement, no gardens between her and the front walls, the dark windows. She heard her footsteps echoing down the street. She knew the echo was her own, but the possibility of someone following, or waiting up ahead, crept out of a corner of her mind. She pushed it aside.

The close-set terraces ended abruptly. The houses were now concrete and clapboard and cold. They were silent, no windows lit. Above her, the lamp-posts were linked with bunting, their pennants hanging dead and heavy in the still air. And underneath her feet, the kerbstones were painted three different shades of grey. Marking out territory.

She slowed down, stopped. Sodium streetlamps and the moon bleached out all distinction. She could pick out no images, no letters that would force the faded bunting and paint to blossom into colour. And around her, in batteries of little rooms, tracing the length of unknown streets, she knew that people were sleeping. The flickering translucent eyelids of the elderly, children stacked in bunkbeds, discrete dark heads of couples on paired pillows: a community in sleep. And she was there awake in the middle of them all, washed up on their pavement, alone.

Maybe not alone. The echo had stopped with the terraces, but the idea of being caught there, where she should have known not to be, still lingered. She had to get out onto unpainted, unpennanted streets before she was spotted. She set off again at a shambling, uneven trot, shoulders hunched and arms wrapped around her.

The street ended, butted on three sides by low blocks of flats. A grass forecourt and a stocky flowering cherry tree, a few clusters of blossom hanging half-rotten. Dark alleyways between the buildings. She slowed, stopped. She was lost. She cast around her. She wasn't sure of the way she had come, couldn't remember the turns and loops and half-guesses that had ended her up there. The squat blocks loomed up above her. Windowpanes reflected back the night. A clot of cherry blossom broke up into platelets and drifted onto the grass. She breathed in, stepped into the darkness of an alley.

Eyes straining to define the edges and content of the deeper dark: no movement. Above her, the sky a narrow strip, starless. Beneath her feet, flat paving stones. She ran her fingers along the roughcast wall. Vague light-edged forms, as she approached, gradually resolved themselves into council dustbins; large, metal, plastic-lidded, hollow-sounding kettledrums when her fingers knocked them, shifting on their wheels.

As she stepped out from between them, there was grass under her feet. The sky above her was open, orange-stained. There were bushes in front of her. Beyond them she could see a road, a row of streetlamps, trees and then rippling dark water. The far bank climbing steeply up into streets and houses, the sweep of parkland over to the right. She felt an unexpected surge of relief. She suddenly knew exactly where she was, and where to go. Across the river, up the hill, and she was almost there. Soon, she would be sinking down on cool sheets, pulling a duvet over her. She did not let herself think what would follow when she woke.

She passed through the bushes, began picking her way slowly down the steep grass bank.

The looseweave curtains let in the light. It seeped through her eyelids, stained them scarlet. Her back ached. Through the thin mattress her hip, ribcage and shoulder pressed against the wooden slatted frame.

She was awake.

Tiny, distorted and pale, she saw her reflection in the mirrored bulb of the spotlight on the ceiling.

She heaved herself up, padded barefoot down the stairs.

The kitchen lino was sticky underfoot. She boiled the kettle, burnt her wrist on the steam, and made a pot of tea. She glanced up at the kitchen clock: half-past seven. The whole long day ahead of her, no chance now of further sleep. Her eyes felt gritty. She rinsed out yesterday's mug, sat down at the dining-room table. Her knee started to bounce up and down underneath the table. She uncrossed her legs. The fingers of her left hand tapped out a rhythm on the tabletop, getting quicker and quicker and quicker. She lifted the hand to her mouth and began to chew on a cuticle. She tugged at the skin. A strip came off between her incisors, and her finger began to bleed. Claire sucked on the finger, tasted the blood, looked around her, at the piles of magazines and the dirty carpet and the clutch of empty bottles in the corner. Grainne would be back at five. Five or six. On Sunday. Land in with a carful of groceries and a heap of exercise books and she would dump them all down in the hallway and come thumping up the stairs and slump down on Claire's bed and talk to her. Just wanted to catch up, she would say, before you head off to work. Just wanted to see how you were doing. And Claire would potter around as usual, smiling as necessary, painting on her lipstick, tugging on her shoes. She would have to listen to whatever Grainne had to say, and she would have to smile. And that smile just wouldn't work. She knew it wouldn't. It would start badly, become shaky, then grind itself to a premature halt. She scraped back her chair and stood up.

She tugged a handful of carrier bags out of the kitchen drawer. She stuffed back the others which had rustled out with them, pushed the drawer shut. She bagged up the empty bottles for recycling. She emptied the kitchen bin, scrubbed it with disinfectant. She washed up, she cleaned the sink and draining board.

Five to eight.

The hoover was tangled in the under-the-stairs cupboard, its flex knotted round the ironing board, its hose twisted through wire clothes hangers and a folded chair. She fished out the dustpan and brush. She climbed three flights of dusty, gritty, hair-matted stairs, knelt down at the top and swept each step as she descended backwards on her knees. By the time she had finished she had filled a Tesco's bag with fluff.

She cleaned the bathroom, scrubbing at the film on the bath, at the mould between the tiles. She watered the plants, dusted the shelves, plumped up the sofa cushions. Her fingers were pink and desiccated and cold. They smelt of bleach and polish. She sat down on the sofa and cried. She cried noisily, convulsively, till her stomach ached and she was left gasping. She wiped her face with her hands.

In the bathroom she blew her nose on toilet roll. The snot was black with dust. She turned the hot tap on, washed her hands, then ran a basinful of steaming water. Leaning over, she scooped the water up, held it to her face, splashed it over her skin. Her fingers felt rough against her face. Squinting, she felt around for her tube of cleanser. She flicked the cap open, squirted a slug of cream into her hand. She rubbed it between her palms, over her face, then rinsed her skin again. She got soap in her eyes. She scrubbed her face with the hand towel, looked at herself.

Eyes smarting and misted by tears and facewash, she saw only a pink smear. She blinked, and it clarified. Her eyes were thick-lidded and pink, underhung with heavy mink-brown shadows, cheeks flushed and hot-looking. She tugged out the plug, rinsed away the dirt and soap scum, ran another bowlful of water. Heron-like, she lifted her foot and immersed it in the hot water, peeling off the gummy blue plaster. Underneath, the cut was pink, wet, rubbed raw.

The bike was cool and damp after a night in the back yard. She wheeled it, ticking like a grasshopper, through the house and out the front door, bumped it down the steps. She pushed her right foot into the toeclip, swung into the saddle. Shuffling the other foot into its clip, she tacked slowly up the hill. The gears clicked into place with the certainty of a problem solved.

On Stranmillis Road the pavements were littered with last night's grease-stained papers, chip trays and polystyrene cartons. On the zebra crossing an abandoned kebab spilled out shredded lettuce and grey scraps of meat. All the shops were shut except for the tiny all-night newsagent's, its purple Cadbury's logo glowing. As Claire passed she glimpsed a yellow-lit perspective of shelves and lino, and a young woman, dark haired, who turned a page, smoothed her newspaper flat across the counter, did not look up.

The road swept her down Stranmillis Hill in a single smooth bend. Squinting into the rushing air, she flew past stolid terraces, leafy villas and a splinter of parkland. She saw just one car, a red Micra, grinding up the hill. The roundabout was clear. She coasted round it without touching her brakes. On the flat beside the river, she caught the rhythm of the pedals again. Blue-and-white, a rowing team hoisted a boat onto their shoulders. Passing the pub she caught the scent of old beer and tarpaulins. She stopped at the towpath gate and slid out of the saddle. She pushed the bike through. Kissing gates they called them at home. At home there were kissing gates, grannies' teeth and fat man's agonies.

The Lagan was high, dimpling through the sluicegate. The towpath curled out of sight ahead of her, shadowing the river. She slid back onto the saddle, pushed off, then stood up on the pedals. Starting in a high gear, she clicked her way further up as she gained speed, heaving the bike along until she was flying, hair blown, eyes streaming, sweat gathering under her arms and on her back. There was something necessary about this, something essential. Claire, aware only of the press, release, of her muscles, of the air that abraded her nostrils and swelled her lungs, of the sweat cooling her skin, the wind wetting her eyes, could lose, just briefly, all other sense of herself. She unbuttoned her jacket and it flapped loosely around her.

The path lost the river, clung to the hedge. On the left, the ground swept away into parkland, hazy, pooled with the shade of massive oak trees. A herd of cream-and-coffee-coloured cattle stood motionless, knee-deep in the long grass. The river swept back towards the towpath. The parkland shrank, disappeared. The river was running just beneath her. Above, the bank was knotted with rhododendrons, dry earth showing through the low tangle of branches. She rounded a bend and the far bank loomed up steep and close. Trees dappled the path with shadow.

Round the next bend, a tight right-hander onto a steep wooden bridge. Keeping up as much speed as possible for the climb, Claire slewed round the corner, slid quickly down the gears.

There was a bench, usually empty, just before the bridge. That morning, someone was sitting on it. She was past almost before she saw him. For a second she thought he was just a jogger catching his breath, but in the same moment knew that he couldn't be. Too dark, too crushed. She pushed her way up the bridge's smooth arc, stopped at its apex, leaned one foot on a low rung of the wooden rail. She turned in the saddle to look back.

Zipped up to the chin in his parka, shoulders hunched against some imaginary or pathological chill. A sparse beard, tucked, with his chin, into the nylon fur of his collar, staring down towards the stone-troubled water, or perhaps just at his feet. Battered, blackened trainers. Claire, havering on the bridge's curve, was just turning away, just resettling herself on the saddle, when he looked up, and she almost caught his eye and the start of a smile. But she was already turning, already pressing down on a pedal, the bike already rolling forward, caught by the slope's pull. It was too late to smile back, because smiling back would now mean wrenching on the brakes and heaving herself round in the saddle to look at him. Claire ducked beneath the overhanging willows, flinched inwardly.

And when she cycled back that way, half an hour later, the young man had gone.

The phone was ringing. She could hear it from the front door. Faint, insistent. Her stomach twisted into a knot. She dumped the bike in the hall, grazing the wallpaper, and pushed through the door into the dining room, crossing it in three paces. She reached the phone, stopped dead, her hand hovering over the receiver. The ansaphone had clicked into gear. Grainne's recorded voice, solemn and precise.

Sorry, there's no one here to take your call right now . . .

Claire felt her stomach twist again, curling up like a salted slug.

. . . so leave your name and number after the tone, and we'll get back to you.

An electronic beep. A pause. Claire imagined him on the other end of the line, receiver held to lips, ear; caught, hesitating, just like her. Except that he had picked up the phone, dialled the number.

The line went dead. The ansaphone clicked itself automatically off.

Claire's hand still hovered over the phone. Slowly, as if afraid of breaking whatever thread still connected it with Paul, she lifted the receiver. Slowly she dialled 1-4-7-1. An artificial English voice, in distant emptiness. The caller had withheld his number.

She stepped into the bath. She had run it hot, filling the bathroom with steam, clouding the mirror and the window. The water was scalding; at first her nerves misfired, and she was puzzled by the brief sensation that she was climbing into cold water. She slid down and the heat soaked through, bringing her skin out watermelon pink, beading her nose and upper lip with sweat. Her cut stung and pulsed, she could feel the blood pushing through her. Her hair stuck to her face, damp with steam and sweat. She closed her eyes. She ducked her head under.

Guilt so bad it made her curl up small and wrap her arms around herself in the water. Memories of last night buckling and twisting with images of Grainne in Paul's arms, her pale naked skin slipping in, displacing Claire's yellowish flesh. Which is how it should be, how it was. Grainne's smooth slim arms round his neck, Paul pressing his face into her hair. Claire in bed, in the spare bedroom, awake, aware. Which was jealousy, not guilt, Claire realised, pressing her eyes shut tighter, feeling sick. His touch still haunted her breast; she could almost taste him still. At least, she thought, surfacing, sucking in air, I didn't say anything.

On the corner of the bath, by Claire's red and wrinkled left big toe, was Grainne's soapbox. Neat, pale green, *Clinique* embossed on the top. She had forgotten it. She would be annoyed, and anxious, Claire knew. Her skin was sensitive, prone to break out in rashes of tiny pale unobtrusive spots. She hated going into work with spots, however unnoticeable. Claire smiled at the memory of Grainne's morning gloom over a slight bump on her chin. Spots undermined the pupil-teacher relationship, she had announced, and Claire had done her best not to crack up.

"What, what?" Grainne had asked, and Claire had been unable to explain why she was laughing.

"What?"

Grainne. She could almost see the unlocked door swing

open and Grainne come in, as she often did, unbuttoning her trousers.

"If you didn't take so long in the bath . . ."

Claire, her back towards the toilet, almost thought she heard the slap of naked thigh against plastic, the hiss and splash of Grainne's piss. Claire splashed her hands in the foamy bathwater.

"Listen, Grainne," she muttered.

The toilet roll would rattle on its holder.

"I have to tell you something."

Soft scuffling noises.

"I fucked your boyfriend."

Trousers being pulled up, buttoned. "Ah, right."

A pause, then the rush and gurgle of the toilet flush.

"So what did you think? He's good isn't he?"

"He was fucking great."

Claire closed her eyes, breathed out sharply, wiped her face with her hands. She didn't know his phone number, or even his address. She had no fucking clue how to get in touch, and even if she had, she realised, lifting her bent knee to inspect the pulsing cut on her ankle, there was no way she would have the balls to phone. But, when he had reached out for her last night, his face cut and hurt, he had looked at her, and had seemed to see someone he recognised. Someone he knew, and wanted. Claire, suddenly caught up by the dizzying knowledge that she was *there,* had been unable to speak. But what she had wanted to know more than anything else, and had wished that she could ask him, and was now glad that she hadn't, was what he'd seen.

She jumped. The phone had burst out ringing. Down the

stairs, dripping, towel clutched round her, leaving heavy dark footprints on the stair carpet.

"Hello?"

"Claire?"

"Yes—"

"Paul."

"Hi."

"Hi."

A pause.

"How are you doing?" he asked.

"Fine. What about you?"

"Fine."

"How's the cut?"

"It's okay. Listen."

She felt her stomach twist tighter.

"Mm?"

"I'm sorry."

"Oh."

"I've been feeling terrible. It wasn't fair of me. You're not over Alan yet—and Grainne, you know—"

"Yes."

"I'd hate to upset her. It'd be terrible if she got hurt."

"Yes."

"I mean, it's not like it was anything serious. It's not like we've had an affair or anything. It wasn't, like, well . . . When you think about it, she doesn't really need to know, does she? It would be kinder, really. Don't you think?"

"Right."

"So you won't tell her?"

"No—"

"Well, listen, you're alright then?" She could hear the relief in his voice.

"Yes. I'm fine."

"And this is just between the two of us? No one else needs to know?"

"Right."

"Well, listen, thanks. I'll see you soon."

"Right."

She put down the phone, stood looking at the receiver's smooth white plastic back. A breath, held.

The white tiles were granular. Flecks danced like static on a TV screen, bright pixels blinking on and off.

It was dizzying. She closed her eyes. Behind her eyelids, the same. Little dancing squares of light and dark. Her picture breaking up. Underneath her, the floor seemed to shift. She slid her feet away, planted her hands on the tiles, leaned her head back against the cold ceramic rim of the bath.

Windy dark outside. The screen fizzing. Dad crouched, twisting the plastic dial, and the Doctor Who *theme tune wailing from the TV set.*

She opened her eyes. The light and dark specks still jostling, dancing. She narrowed her vision, stared at her wineglass, trying to grip it with her attention. A tiny pool of liquid red resting in the deepest pit. A bubble caught in the thick greenish glass, near the lip. Her hand lying near the rippled base. Pale skin, tiny lines crossing and recrossing like a map. Tendons and blue vessels pushing against the surface. Creased swellings round each joint. Two silver rings, the smaller holding the larger one in place. Scarred, abraded, old-looking.

The flash of silver from his hand when he skimmed a stone across the flat of the reservoir. The stone flickering into the distance. Always uncountable, unbeatable.

The thumb was bent, pressed down against the index finger, a tiny mole in the crook. Blood had crept underneath the nail, dried into a brownish-red half-moon. The blade lay beside her hand, one corner moist, red.

Soft black fabric pulled up in folds. Dips and curls and invaginations, dark shadows. Pale skin, puckered with goosepimples, pale hair bristling. The left knee bent. Ankle resting on the right knee. Profiled foot, the reddened pachyderm hide of a heel, the bulge of a calf muscle laced with old pale scars, dripping with new blood, cut.

She had drawn a spiral round a mole, traced a five-pointed star into her skin, she had shaded and cross-hatched a tiny parallelogram. She bled onto the bathroom floor.

The car engine sighed off. The car door slammed. A key rattled in the lock and the curtains moved in the draught. The front door banged shut.

"Claire?"

Grainne thumped up the stairs.

"Claire?"

"I'm in my room."

She heaved herself up from the bed and stumbled over to the dresser. She scrabbled around in the clutter as if looking for a lipstick, mascara, eyeliner. Anything at all rather than look up. She grimaced at Grainne's reflection in the mirror, then looked back down at her scuffling fingers.

"Good weekend?" Grainne asked. She eased herself down onto the bed. "I had a great time. Met up with Roisín and Anne. You know, them ones I used to run around with at school. Hadn't seen them in, oh, months and months. Not since Christmas, anyway. Went to Charlie's. Got completely blocked. Haven't been there in ages. D'you know what we used to drink? I'd forgotten this. Cider and Lucozade. Can you imagine? Jesus."

"I—"

"Were you working? Course you were. I knew that. Paul said."

"Oh—"

"He's some boy, isn't he? Can't take my eye off him for a minute. He's healing up nicely, though. You did a good job looking after him. What did you think of his house?"

"I didn't really notice—"

Grainne paused, sat up a little.

"You know, you look exhausted. Gareth has you run off your feet. You'll wear yourself out, so you will."

"I am a bit tired."

"You should take some time off."

"Maybe."

"I would if I were you. No point killing yourself. Get yourself a night off, at least. Come out with us. We haven't been out for a drink together in ages. Here, what about Thursday? We were planning on heading out for a few beers anyway. Come on. It'll do you good."

Claire woke. A door had slammed. She heard Grainne's car start up, the fanbelt whine. She lay flat. The air had got thick. It pressed her down onto the bed, pressed the duvet down on top of her. The central heating sighed off. A stair-tread eased itself back into shape. Her feet were cold. Her bones seemed sore. Her cuts were sticking to the sheets.

There had been an orange nylon quilt when she was sick. It had crackled with static. Flattened out on the sofa, she had leaned against her mother and looked down over a soft tangerine landscape. She had bent a knee and watched the earth ripple. An orange stream would run down that gorge; tiny orange forests would cling on the slopes, and in the dip a perfect orange lake would settle. The photograph album was dark and heavy on her lap. Slowly turning pages, her mother's grained finger drew Claire from orange into grey. Beards and waistcoats, glossy bosomy cars, thin-dressed women and boys in baggy shorts. Uncle, granddad, aunt and cousin. Aunt, cousin, granddad, uncle.

Upright and her head spun. She waded, pushed her way through to the bathroom. Like trying to run in a dream. Like the blankets still covered her. She felt brittle, sluggish, but her heart was going fast, fluttering.

She stood under the shower. The water ran over her until it ran cold. She bent to turn off the taps, then stepped stiffly out of the bath. There was a towel. She pulled it round her shoulders, slumped down on the tiles, dragging it over her skin. Underneath her breasts, on her ribcage, a few pale soft hairs, like baby hair, were growing. She hadn't noticed them before. She gripped one between her thumbnail and her finger. It came out easily, and didn't hurt. She grew cold watching the goosepimples prickle her arm. The curve of her upper arm was steep and round, the crook of her elbow a fold in moorland.

The electricity bill was open on the dining-room table. A note in Grainne's big round handwriting. *Asap, please. This is the reminder.* Claire leaned over it, rubbed her face.

❖

I fucked your boyfriend.

Claire brought the biscuit to her mouth, bit it. The short-bread was thick and sticky in her mouth; she couldn't swallow. She looked down at her teacup, blew unnecessarily on the liquid, watched a shower of spit and crumbs land in her tea. She couldn't drink it anyway. Grainne had put milk in it.

"But you should. You should take some time off and enjoy yourself. Can't be any fun at all watching the rest of the world get drunk every night. Let's face it, it's your turn. You've cleared up after everyone else often enough. Come out on the tear. Get pissed. Snog a stranger. Do you good."

I fucked your boyfriend. His mouth was on my breasts. His hands nearly met around my waist.

"Don't you think? I'll get Paul to bring along some of the ones from work. And there's Jim and Colm from school. We'll bring the lot of them. You can have your pick."

But I fucked your boyfriend. His skin smelt like treacle toffee. Sweet and smoky. When he came, he closed his eyes, but mine were open. I fucked your boyfriend.

"I'm sorry. That was really stupid of me. I didn't think. It's Alan, isn't it? I know how you must feel. It's not easy, getting over something like that. Alan's such a lovely bloke. And you two had so much in common."

Claire looked up. Grainne's eyes were clear. Paler than she remembered. You don't have a clue what I'm like, she realised, not a clue. And if you'd just ask, just the once, I'd try and tell you.

"I do know how you feel. When I split up with Sean, I thought it was the end of the world. But it wasn't, was it? If

I hadn't broken up with him, I wouldn't be going out with Paul now, would I? And when it comes down to it, that's the most important thing. You never know, your Paul might be waiting just around the corner. Did I tell you he phoned me in Armagh? He never usually does. And to tell you the truth . . ."

Claire took another bite of her biscuit. Her mouth felt gluey. She tried to smile.

"What are you having?"

"Gin and tonic."

"Right."

And that was it. All he had said to her. Hours ago now. Claire squinted at her watch. Half eleven. Hours ago.

At least they weren't at Conroys. She lifted her glass to her lips, drank. The glass seemed uneven, unbalanced, slightly slippery. She couldn't taste the gin. Her head felt as if it had been hollowed out and filled up. Her ears had been plugged. She squinted at Jim, who seemed nice, and tried to work out what he was saying. It was too noisy. She had lost the thread ages ago. He looked quite distant, much further than a table-top away. He looked like he might be on a TV screen, slightly out of focus, slightly grainy. She reached out towards him. Her hand touched cotton; beneath it, his arm was warm. She let her hand rest there. It was quite reassuring. It seemed to anchor her.

Grainne had, she thought, been right. It *was* doing her good. Grainne was bound to be right once in a while. Statistical certainty, Claire thought, pronouncing the words carefully in her head. Statistical certainty, given the amount of stuff, the sheer volume of stuff that she said. Like monkeys and typewriters. Like chalk and cheese. Like dandelion and burdock. She rubbed gently at the cotton, feeling it shift and slide against the muscle beneath. She watched Jim's face—it was Jim, wasn't it, or was it Colm—she watched his face, his lips moving as he talked to her about Kenya, was it, or was it class sizes, or was he going on again about *Captain Corelli's Mandolin*.

"D'you know Milton?" she asked slowly. "D'you know *L'Allegro?*"

Because just beside her, half turned away, Paul was still sitting, his thigh against hers, his arm pressing against hers, the back of his neck a too-close blur in the corner of her eye, and she had to say something, even though the words sounded thick and ugly, and she had to smile, even though her face was numb. And she had to touch this man on the arm and look at him, and try to hear what Paul was saying, because he was talking more than she had ever heard him talk, but she couldn't hear a word, just feel the rhythms of his words in the air, feel the thrum in his bones, and it made her want to smack her hand down on the tabletop, and shout for silence, because she couldn't hear what he was saying, and soon he would stop. And then it would be too late.

Knocking. On her door. She blinked awake.

"Yes—"

"Just reminding you. Rent day."

Filth in her mouth. Her head sharp, her stomach boiling. She'd kissed him. She could feel the dried saliva on her skin. She'd kissed him and asked him to stay and he'd said no. She'd only wanted someone to fall asleep with. What was his name?

❖

Someone laughed. She flinched. She pushed her card into the cashpoint, keyed in her number. Waited. The balance flashed up on the screen.

Shit.

She stood looking at it. Behind her, someone shuffled impatiently. *Shit shit shit.* When is pay day, end of the month, how many days till then, how much did that leave her a day— the machine let out a string of angry beeps, spat out her card. *Shit.*

She stood on the raised terrace, behind the twisted iron bars. Her cuts had not been dealt with. They oozed and trickled. The fabric of her grubby trousers stuck to them. Her jaw was locked, her headache swelling, neck and shoulders stiffening. Through the peripheral flutterings and grainy interference, she looked out across the bar.

She had seen them arrive together, walk together across the bare gritty boards. Their faces frozen in profile, they seemed careful not to see her. Grainne had slid gracefully onto a barstool, Paul leaned up against the marble counter. Alan heaved himself up onto another stool.

Then Gareth was leaning over to give Alan a friendly punch in the shoulder, and Alan grinned his quick, evasive grin. Paul, three-quarters profile, pulling out a pack of cigarettes, a calm, reflective smile on his mouth. The curve of Grainne's cheek, dark glossy back of her head. Half-heard snatches of speech. Claire could not quite catch what they were saying.

She turned, walked unnoticed through to the kitchen, sat down in the dark in the back of the store cupboard. She rested her head on her knees, closed her eyes. Her heart seemed to be beating erratically, skipping, stuttering. The dark smelt sweet with spilt aspartame-rich sauce. How the fuck, how the fuck did I get here, she thought. And what the fuck do I do now.

The door creaked open. Claire looked up. Gareth stood in the chink of light, his face dark. She smiled vaguely at him, peering through the jostling shadows.

"I was looking all over," he said. "What's the matter?"

"I think I need some time off," her mouth was dry; the words sounded strange to her, sticky.

"Are you okay? What is it? Is it Alan?"

"I want to go home."

FOUR

Alan soon came to look back on that moment with nostalgia. The shade of a naked, candlelit, silent Claire reclining on his sofa haunted the whole of the relationship for him. The memory carried with it the scent of childhood Christmas Eves, the presents under the tree still in their glossy, shiny wrappings, still mysterious and exciting. The rest of the relationship was, Alan had come to think, really just one long disappointing Christmas Day. Even when you got what you wanted, it was never as good as you thought it was going to be. The shiny wrappings were soon torn and shredded all over the Axminster, you were tired and ratty from lack of sleep, and your Evel Knievel motorbike was in bits. Alan, twenty-five years old, experienced the kind of deflation that he had not felt since Christmas morning, 1982, when he had gleefully peeled the reindeer-wrapping off a big flat box expecting to find a Scalextrics, only to see the cool blue and white lettering of a chemistry set.

But, briefly, things had been perfect. He had felt warm with wine and lust. And as she had opened the door and walked naked into the room he had, briefly, been unable to breathe. Candlelit, she was smooth and slender and seemingly flawless. Her breasts had shaken slightly as she came towards him. He saw her buttocks fold and crease against her thighs in turn as she passed him to get to the sofa. He became aware of a reassuring tumescence in his underpants. He might not, he realised solidly, ever need to visit Northgate Hall again.

He had taken time over the picture. There was no point, he thought, in rushing things. He had settled the drawing board more comfortably in his lap, and, not looking up, he had marked her down on the paper. He drew confidently, easily. Sketching out the shapes and shadows of a female body. Thick dark lines and scratchy shading. Oblivious, he had dragged his fists across the picture as he drew, smudging and blurring. He had put down his charcoal, rubbed his smutty hands together, smiled, satisfied.

"How's it coming on?" she asked.

"Fine," he said. "Finished, in fact."

He leaned forward uncomfortably, passed her the picture. She propped herself up on one elbow and the candlelight caught the underside of her breasts. There was, Alan noticed as he handed over the A3 sheet, a mole on her left nipple. His erection pushed and twitched against his jeans. He sat back, shuffled around, unable to get comfortable.

"What do you think?" he said.

She shook the paper straight, did not reply. Alan felt the first hiss of deflation. He should not have shown her.

"Not that bad?" he asked.

Still she didn't say anything, just lay there looking at the picture. There were goosepimples puckering her skin. Her silence now seemed critical, no longer simple and welcome. And who was she to judge. She had said herself that she couldn't draw. That she was useless. After what seemed to Alan far too long, she opened her mouth and said, slowly,

"Is that what I'm like?"

"Pretty much." He leaned forward. The head of his penis had slipped out of his pants. It chafed against his jeans. Uncomfortable and annoyed, he snatched the picture off her.

"It's very good," she said, shifting round, sitting up. Her bare feet hit the floor with a gentle slap. "It's just it's strange to see it." He heard the springs creak as she got up. She came and stood behind him, looking over his shoulder. Alan, still offended, did not look up.

"It makes sense," she said. Which didn't make much sense to him. He wasn't sure if it was an apology or not. His eyes flickered up towards her, his head didn't move. Her mole-marked breast was close to his face. Angry, he laid the picture carefully down on the floor.

He realised afterwards that he should have known all along that nothing would ever be quite as good as her silent, still nakedness, and that it would be better to let it go, not to touch. But he did touch her, and was surprised to find how cold her skin was, how rough it felt, pocked and puckered all over with goosepimples. It had looked so smooth in the candlelight. But she smelt good, and when he kissed her dry lips her cool silky hair brushed against his cheek, and her eyes when she looked at him were dark and wide and beautiful, and his balls ached for her. He pulled his jumper over his head, kicked off his trainers, unzipped his jeans, bent to pull off his pants. She stood, prickling arms wrapped round her, not watching. When he tried to lay her down on the sofa, she seemed stiff and unsupple, and they struggled for a moment, staggered, crumpled onto the cushions. Her breasts were firm to his mouth, the nipples hard. She was cold and dry between her legs, so he licked his finger. He realised then that he should have cut his nails.

He leaned away from her to rummage in his jeans pocket for a condom. She watched him tear off the foil, roll the latex down his penis. He smiled at her, leaned in to kiss her, and there was another awkwardness as skin adhered to rubbery skin, as limbs were shifted and rearranged. He pushed into her with some difficulty, and it occurred to him that she might have been a virgin. She was quiet underneath him. Perhaps she was nervous.

"It's okay," he said.

He closed his eyes and came, shuddering. He felt his whole body go slack, his mind melting with relief. Winded and delighted, he felt he could almost laugh out loud. A whole different arena, he thought, from masturbation. A whole different world. He had almost forgotten. He sighed deeply, satisfied, and reached down to grip the condom, and withdrew. He sat up, began to ease the condom off.

"You okay?" he smiled at her.

"Yes," she said, "fine."

She sat up awkwardly. He knotted the condom, dropped it on the floor. He put his arm around her shoulders, but that felt awkward, so he drew her to him, held her a moment. He felt the curve of her breast against him, felt her breath on his chest. He felt himself expand.

"Bit cold," she said, and drew away from him.

He rubbed her arms, chafing them.

"I'll put some clothes on," she said.

He smiled as he watched her go through to the other room. She walked stiffly, arms wrapped across her breasts. He slumped back into the sofa, and closed his eyes. He could hear her moving around in his bedroom. Her scent hung around him, reminding him, oddly, of pink wafer biscuits from Christmas tins, that weren't quite a mouthful, were there-and-gone, leaving just a sweetness on the tongue.

She was sharp, too, had to be. Nineteen, she would be. Nineteen or twenty. Good looking, an Oxford undergraduate. Wait till he told Paul. Alan's eyes opened, he reached round for his pants, his lips still tender with the memory of her nipples, like raspberries they were, dark pink. He stood to pull his pants on, picked up his jeans. Her eyes had sharpened, he remembered; he had seen something click into gear when he'd started talking philosophy. Heidegger. Where had he put his Heidegger? Alan settled his softened cock into place, padded across the room as he zipped up his flies. He ran his hand over the dark spines of his books, tugged *Being and Time* from the shelf. He turned at the sound of her feet, smiled.

She was dressed, her hair long and loose, a slightly bruised look about her eyes. She tucked in her lips, pushed her hair back from her face. He came close to her, put his arms around her, kissed her, unexpectedly, on the ear. She shifted, made a small sound: he released her, walked back to the sofa, filled his glass. He smiled at her. Draining the lees of the wine into her glass, he began to talk. In philosophical terms, he said, it was impossible to prove that either wine or glass existed. She perched on the arm of the chair, tugged her hair back into a ponytail, secured it with a band. He outline the proposition that the Universe exists because man perceives it, that man exists in order to perceive the Universe. She swung her feet slightly. Her toes, cold and bare, just scuffed the floor. Smiling, he expanded upon the implications of quantum theory for Judeo-Christian theology. She had to go, she said. She stood up, shuffled on her shoes. She had a tutorial in the morning. She had books to read. As she heaved on her ugly outsized overcoat, he held out the book.

"It's amazing," he said. "It will change your life."

Her rucksack was already weighted and angular with books, but one more wouldn't make it that much heavier.

Over the following days Alan became aware, with mounting surprise, of his need for Claire. He found himself daydreaming. In front of the pale luminous computer screen swam the image of her; silent, naked, and still. His hand, as it turned and flattened a page, was haunted by the curve of her hip. The distraction, although pleasant enough in itself, was currently inconvenient. He was busy, very busy. He didn't have time to daydream. Especially when the daydreams were so engrossing that he ended up having to masturbate, and even that was never quite enough to clear his mind. At the weekend he would call her, he decided, and ask her to come round. It would be nice to see her.

She had pushed the folded picture into her desk drawer, but kept opening the drawer to look at it. Angular unfamiliar limbs stretched out across the grey textile surface. The belly was flat and grey, the navel a deep black pit, big as a fist. The

breasts were heavy and sore-looking, the nipples harsh and scratchy. But it was her face that had unsettled her most. An unevenly sketched shape, featureless as an egg. Eyeless. The picture was incredibly insightful. It was terrifying.

It must be because he was so perceptive that he was offering her his help. He had seen what she was like, and sympathised, and wanted to show her how to be. He continued to invite her round, make her coffee and sit with her on the sofa, and all the time he seemed to be offering her oblique clues to survival. She sipped her thin black drink and felt that he was describing to her the route she must follow. The only way to be.

Already tired with study, she tried to read the books that he lent her, but they left her feeling dizzy and bloated. She would wake up in the morning to find a dark hardback splayed across her chest, where she had laid it down last night as she drifted off to sleep. When he spoke, she always tried to listen attentively, drinking up as much of each disquisition as she could. She often became confused by the arcane vocabulary and devious logic.

It took her quite a while to admit to herself that she doubted. She tried to ignore her suspicions, to push them away, but they hung around her like guilt. She suspected that Alan's way of thinking resolved nothing. It seemed as if all he did was navigate his way around mazes. He wound his way through to the middle and he twisted back out again, and that was all very impressive, but that was all. She couldn't help but feel that there might be better things to do than solve mazes, but these doubts only served to make her more unsure of herself. Alan did, after all, have a B.Phil., he was doing a Ph.D. He did, after all, know what he was talking about. And Claire, for all her As at A level, was only an undergraduate.

She began to find it hard to be alone. An uneasy feeling descended on her whenever she realised that there was no one else around. At night, working under the parchment-shaded lamp in her college room, desk crowded with old books, she would grow suddenly cold and tense with the suspicion that she was not there. Unconnected and unperceived, her mind wrapped up in the knots of someone else's thought, she half believed that she was slipping out of her own and others' consciousnesses, growing hazy, fading. She would disappear.

But nonetheless she found herself unable to enter the college bar and common rooms. To walk into a crowded room was like walking down a hall of cracked mirrors—Claire saw herself reflected in a hundred different ways, distorted, fragmented, multiplicitous. In company, she could not resolve the myriad reflections of herself. She couldn't begin to know them. A crowd made her mind feel like a rubbish bin, stuffed full of discarded, throw-away ideas of Claire.

She practically crawled into lectures. She always got there early while the room was still empty. She sat at the back, wondering at the ease of the habitual latecomers: the calm nod to the lecturer, the grin and half-wave to a friend.

She felt safe in the library. There were people around her, but they were buried in their work. She felt she might be lodged somehow, barely noticed, in a corner of a mind, just another bent body amongst a barely noticed row of bent bodies. As she sat hunched over her own work, she fluttered from total absorption, total absence from herself, to extreme, painful self-consciousness. She hated the walk past rows of occupied desks to go to the ladies' or to get a cup of coffee. It seemed like a tightrope. She wobbled, faltered, blushed, as if everyone was staring. Reluctant to move, her mouth became

gluey, her bladder ached. By eight or nine at night she was exhausted and faint and her eyes hurt, and still she did not want to go back to College. Back to her empty room, or the noisy press of the college bar.

The best place to be was at Alan's set. As he worked on his thesis, she could sit on his sofa drinking black coffee and either reading or scratching away at an essay. He would glance around every so often and notice her. That was necessary.

Sex, frequent, quick and uncomfortable, was also necessary. It left her awake after he slept, frustration chewing at her gut. She toyed with this vague unsatisfied desire, unable to leave it alone. She prodded at it as a tongue explores a broken tooth, irritating both the exposed nerve and the tongue. And it was this post-coital wakefulness, not the sex itself, that was so necessary. It reassured her, even as it troubled her. If she was alone, and wanting, if she had an impulse so strong that it actually kept her awake, then surely, somewhere, there must be an individual experiencing desire. However frail, however fledgling, however unlikely, her own perception of her own desire, untold to anyone, was enough to guarantee her existence. And the best of it was, she couldn't tell Alan, so he couldn't question her logic. She couldn't tell him, because that would mean telling him how bad sex was with him.

She had stopped drawing altogether.

A Sunday afternoon in February. They walked out across Port Meadow. The raised track across the flat green waste was potholed and abraded by the winter weather. The sky was wide and grey. Ahead, the riverbank was marked by a row of bare willows. Riverboats were moored along the bank. Peeking

up above the edge of the grass were smoking chimney pots, flat roofs, a splayed-out bicycle. As they came closer, Claire could smell the smoke in the air, and the soft sour scent of bread. She followed Alan through the gate and onto the footbridge. A small dog, gingerbiscuit-coloured, scrambled up onto a cabin roof and barked at them. From inside the boat a name was called, then there came a muffled whistle. The dog stopped barking, turned its neat, otter's head. Another call, and, tail wagging, the dog leaped back down onto the deck, out of sight. Claire heard a woman's voice, quieting the dog, and ached for the unexamined comfortableness of it all.

"I want this," Claire said thoughtlessly, then flinched, afraid of Alan's reply.

Alan shrugged, not understanding, and began instead to tell her how beautiful the North of Ireland was. The steep hills, the sandy beaches, the basalt cliffs. The names sounded melancholy, slow. Glenarm, Glenarf, The Mournes.

"You should come," he said. "I'd like to show you."

Claire took her finals in June. She stayed up at Oxford until she got her results. Skint, she stayed with Alan. She had to sneak out early every morning, before the cleaners arrived. She had to make sure she left none of her clothes or make-up lying around. She was not, officially, there. If the College found out that she was staying, Alan said, they would throw her out, and send him to the Dean.

Alan was working on his thesis. She walked down to Schools alone. The results were pasted up on a grey fibrous board. She scanned down the list, found her name. Somehow, it didn't look like her. Afterwards she walked down to the

Botanic Gardens and sat watching the fountain, sniffing the traffic fumes in the air. A duck dozed on the side of the pool, its bill tucked into its feathers. A woman in an anorak leaned over a silver-grey shrub and read out its name in Latin to her husband. Claire couldn't stop shivering.

Later, on the High, she heaved open the door of a phone box and stepped inside. She lifted the handset, dropped a coin into the slot. She tried to keep her voice from shivering too.

"That's wonderful. We're so proud of you love. You'll be off out to celebrate tonight then?"

They didn't go out to celebrate. Even if Alan hadn't been so busy, and they hadn't been so skint, she was in no mood. Nothing to celebrate, really. Not much you could do with a 2.1 that you couldn't do without. That weekend, she started work at Culpeper's. The heavy scent-laden atmosphere of the place, coupled with the traffic fumes and heat of the streets outside, gave her a constant headache.

When she left for work in the morning, he was just switching on the computer. When she came home he was still there staring at the screen. Exhausted, she would go to bed at ten, ten-thirty. He would come to bed hours later, waking her as he moved around the room, opening and shutting drawers, cleaning his teeth and hawking into the wash-hand basin. In her lunch break she bought sandwiches and walked down to his building, out of breath, heart pounding. He would consume his lunch wordlessly at the computer, careful not to drip mayonnaise onto the keyboard.

They hardly spoke for a month. She felt that she was barely there, that she went through her days like a ghost. Her lungs felt permanently sore, her chest cramped up into a knot. She had to get some fresh air. She would go home.

❖

Alan was furious. He had never felt so angry in his life. His rage choked him. When she slung her bag onto her shoulder and kissed him, he just said, "Yeah, see you," without turning away from the computer. He heard her footsteps on the stairs, then the street door slam shut. He half stood up from his chair, squinting out of the window. Her hair was glossy in the sunshine. Her bag didn't seem to be weighing her down at all. He slumped back down at his desk. How could she abandon him like this, right now, when he needed her more than ever? How could she behave like this, making him so angry, so fucking furious that he couldn't see straight, much less concentrate on his work? He banged his fist down on the desk. The screen blinked. His hand hurt.

A single-track road wound round the edge of the reservoir, slipped out through the pass in the fells. A car had passed a moment ago, skimming headlights across the water, defining it, coating it with a smooth silvery meniscus. As the lights swung across them, Claire had seen Jennifer clearly, blinking sootily in the light, shifting slightly in her plimsolls. Since then, they had been standing there in silence. Claire had run out of questions. She was desperately raking through her head for something, for anything else to say. Soon, if she wasn't distracted, Jen would ask a question, and she would have to reply, and she wouldn't be able to handle it.

"Well, what about it?" Claire said. Her teeth were aching.

"I don't know. Can't we just go down the pub?"

"If you want to."

"You don't, I take it."

In the darkness, Claire pulled her lips in against her teeth. "I'm sorry."

"What's the matter with you, Thomas? You've done nothing but apologise since you got back. What's up?"

"Nothing. It's just. This was your idea, you know."

"Five years ago, it was my idea."

"Well. I thought you liked it."

"I always thought it scared the pants off of you."

"No. Not really."

"Well then. You go first."

Claire, unbuttoning her coat, shrank at the thought of ploughing out across the dark water. On an old map, somewhere, she had seen the dots and lines of habitation, the simple cross that marked the chapel, a whole village deep within the swelling water. Pike hanging in the dark fireplaces, eels slipping down the stairwells, minnows clouding the branches of drowned trees. The dark beneath her always felt, somehow, populated. She saw herself thrashing through someone else's sky, alien, ungainly, and it made her panic. Every time.

So why, she thought, grimly untying her boots, do this now. Why not go down the pub and sit by the fire and drink a couple of whiskies and just listen to Jen talk. And if she asks about Alan or Oxford or what next, spoof it. Lie. Because crying, Claire thought, tugging her jumper over her head, was a lot like kissing: it should never be done in pubs.

Halfway up the hillside a sheep let out a rasping, belch-like bleat.

"Are you ready?" Claire asked.

"I'll follow you."

The grit bit into her feet. Her skin puckered with

goosepimples. She hugged herself, felt her nipples hard against the softness of her inner arm. From the edge of the dam you could wade out slowly, stepping down from rock to rock, letting the water rise up from ankle to knee to hip with each step. That was on summer afternoons when there were damsel flies and sunbathing with an arm across your eyes, and the water taking the sting out of sunburn. But when it was cold, you just had to jump.

Claire jumped. In an instant she was deep, her hair lifted, legs and arms wide, breath knocked out of her, eyes open in the streaming bubbling dark. She crashed up through the surface, gasping, her lungs squeezed small. She pushed the flattened hair off her face.

"How is it?" Jennifer called.

"Fine."

Claire, winded, treading water, heard Jen laugh. She peered through the grainy dark, saw the pale luminescence of Jen's skin, the curve of her back as she bent to pull off her plimsolls. The water tugged at the unshaven hairs on Claire's legs, slid between her fingers, dipped into the hollows of her knees. She stopped treading water, lay suspended, still. Around her, a thin film of water grew a little warmer from her skin. Faint and pale, Jen picked her way down to the water's edge, paused.

"Cold?" Jennifer called.

"Just a bit."

The figure on the bank shifted a little, finding a sure footing, then dived. The crash of body onto water, then quiet, and the backwash slapping against the bank, against Claire, washing her slight warmth away. Then a nearby splash and splutter as Jen surfaced.

"Jesus. It's so cold."

"Told you."

"Jesus." Claire felt the water move as Jennifer rolled into the crawl, swam a few strokes. Tiny flecks of water hit her face. Then suddenly the surface was dazzling, concentric ripples overlapping, interlacing, the spray flung from Jen's movement bright, suspended, frozen. Claire looked round: car headlights swept across the sky, then the rattling splutter of a diesel engine.

"Car!" she said, unnecessarily.

"Shit."

A couple of strokes back to the bank. Claire's hands found the edge of a low rock, and she levered herself up. Jen was already ahead of her, on the top of the dam, crouching, fumbling for her clothes. The headlights swung again, focused, and the car rounded the bend. Spotlit, they looked at one another, Claire crouching down near the water's edge, Jen up on the dam, hand on mouth, naked. Then the car turned and coasted along the lakeside road. The light swept away, up across the fellside and over the runoff channel. Claire's eyes swam with ghost lights.

"Ooops," Jen said.

And Claire, standing up on the damp rock, putting out a hand to steady herself against the bank, began to laugh.

Dressed, their clothes dampened from their skin, they slid back down the hillside through the sharp old bones of bracken. Loose pebbles skidded out from underfoot. Jennifer's heavy breath in the dark; yellow lights from the houses below. Claire could pick out Jen's house, and the vicarage, and the darkness where the parish hall was, and nearer, the back windows of the pub. But she couldn't see her house, not from there. Other end of the village. Dad sitting by the fire and Mum with half an eye on the telly and half on her knitting, but she couldn't go home and sink down by Dad's feet and slip into whatever it was they were watching, because there was nothing there for her now. Her mum had said so. Said so time and time again. Claire, stumbling on the sheep path, swallowed the thought, refused to think it, because if there was nothing there for her now, then there was, really, almost nothing at all.

Her foot found a toehold in the drystone wall; she gripped the top and swung herself over, into the carpark. Braithwaites' battered Land Rover, Nick's motorbike, dark against the pale gravel. Claire, half a pace behind Jennifer, crossed the carpark, slipped in through the back door. They pushed past the door into the ladies' toilet.

A small, cold, familiar room, one cubicle with a dodgy lock, a mirror, an electric hand-dryer on the wall. Liquid soap oozing like mucus, encrusting the pink ceramic basin. The air smelt of air-freshener and cold peat water. Jennifer switched on the hand-dryer at the wall, then crouched underneath, reaching up from time to time to bang the chrome button again, then sink back into the hot air. Claire turned on the hot tap, let the water run over her fingers. The cold had left them numb. They looked like they belonged to someone else.

Jen slipped out from underneath the dryer, uncoiling herself cautiously in the narrow space.

"Your go."

Claire shuffled past her, squatted down under the hot air. She watched, deafened by the noise of the dryer, as Jen tugged a plastic tube from her pocket, spun the lid off. She dabbed creamy-coloured liquid onto her skin, smearing over the cold sheen of her cheeks and nose. She fished out a kohl pencil and lined her eyes. She coloured in her lips with plum-coloured lipstick. Her features became defined, clear, bright. She smiled neatly at herself. Claire edged in beside her.

"Can I have some?"

"Help yourself."

Claire blotted on foundation, smudged her eyes, greased her lips with lipstick. She could feel Jennifer's warm and smoky breath beside her. She blinked at herself in the mirror. They had nicked Jen's mum's new lipstick, she remembered. It had been placed neatly on the doilied dresser; a sheeny cylinder of blue and gold. They had lifted it down for a closer look, and found it irresistible. The name, printed neatly on a little golden sticker on the base, was what did it for them: *Pink Paradise.* They peeled off the cellophane, unscrolled the stick of vivid magenta and drew it thick across their mouths, kissed tissues just to have the kissprints, kissed each other and admired their pink-smeared cheeks in the mirror. Then Mrs. Rothwell hollered their names up the stairs and suddenly everything shifted, and Claire saw the stained cotton doily, the spilt talcum, the mushed and broken stem of the new lipstick and wondered, briefly, how to disappear, considered hiding under the bed next to Mr. Rothwell's slippers.

"A Rusty Nail, I think," Jennifer said. Claire smiled.

"A Rusty Nail would be fab," she said. Her lips felt tacky.

Tom and Nick were sitting at the bar, half-drunk pints of bitter in front of them, each with a packet of cigarettes open on the counter. There were no other customers. Mrs. Hall was watching TV in her sitting room upstairs. Claire could hear tinny American voices, synthetic music, drifting down the stairwell. Mrs. Hall didn't much like having customers in her pub.

Jennifer hitched herself onto a barstool, Claire climbed awkwardly onto the next. They waited. Tom nodded at them, smiling:

"Alright?"

"Fine," Jennifer smiled back at him.

"Cold night."

"Cold enough."

Claire, conscious, pushed a strand of hair out of her face. Tom continued grinning at Jennifer. Nick blinked at them, swilled his beer round the glass. Mrs. Hall appeared behind the bar, the adverts being on.

"Well?"

"Two Rusty Nails please." Jennifer smiled at Mrs. Hall; Mrs. Hall grunted and turned towards the optics. Nick put down his glass, asked:

"You see anything of them mermaids then?"

Jennifer raised an eyebrow. Claire shifted, waited. Nick went on.

"Tom here's been saying how he saw two of them up the reservoir. Completely starkers. Wondered if you'd caught sight of them."

"Hide nor hair. You've been at them mushrooms again, eh Tom?" said Jennifer.

Tom laughed, apologetic, shook his head at her, smiling.

Mrs. Hall placed two glasses of greenish-gold liquid in front of them. Jennifer paid and Claire followed her to the table nearest the fireplace. A crumbling log fire glowed in the hearth and Mrs. Hall's old lurcher was roasting his skinny body in front of it. Claire squeezed in between the table and the wall, sat down on the wooden bench. She brought the glass to her lips, just touched them with the liquid, then licked them. It burnt her lips and tongue, but was sweet. She leant against the warm flank of the chimney breast and inhaled deeply. The sharp smell of burnt doghair, peaty whiskey, woodsmoke. There was a faint perfume from the lipstick. She could almost taste it.

Jennifer had taken out her tobacco and was flattening a cigarette paper.

"My arse is frozen," she said. "Colder than the rest of me." She gave Claire a smile. Claire felt as if she'd been scooped up and held close. Jen's smiles, Claire thought, when she gave you one just for you, let you know where you were, what you could do.

"It was your bright idea anyway," Claire said.

"Aye, originally." Jennifer looked up grinning, her fingers still teasing out tobacco threads. "But it was yours, tonight."

Nick called laboriously over from the bar:

"We've got to drink that water, you know."

"Shame we pissed in it then," Jennifer sang back. Claire snorted.

"And when did you last have a drink of water, eh?" Tom asked. "I've never seen you drink anything but Mitchells."

"Aye well I'll be sticking to it from now on."

Tom lifted his pint from the counter and wandered over. He put the glass down but didn't sit. He placed his hands on the tabletop, on either side of his beer, leaning in beside Jennifer, his head crooked round to look at her face, one thick dark forefinger slowly tapping the wooden surface of the table. His fingers were scraped and scarred, the skin harsh. There was permanent dirt beneath his nails. Claire looked up at his profile. He was smiling, his face creased. Tom Braithwaite was a stonemason. He had washed the dust out of his hair.

"So you're finished at university then," he observed. "What's next? Any plans?"

"Loads," Jennifer began. "I've been offered a job. A friend's opening a club in Birmingham. He wants me to come down, help him run it. Or I might go travelling. My friend's off to Indonesia and I . . ."

Claire leaned back against the warm stone. She slowly closed her eyes until she could just see Jen through her lashes; bright, happy, gesturing as she spoke, waving away Tom's stumpy Embassies and rolling herself another cigarette, her attention caught between Tom's face and the tiny roach she was tearing. The whiskey was making Claire's cheeks burn; her eyes felt gritty. Cigarette smoke caught at the back of her throat. Claire listened to the deep vowels of Jennifer's words, heard the glottal stop she had caught from new friends. She shivered.

Alan didn't ask Claire to come with him. He didn't even tell her that he had been called for an interview. He didn't think that she deserved to know, quite frankly. It was a rush job, anyway. He had to work on the thesis right up to the last minute, and he would, he knew, have to start preparing for the viva on the way home. It was only on the long and devious bus journey from Oxford to Stranraer that he had a chance to organise himself for the interview. He sat two rows from the back of the bus, muttering his presentation to himself and eating sour-cream-and-chive Pringles, four at a time.

The interview was in the central teaching block. They had

done it up since he was a student. The corridors were clean and echoed as he walked along them. The room was on the third floor. There was an empty seat outside. Alan could hear low voices from behind the door. He sat down, glad for the chance to catch his breath, and waited to be called. After ten minutes had passed and he was beginning seriously to wonder if he was in the wrong place, the door opened and a young, tired-looking woman came out, a leather folder clutched under her arm. "Good luck," she said. Alan smiled at her.

There were five people on the panel, three of whom he didn't recognise. Professor Hughes was there, and Dr. McIlveen, but they seemed to be pretending that they didn't remember him. Professional distance, Alan thought, persuading himself not to be offended. Only appropriate in the circumstances. He settled down into his plastic chair, crossed his legs, listened attentively to their questions. He described his thesis, his articles, and the imminence of their publication. As he spoke, his eyes flickered from face to face, to the cream-painted wall, to the blue squares of carpet on the floor, back to the faces.

The interview passed quickly. He enjoyed it, on the whole. It was good to flex his new-won qualifications in front of his former tutors. He hadn't quite forgiven them his 2.1. If he had got the results he'd deserved back then, he would have almost certainly been awarded full funding for the Ph.D., if not for the B.Phil. He wouldn't have had to scrape by all these years on his parents' meagre allowance.

It was a bit of a rush to catch the bus back. He didn't have time to visit his mum, so he didn't call her. It would only complicate things. And things were complicated enough already. Claire was preying on his mind. Whenever he thought of her, he found himself gritting his teeth. It had started to give him headaches. He had been good to her, he thought, so she should, in return, be good to him. And she most certainly wasn't being, not at the moment. He was going to have to put her straight. She couldn't go on neglecting him like this. But that row would have to wait. Right now, he had to get straight back to Oxford. He had to knuckle down and concentrate on the viva. That had to be his priority. He could deal with the Claire thing afterwards.

He bought refreshments at the Spar on Bradbury Place. Striding down into town, towards the docks, a green-red-and-white carrier bag swinging from his hand, he smiled to himself, smiled at the women that passed by him. Travelling light, Claire-less, he felt cool and confident and sexy. He passed new cafés, new bars that had opened since he'd left for Oxford. He noticed the customers: affluent, chic, besuited, and he thought to himself, Belfast, at last, is catching up with me. Belfast is getting ready. It is almost time to come back. In the low autumn light the city looked, he thought, almost beautiful.

During the crossing, he munched Tayto cheese-and-onion crisps and swigged brown lemonade from a two-litre bottle, oblivious to the rock and swell of the boat. He ate and drank as a salute, a communion. He found himself feeling tearful, and even a little holy. He would, he knew, be coming back. He would be coming home.

"Of course, it depends on the viva, but there's no worries there. Unless they completely fail to understand what the thesis is about." A moment's pause. "Wouldn't put it past them."

"So you're taking it? The job?"

"I thought I would. Why not? No reason not to."

The voice was deep, unfamiliar. Alan on the phone. Perhaps for the first time. She leant back against the stair rail, swallowed.

Jen would be off, soon enough. As soon as she'd got bored with Tom. And that wouldn't take long, Claire thought. Jen was too bright, too brilliant, too beautiful for Tom. There was very little to keep her there, and so much luring her away. That job she'd been offered, the friend who'd asked her to go travelling. Either way, whatever she decided to do, Jen was out of there. Leaving, and never looking back.

And what did she have? A headachy uneasy job in a shop that hardly paid the rent, and a 2.1 in reading books.

What about me, she thought.

"What about me?" she said, and immediately felt hot and wrong.

There was a moment's static silence. Alan cleared his throat. He said:

"You can come too. If you want to."

FIVE

ॐ

It was a small bag, nearly empty, but nonetheless it had to go through the X-ray machine. Claire watched the security guy watching the screen, imagined the picture. A cat-scan of her brain. Soft, tangled stuff. Nothing clear or identifiable.

She had packed it last night, in Grainne's house. Stuffed in what clean clothes she had left. A couple of pairs of socks, pants, her balding cords. The bag had remained flaccid, expectant, lying open-mouthed on the bed. It had looked hungry. It had made her feel guilty. She should have more stuff. Surely she should have more.

Claire shivered, pulled her jacket tighter round her. The lights were harsh, cold. They buzzed. She gritted her teeth, ducked down inside her collar.

On the way down to the docks, she had noticed a sign. Blinding bright in the early-morning dark, illuminated by the taxi headlights. Never seen before. The word HEYSHAM and, underneath, a silhouetted lorry. She had realised, with mounting delight, that the way home was signposted. Not that Heysham was home, but it was close. Just a bus ride away.

But she should have known that already. She had leaned forward in her seat, grown tense with irritation. Stupid. All this time she had thought home was so far away. That it was across the sea to Scotland, then a long meandering coach journey through tiny Scottish towns, along the carious sea-coast. Home had seemed so immeasurably distant and remote. When in fact home was there, just across the water. A glowing sign had been there all along, pointing the way. Stupid.

They had pulled up outside the terminus and she had paid the taxi driver, walked into the bright-lit reception area, joined the end of a queue. When the woman behind the counter asked her, smiling, "Single or return?" Claire had suddenly realised that she didn't know.

"You're travelling this morning?" the woman had asked, helpfully.

"Yes—"

"And you're coming back . . . ?"

"I'm not sure."

"Well, you could get a return, and leave it open-ended . . ."

Claire had nodded.

"That's thirty-five pounds. Or you could just get a single."

"How much is that?"

"Seventeen fifty."

Claire had stood gnawing her lip. The woman had stared up at her, waiting. Claire had pulled her purse out of her back pocket, opened it.

"I'll take the single."

And she had paid, taken her boarding card, and walked through to Security.

"You can come on through." The luminous-jacketed woman was smiling at her, beckoning. Claire stepped through the empty electronic doorway, did not set off any alarms. She walked down the short, sloping corridor.

The chairs were blue. Except where they were red. Red seats were set out in a square at the far end of the room. If you smoked, you sat on a red seat.

Claire walked awkwardly, hands pushed into her pockets, bag bumping against her back. Her jaw was tight, her shoulders high. She kept her eyes out of focus, did not turn her head at all. She was aware that the room was populated, did not want to see if she was being watched. A soft uninflected murmuring, the high shriek of a child, the hiss and trickle of a hot drink being made. The far corner was empty. She sat down, slid the backpack off her shoulder, dropped it at her feet.

The sky was greying outside. The pot plants were plastic. A crumpled metal ashtray had a cold dead filter in it. She slumped deeper into her coat. Going home, she thought. Trying to get home.

Sitting on their new concrete doorstep. She pregnant and miniskirted, he moustached and smoking a cheroot, reaching out to grab the dog, to turn its attention to the camera. Faded to a pinky-orange now, as if turning, as the years passed, from colour into sepia. There were two copies. One in a clipframe on Claire's shelf, the other in one of the photograph albums at home.

The photograph albums. They shuffled them quietly out from amongst the shoes and shoeboxes at the bottom of the wardrobe. Her mother lifted one up onto her knees. The sharp edge pressed into her soft round belly. They turned the pages cautiously, speaking in whispers. Dad mustn't know what was going on.

Her mother pressed a finger down onto the dimpling clear plastic. A little girl, her knees showing beneath a short green dress, a thick fringe across her dark eyes, frowning. Standing on the sun-hot pathway, in front of the doorstep.

"That's the day we took you to the Butterfly House," Claire's mother said. It was a familiar story, warm. Claire drifted along with it. "A great big blue butterfly, the size of a swallow, landed right on your nose. You went cross-eyed trying to look at it. I wish we'd got a photo, but we'd left the camera in the car. The old Instamatic was no good indoors."

Claire remembered blue-green iridescent eyes blinking at her, the tickle of tiny feet printed on her nose. She saw the untaken picture. A leafy archway above, the glass dome of the Butterfly House. Shiny ferns brushing against bare arms. A round nub of a chin, forehead creased, frowning with concentration. The rest of her face unseen, covered with the dark, papery, unfolded butterfly mask.

And when the butterfly blinked and was gone, Dad had scooped her up, his big hands meeting round her ribcage, holding her up towards the misty glass dome. And, exhilarated, laughing, her red shoes dangling in the air, she had stretched out her arms towards the butterfly. It flew stiffly away, bobbing along as if powered by a wound-up rubber band.

Alan had been good with Dad, and it seemed as if he had

liked Alan. Did he realise Alan wasn't coming back? She wondered whether it bothered him, whether she could ever know. When he spoke, his intonation was perfect. He mumbled familiar skeins of sound, in phrases, statements, questions. The rhythms told you what kind of thing he was trying to say: there were no longer any words. Bubbles formed at the slack corner of his mouth, spittle gathered behind his lips. He held tissues to his face with thick, shaky fingers. Claire had, for years now, kept a clean tissue folded in her pocket.

When Alan had come to stay that one time, the rowan berries had been bright red, peppering the hillsides. The first sign of the end of summer, they always made Claire feel sad. She'd picked Alan up from the station in her mother's buoyant battered Fiat 128, and she tried not to be irritated when she saw him flinch at the sight of it.

"Don't worry. No one round here to see you."

While Claire peeled carrots, she kept half an eye on Alan through the open kitchen door. He lowered himself into the chair beside her father. He made some low, meticulous observation. She could not see her father, but heard his reply, a fluttering, wordless, quiet phrase, and Alan nodded, his uneasy grin flickering across his face. She felt warm with guilt and forgiveness. Her mother, hearing, glanced round from the sink at Claire, lips puckering. They smiled at each other.

In the waiting room, her nose prickled.

Her mother turned the page, closing the album. She placed her hands down flat on top of it.

"Let's look at the special one." Her voice was low, conspiratorial. The special one held the old family. Mum's family. The ones who were gone long before Claire was born, when her mother was herself a child. The ones who had come before the adoption, before Ray and Fran, themselves now yellowing in a different album. Claire knew her father mustn't find out what they were doing. She never quite knew why.

Her mother leant down, dragged out the old familiar photograph album from the bottom of the pile. It trailed cotton-silky threads. She lifted the scuffed fake-snakeskin cover and the pages inside lurched, tugged up by the tight binding. The paper was brown, powdery as mothwings. Tiny white triangles cupped the photographs' corners, held them in place. Some pictures had slipped their moorings. They left blank black rectangles where the paper had not faded. The strays slid and shifted, loose between the leaves. Familiar images. Claire's mother began again to name them, repeating things Claire knew so well that they no longer needed to be said.

A bushy-white-bearded man, watch-chain across his waistcoated middle. A grave, grey-suited little boy at his side. Their collars soft, shapeless. Behind them, a stack of splintering wood, a high fence. The old man was her great-grandfather, her mum's dad's dad. Over from Poland at the century's turn, leaving his name behind him. In England, he had taken his name from his trade, and called himself and his family Taylor. The boy, eyes shadowed, was her mother's father. Granddad.

On the next page, the muddy pair of kids in shorts so big they had to be held up with thick buckled belts, were Granddad and Great Uncle Sid. Great Uncle Sid was the older, bigger boy, who had his arm round Granddad's shoulder, and who would grow up to drive a Vauxhall Velox and work for the

Electricity Board, and die, quite suddenly, aged forty-two, of a heart attack, whilst hanging up new net curtains in the parlour.

The young woman in a pale patterned dress, her lips folded in against her teeth, her arms folded behind her, looking cut off at the elbow, was her mother's Aunty May, and Clare took after her. Her two sons, Ben and Sam, were older than Claire's mother, and brought up Jewish, not like her, and were only little when the Fascists marched through their part of town. Aunty May locked the front door, pulled down the blinds and hid her boys in the kitchen dresser, and Mosley's mob passed them by unharmed.

And that was all there was. Loose, slithering photographs; her mother's stories. These pale imagined people, who were hers, and to whom she almost belonged. Offcomers, all of them, she thought. Never a generation born in the same place as the last.

A queue had formed. Its tail was just slipping through the doorway. Claire grabbed her bag, leapt to her feet. Her footsteps were unexpectedly loud; the floor sounded hollow as she walked across the empty waiting room. Up two flights of stairs, then across a gangway. She handed over her boarding card, stepped onto the blue metal deck of the Seacat.

It was a grey morning. The lough was smooth, flat, but for the ship's wake. The air was wet with drizzle and spray. Claire leant on the railings, breathing in the cool damp air, the smell of oil. It was good to be on board, to be moving.

She had walked round the interior of the catamaran, past aeroplane-style seating, past the giftshop, the newsagent's, the video-screens, through the piped music and the smoky, already alcoholic atmosphere of the bar. She couldn't settle. She had come back out on deck, into the damp grey morning. Passengers pushed in and out of the heavy glass doors, leaning on the railings just long enough for a breath of fresh air or a cigarette. She had stayed.

From out on the lough, the city, wedged between the flat dark hills and the lip of the sea, seemed to take up very little space. Streets ended abruptly halfway up the hillside, then there was nothing but a steep dirty climb, patched with scrub and bright gorse, right up to the radiomasts and listening stations on the crest. A helicopter hung in the sky, silent, distant. Claire couldn't guess which part of town it was hovering over, but knew well the soft, insistent, unobtrusive throb of rotorblades. Unnoticed, it would fill heads and homes and streets for miles.

Alan had known that kind of thing. Looked in the sky and seen a helicopter and told you, confidently, which part of town they were watching. Back in Oxford, his arms around her as they lay in his bed, the rain spangling the window, he'd told her about Belfast, made a map of the crook of her arm and the pillow. That was his street, that was his house, he said, and that was where they left the bomb. The front windows had got blown in and the sofa was stuck all over with broken glass, and when his mum tried to claim compensation, they just told her to go and pick out all the bits of glass, and not to make such a fuss over nothing. Alan, running a finger down her arm, told her how the city had been built on its own refuse; built out onto the lough on mud, on muck. Drowsy, she'd imagined the streets slithery and sticky underfoot, seen the city traced all over with the white outlines of the dead.

From the first, she had been delighted with the names, fascinated by the destinations on the front of passing buses: Four Winds, Silverstream, Cherry Valley. She would, one day, jump on board and be whisked out to one of these mythic places, just beyond the city limits, where there was cold bright air and clear water and thick clotted blossom. When a taxi ride took her under unexpected bunting, swept her past flags and painted kerbs, half-seen murals and graffiti, she had to fight the urge to duck down, ashamed and anxious, her eyes closed, into the seat well. Seeing that stuff always made her feel like she was eavesdropping.

"On your holidays?"

An elderly woman, her wispy hair glistening with spray, was leaning on the rail. She wore a grey dogtooth-checked coat. Her skin was pale, heavily lined. No make-up, except for some strong dark eyeliner and mascara. It made her eyes look oddly young; made her wrinkles look incongruous.

"I'm going home," said Claire, grudgingly.

"Me too," the old woman said with warmth. "Be glad to get back." She leant more of her weight on her arms, stuck out her behind and crossed her feet. She was wearing startlingly white trainers.

Claire smiled involuntarily.

"Got a train journey on the far side. Just as far as Oxford. There's a straight line from Lancaster. Takes me almost to my doorstep."

"That's handy." Claire turned back, looked out across the water, at the shore of the lough. They passed distant houses, yachts, seafront caravans. And, eyes following the Seacat's furrowed wake back towards the quays, she saw gantry cranes and harboured ships, and behind, the distant green dome of the City Hall.

"I was over in Belfast visiting my son. He's an engineer."

"Oh."

"He hasn't half got boring!" The old woman laughed; the sound was sudden, guttural, engaging. "It's all house prices and school fees and the new car with him nowadays. His wife! I've never heard anything like it. She sat one evening and talked, I swear, for an *hour* about whether she was going to get the front room painted lilac or yellow. Yellow's *so* much warmer, but she thinks lilac is more *elegant,* apparently. Like it matters! Like it's actually important! But you can't be too rude, can you?"

"No, you can't," Claire said, a smile twitching at her lips, aware that she was being lured in. "So what did you say?"

The old woman laughed again, folded her papery hands on the rail. "I told her I always went with white." She looked round at Claire, narrowed her eyes. "Are you going far?"

Claire shook her head. "Not far."

"Where are you coming from?"

"Belfast."

The old woman grinned, showing pink plastic gums and neat white false teeth.

"You're not a very forthcoming young lady."

"Do you think?" Claire asked, unsettled, considering this.

"I'd've said so."

"Whereabouts in Oxford do you live?"

"On Port Meadow, not far from Binsey. Do you know it? I have a narrowboat moored there."

"You live on a boat?"

"Oh yes. Why not? I love it. Compact, bijou," she grinned again. "I don't even own a hoover. Don't need one with wooden floors. It's ideal, really."

"Doesn't it get cold? Oxford's freezing in the winter."

"No, no, it's lovely. I've got my wee stove and the girls—my dogs—they get onto the bed with me at night. Bit stuffy perhaps, but not cold. I don't like leaving them, tell you the truth. They're staying with a friend, but she's got three of her own and she isn't as mobile as she was, bless her. But Poppy and Sue would never put up with going in boxes for the crossing. Chris wouldn't have them in the house anyway." She pushed herself upright from the railings.

"I'm going in for a cup of something," she said. "Will you join me?"

Claire hesitated.

"You look like you could do with it."

Which was, Claire realised, true. She bent to pick up her backpack, straightened. The old woman jerked her head towards the door.

"C'mon," she said. Claire followed her inside.

In the bar a handful of men were drinking their early-morning pints. Claire sat, enjoying the buttery flakiness of a crois-sant, the hot black coffee. At the counter, the old woman had ordered for Claire, and then asked for half a cup of tea ". . . and top it up with coffee would you?" and the steward, wide-eyed, had complied. She now sat facing Claire, sipping her drink with apparent enjoyment, her lips pursed and creased. Claire rested her head back against the soft upholstery, listened.

The old woman's name was Margaret.

She had been born in Kerry, at some unspecified point in what sounded like the remote past. There had been a big house, which she could only just remember: "Cold, high rooms, not enough furniture, no bathroom." It had been sold while she was still young. She'd gone to boarding school and then college in England, qualified as a teacher. Frank was the Latin master at her first placement. He'd had polio as a boy; it had left him with a limp and a weak chest. He couldn't serve in the war. He'd had such a sense of fun, could always make her laugh. The year they were courting, he had her constantly in stitches. They had married, he got a job in a school in Kashmir, and they moved over. Their daughters were born there. That was before Independence. Then it had all got complicated and messy, and they had to leave. They moved to Kenya. He taught in a school there. They had a late, unexpected son, Chris. Then it all got complicated and messy in Kenya too. It wasn't just the trouble. It was the way the trouble was dealt with. Terrible. So they came back to England and finally settled in Kent. Their children were growing up, so Margaret returned to work, both she and Frank teaching in a small, girls' grammar school. The children left home. Then, slowly, Frank died.

"It was terrible. He was ill for so long, and in such pain. Watching him suffer like that was awful. He just wasted away. He was never a big man, you know, but when we came to bury him, I could have almost carried the coffin by myself." She paused, lifted her cup to her puckered mouth, drank. "I stayed on at the school for a few years, but it wasn't that much fun anymore. I missed him. I missed him at work, and I missed him when I went home. So I thought, time for a change. Not to get away from Frank, now, you understand.

Not a bit of it. But me hanging round unhappy, just pining away, it would have really upset him. It would have made him angry, you know. So I sold the house, and bought the narrow-boat." She snorted. "Went off to have adventures. Chris went mad. Thought I was going to blow his inheritance, I suppose. Well, I didn't. Not all of it anyway." She lifted a paper napkin to her lips. "I used to get all over the place in the boat, but the locks are too much for me on my own, these days. Permanent mooring for me, now. But still, sometimes I think I might up sticks and move on. I'd buy a caravan, if the traffic wasn't so bad nowadays." She turned the cup round on the table, setting it straight. "I still miss him, of course. I soon realised that I didn't want to stop missing him."

Claire, warmed by the coffee, by the buttery pastry in her stomach, blinked once, twice, smiled gratefully. She wanted to ask something, but wasn't quite sure what it was.

"It's lovely and warm," she said.

"It is, it is," Margaret said. Then, after a moment, added quietly, "Yes."

Under her cheek, the rough canvas of her backpack. Her shoulder crumpled up towards her ear, her arm squeezed flat underneath her. In front, the scuffed aluminium edge of the bar-room table. She had been dreaming. Darkness and warmth and someone close, someone holding her close.

She heaved herself upright, slid her legs off the bench, pushed the hair back from her face. The old woman had gone, their cups and plates had been cleared. She glanced round the bar. No sign of her.

Claire grabbed her bag, stood up. She staggered, steadied herself against the table. The floor was rolling; the walls lurched and shifted. They must be out of the lough, out onto the open sea; choppy slate-blue waves hammering at the twin hulls, making the Seacat lunge and pitch. Spray rattled against the windows.

Singing. Chanting. It must have woken her. A crowd of kids in shiny brand-label tracksuits gaping open-mouthed and thumping the table with the flats of their hands. Plastic beerglasses dancing and slopping on the tabletop. Claire stood, unsteady, swallowing saliva, conscious of her sleep-messed face, her crumpled slept-in clothes. She stepped forward a few paces, stopped, swaying. A warm soupy mix of coffee and pastry heaved up her throat. She swallowed it down, shivered. She wanted to find Margaret, to keep her talking, to listen to her talk, until she could find her way back to whatever it was that she wanted to ask. She staggered out of the bar, down into the seated area.

The floor pitched and heaved beneath her. She gripped hold of the chairbacks, glancing left and right down each row of seats as she passed. Mostly couples curled against each other, children asleep in parents' laps. She came to the last row, glanced down. A young woman with a small child leaning against her. The woman's face was pale, she looked up desperately.

"Will you go and get help?" she said quickly. "My baby's been very sick."

Then Claire saw the woman's cupped hands were full of pale milky vomit. It slopped and swelled with the motion of the craft. The child was draped over her. There were no sick bags, newspaper, nothing to hand. Then Claire caught the sweet bitter smell of the child's sick and felt the oily acid rise in her own throat again. Pale and sweaty, she nodded and turned back the way she had come. There was a stewardess standing near the stairs. Perfectly balanced, one hand resting lightly on a handrail as the Seacat pitched and rocked. Bright hazel eyes, kohl-lined.

"There's a woman down there at the front. Her baby's been sick. Can you give her a hand?"

Then Claire ran, reeling, to the ladies' toilet. She shoved urgently against the closed cubicle doors, retching. Her mouth filled with bitter, bitty liquid. From behind the doors she could hear the coughing, spluttering, spitting, as other women vomited. Her stomach heaved. She shoved the final cubicle door. It opened. She fell in, rattled the bolt into place behind her. She flung the toilet lid back, opened her mouth. Brown foamy liquid fell out of her, slopped around in the toilet bowl. She saw flakes of pastry, strings of mucus. Her stomach spasmed. She heaved again and again, muscles aching, bringing up greasy yellow bile. The spasms subsided. She spat hard, dislodging wet particles of food from the back of her throat. The taste of bile, stomach acid, bitter coffee and sweet pastry in her mouth. Exhausted, she slumped against the partition wall, blew her nose, wiped her eyes, waited. Her stomach, emptied, began to settle.

Leaning on the washbasin, she rinsed her mouth, splashed water on her face. Her eyes were wet, bloodshot. She felt light, empty, better. The weave of her canvas bag was still pressed into her cheek.

Cold air blew through the ventilators. Over the tannoy, a Nordic-sounding voice was patiently explaining the docking procedure. Through the glass, through the grainy grey dirt, Claire could see the rain-curtained crags and knotts, the flat grey sands. Warton, Arnside, Grange. Three rows in front of her, the young woman read her magazine, the child slept on her lap.

In the bustle and rush to disembark, she glimpsed a fold of dogtooth coat, a flash of white trainer, then for a moment saw Margaret fully. The old woman was deeply engaged in conversation, her grey head bent back to look up at a tall, balding man. Claire started forward, faltered. She didn't push her way through to speak to her. She still didn't know what it was she wanted to ask.

The bus dropped her at the crossroads and pulled away. The drizzle had thickened to steady rain. After the warm muggy atmosphere of the bus, Claire breathed in cool clean air. A car passed, its tyres sounding sticky against the wet tarmac. Claire turned up the laneway, towards the village.

Uphill between high banks, old hedges dripping. She hitched the bag up her shoulder. The road had been pressed into the earth by years of passing feet and hooves and wheels. Every evening, seven years, that same weary walk up the hill. Schoolbag over her shoulder, games kit, hockey stick shifting and slipping under her arm. It was all too big for her, her school stuff: she could never get a good grip on anything. And Jennifer loping along, half a pace ahead, lean legs in sheer, forbidden tights and miniskirt, carrying her bags as if they were inflated. Claire, water trickling down her nose, could almost see the young imagined Jennifer striding along beside her. She flickered, shimmered in the corner of her eye. Claire didn't look directly. She muttered at her out of the corner of her mouth.

"You know what I've always hated about you?"

She trudged on, not looking round. Mud ran in brown rivulets across the tarmac.

"You've always had it so fucking sorted."

She stepped over a fallen branch.

"I mean, right from word go. There was never anybody that you couldn't make love you. Anything you did looked cool. You'd buy a manky old jumper from Oxfam for a pound, and next thing you'd know, there'd be manky old jumpers just like yours in all the shops at fifty quid a throw. Manky old jumpers would be the next big thing, just because of you. Everything you touch—"

The bag slipped down her arm again. She tugged it back into place. She could almost see the imagined girl falter, as if hurt. Claire felt ridiculous, mean, but couldn't stop.

"Every single thing you touch turns to twenty-four-carat solid fucking gold. But it's not that that pisses me off," she continued. "What pisses me off is that you don't even notice. You swan around wearing your manky old jumper and your wonky smile and your glossy confidence and you never once realise how lucky you are. You have no idea how easy it is, being you."

She glanced round. Grass verge, hedge. Dripping leaves, nettles, a clump of sodden harebells.

"And it's not as if I'm going to tell you."

She wiped the rain off her face. Her skin felt cool to the touch. She walked on.

At the top of the hill she paused to catch her breath. She leaned on a wooden fencepost, felt the damp soak into her sleeve, and looked out across the known, familiar place. Ahead, the flat rich watermeadow, long grass dotted with Friesians. The river was hidden by its banks and a lacy screen of coppiced willow trees. It would be low, despite today's rain. The rocks would be green and slippery with algae. Ahead, the old road, lined with thick dripping oaks, hugged the base of the hills. The Robin Hood tree was still there, up ahead, dark with foliage, but the Krynoid was now just a weather-bleached stump, cut down while she was still a child. Heavy grey clouds lay like a lid on top of the encircling crags. At the far end of the valley the hills rose again, and there, on the far slope, were the first houses of the village, clinging, crumbling, slipping.

The last house in the close. Its pitched roof was bright with moss and lichen. Smoke swelled slowly from the chimneypot, did not rise. Every evening on the way home from school she had glanced up, picked out that house amongst all the others. Number eight.

Home.

Claire knew, so well that she couldn't remember a time before knowing, that her parents had come there because of Joseph's new job. They'd packed their wedding-present tea sets and dinner service, and the orange nylon quilt bought with Green Shield stamps, into the boot of the Hillman Imp, and driven up the empty motorway in hot July sunshine, Moss with his head out of the open window, Anne with an arm around his barrel chest. Moss, Claire knew, had been a wedding present too; he had left pawprints down the front of her mother's white dress. Moss and the tea sets were now long gone, but the dinner service remained, minus two plates and a coffee cup, in the sideboard.

Claire also knew, though didn't know why she had been told, that when her mother had gone to the doctor back in London, three weeks late and giddily nervous, the doctor, gruff and unconcerned, had waved her away. She should come back, he had told her, in two months' time, if she still hadn't bled. Then, and only then, would they see about a test, any earlier being a waste of everybody's time. And Anne had resolved, then and there, never to go back, and to find a new GP, a nice GP, a *family* doctor, up north.

It wasn't that the north had smelt different from the south, but there was a different timbre to the air, a distinct quality to the light, Anne had always said; and Claire, struggling back and forth from Oxford, had soon come to the same conclusion. Southern air, she thought, was stifling, dulled, and the light seemed overused. And there was, she thought, her feet slapping down on the wet tarmac, the jolt of each step resonating through ankles, knees, hips, this same quality of northernness to Belfast; the air fresh with rain, light sheering down through broken cloud, the hills suddenly miraculous with sun. Which was why, perhaps, it sometimes almost felt like home.

Claire's father had worn his desert boots tied with string, and her mother had met him first in Rag Week, at a pyjama party. Anne had studied geography, loved best the close measurements, the precise lines of mapmaking. Her black cartography pen, unused since graduation, had long since been passed on to Claire. In the photograph, Anne's fingertips are inkstained. She is smooth cheeked, smiling, white-pyjama'd. Her eyes are blinked shut in the flash, and Joe's arm lies lightly on the table in front of her, his striped sleeve rolled to the elbow, the muscles in his forearm clear and strong.

Through the wire fence, Claire looked out across the thick

wet grass of the meadows, and thought of her parents driving up that road together for the first time. A summer evening, the light low, and the grass dry and pale. And it would have seemed to them, perhaps, that it was always summer there. Later, sitting beside her husband on the slate bench in front of the pub, with Moss lying stretched out like a rug on the sunwarmed paving slabs, Anne had sipped flat pub lemonade, and noticed for the first time the creases and ridges in the summer-scorched grass, the parch-marks patterning the whole breadth of the valley floor. These, she had told her daughter, Claire didn't know how long ago, were fieldstrips, old boundaries, pathways, far older than the ancient drystone walls. This land was written on by generations, she had said. And Claire, glancing back from the rich wet grass to the tarmac beneath her feet, watching the water flick back over her shoes as she walked, dampening the suede, leaving behind a trace of grit and road-dirt, wondered what it would be like to see this place unmediated, for the first time. To not have been told.

Because the people who had walked this road into the earth, worn the pathways across the land, held each glacier-scattered stone a long moment while considering where best to place it in the composition of a drystone wall; their lives had made these marks; they had not been told. Lives lived in the old village, up the valley, generation upon generation. And when the decision was taken to build the dam, they had carried on, shifting their lives to the new village down the valley. They must have gone back, now and then, to look for something lost or forgotten, or to lift the potatoes when they came into season, but as the water rose, swelling the tarn, seeping over the banks to wet the earth, lifting the dust from the cobbled street, slopping over thresholds, hearthstones, windowsills, creeping up stairwells, would they still keep climbing the hillside to watch? When it eased over the last chimneypot and drew the chapel weathervane forever due west with the current, was there anybody there to see it, or were they all already settled in their new dry houses down the valley, with their electric lights and electric fires and carpets that reached all the way to the walls, fiddling with the TV aerial instead? And why not, Claire thought. Because, when it came down to it, it was just a place, and they were the village. They still are. And then there's the offcomers like us.

Claire, feeling a catch in her lungs, a numbness in her legs, turned the last bend before home. The climb had, she realised, almost been too much for her. At the garden wall she put a hand out to rest herself. Her heart was skitterish, her breath harsh.

Through the gateway, she could see the front room. The light was on, and she watched, uneasily, the small familiar form of her mother moving, bending, straightening. Setting things to rights. She was always setting things to rights. Plumping up cushions, piling up newspapers, offering whispered explanations. For her mum, Claire knew, there was always a neat, orderly way things should be arranged, an answer for everything.

The rain was still falling steadily. Her jacket felt cold and heavy. Her trousers, from mid-thigh down, were drenched; they stuck clammily to her legs, irritating the cuts. Her hands and feet were numb with cold; her whole body seemed to be bristling with goosepimples. She put a hand on the gatelatch. She saw her mother cross the room, dip down in front of the fireplace. Stoking up the fire. Keeping the place warm. Dad, immobile, got cold easily.

Claire hesitated, slipped back behind the wall again and

hunkered down, her bag between her knees. She should have phoned. She couldn't just march up the drive and ring the doorbell. And she couldn't wander round the side of the house to the back door and slip in through the kitchen either. A revenant, her sudden, sodden appearance would send her mother's blood pressure sky-high, might blow another fuse in Dad's brain. Claire stood up uncomfortably, wet clothes clinging to her skin, and dug a hand into her trouser pocket. She held out a palmful of cold change, picked out a 10p piece, walked up the village street to the phonebox.

"Hello, Mum?"

"Claire? This isn't your usual time. Is everything all right?" Claire heard for the first time the Englishness, the southernness, in the familiar voice.

"Fine." Claire kept her voice level, cheerful. "I just thought I'd call you. Let you know. If it's okay with you, I thought I'd come home for a bit."

"Of course it's okay. It's wonderful. When are you coming?"

"Well, now, really." Claire laughed uneasily, pushed the hair off her face.

"I'll pick you up. When are you due in?"

"Mum, I'm in the phonebox. Just up the road."

A breath.

"What are you doing there?"

Claire bit her lip, said nothing.

"Listen, I'll come and meet you."

The phone went dead. Claire hooked the handset back in place, pushed out of the phonebox. Still gnawing at her lip, tugging at a slip of dry skin there, she shrugged her bag up her shoulder, set off slowly back towards the house. This could not, she realised, go unconsidered, undiscussed. This was all too dramatic to avoid comment. Her pace slackened. She could have handled it so much better. She should have thought ahead.

Her mother was coming up the slope towards her. She hadn't put a coat on. She was steaming along in her sweatshirt and jeans, her grey hair limp and heavy in the rain. Obviously she had decided that this was a crisis. Claire stopped. For a moment, she considered turning on her heel and running full tilt, rucksack bouncing on her back, up past the phonebox, past the pub, up to the reservoir and along the bank, up Rise Hill and over the horizon, while her mother followed relentlessly, like a Terminator, rattling out questions like machine-gun fire. But instead she stood there, soaked, as her mother marched doggedly up the slope towards her. She stopped just in front of Claire, her face a puzzled mix of delight and worry. Claire reached out and hugged her, her cheek pressing against the wet grey hair.

"What's all this about then?"

Claire let her go, tugged her bag up her shoulder. Stopped biting at her lip.

"My God, you're so thin. I can feel all your ribs. And you're pale. I knew you wouldn't be eating properly. We'd better get you indoors before you catch your death. Come on." She grabbed hold of Claire's bagstrap, tried to take the bag. "Give me that. I'll carry it."

"I can manage, Mum. Really."

"Why didn't you call sooner?" Her mother set off down the street, disappointed. "Your dad's in a right state."

"Sorry."

❖

He wasn't. He was sitting in his armchair, grinning lopsidedly, a pool of spittle gathering inside the slack corner of his
lower lip, holding out his hands towards her. Claire felt an
unexpected surge of relief. He knew her. She realised she'd
been afraid that he wouldn't. She leaned down and hugged
him awkwardly. He laid his heavy arms across her back, kissed
her clumsily on the cheek. She felt her face crease up with
pleasure.

"Hello, Daddy."

He nodded, said something. She could tell from the inflec-
tion that it was a statement, not a question. She grinned at
him, sat down on the floor, leant against his warm heavy legs.

"Go and get changed, there's a good girl. You'll make your
father wet too."

When she came back downstairs, in her dry cords and
T-shirt, the TV had been switched on. It remained on throughout dinner. Her mother heaped Claire's plate high again and
again. Television continued throughout the evening. Local
news, a game show, a wildlife documentary. While her father
was still in hospital, Claire had mostly stayed at Jennifer's,
her mother had mostly stayed at the hospital. Both of them
waiting in their solitary bleached-out exile, desperately wanting to be told they could go home. It was only when they got
home that they recognised fully the change that had occurred.
Not in Joseph, not in each other, but in home. It had suddenly
seemed stuffed full of absences. From the moment Claire
entered it again, she found herself stumbling and suffocating
on the big soft bubbles that filled the place.

One evening, tired from school, Claire had found herself

standing over him, talking to him slowly, simply, as if he were a child. He had looked up at her in silence, blinking lopsidedly. She had seen herself suddenly, from where he was sitting, and had had to run off upstairs without finishing her sentence. She had beaten her head against her bedroom wall. *"Arsehole. Fucking arsehole,"* her nose bubbling and tears running down her face. The thick breezeblock and plaster wall was percussionless. No one heard. She had come back downstairs dry-eyed and sore and smiling. She sat at his feet in silent apology. His heavy hand had rested on her head, clumsily stroked her hair. Whenever she remembered it, how ever long it was afterwards, that moment could still make her crumple up inwardly, make her want to hurt herself.

The three of them had come to a tacit agreement. They had filled up the soft unmanageable emptinesses with constant TV. The incessant voices, music, flickering light had come to fill up the wordlessness and stillness that surrounded them. It made all three of them feel easier, all three of them feel guilty.

And tonight, Claire was again glad of the constant noise, the false focus to the room. Ever since she had arrived, her mother had been flicking her sidelong questioning glances, and she knew it was only a matter of time before the actual questions started. After dinner, Claire installed herself on the sofa, remained resolutely in profile, pretending to be engrossed in the news. She knew there was washing up to be done, but if she was cornered in the kitchen there would be no way to avoid her mother's gently persistent enquiries.

"Mum, leave it. I'll do it in the morning."

"You could give me a hand now."

"I want to see the news."

Belfast was on TV. A half-filled debating chamber, a glowing digital clock, the minutes ticking by. Angry laughter and polite fury. Then cut to elsewhere. She recognised the brownbrick building near the bus station. Square spectacles, a boiled, thin-eyed face, and clustering around him, men familiar from local news back in Belfast. The one who looked like Mr. Burns from *The Simpsons,* the brushy sergeant-major type, the swelling spreading Jabba-jawed one. Claire could never remember their names. All of them with narrow smiles. They would not be taking their seats.

In Belfast she had never felt entitled to an opinion. Now, across the water, she felt a sympathetic ache for the city. Things had faltered, halted, broken down. She felt a sudden urge to go back, to be there. Not to have run away.

"It'll only take a minute."

"I'm tired."

She was tired. Her stomach was full of roast potatoes and casserole, the fire was hot and her face had started to glow. She felt shivery.

"I'll do it in the morning. I'm knackered, honestly. I think I'll just head on up to bed."

Claire lay in bed underneath the uncurtained skylight. Darkness had not yet fallen, and tonight, there would be no stars. The sky was covered with a thick grey crust of cloud. The rain picked up soot from the chimney smoke, and left streaky dark marks down the sloping glass. She pulled her duvet up to her chin, rolled onto her side, closed her eyes. She did not want to look around the room again. It was not as clear as she'd remembered it.

When she stuffed her bag in the wardrobe, she had noticed the few forgotten clothes left there: her school tie and skirt hung next to the overcoat Alan had hated so much, which was on the same hanger as a top she'd borrowed from Jen and never got round to giving back. The bookshelves were incoherent too: they rambled. *Ape and Essence* sat between *Fantastic Mr. Fox* and *The Magician's Nephew,* and she couldn't remember what it was about. There was a *Bunty* Annual for 1968, *A History of The English Language,* a copy of *Romola* that she knew she'd never finished, a pop-up version of Jack and the Beanstalk and *Beowulf* in the original. She'd seen them: she didn't want to look again. The room was wrong, it was misleading. It was full of anachronisms.

And on the walls, her pictures. A few had fallen down, slid between the divan bed and the wall or behind the chest of drawers. They left torn scraps of paper on the wall, and blobs of blu-tack which had stained the wallpaper with grease. Many more were still stuffed into her old art file. A corner of it projected from behind the wardrobe. Mostly GCSE stuff, some sixthform. Nothing later. Inky outcrops, tangled roots, torn and twisted stubborn moorland trees. Claire had known what they would be without looking at them. But by her mirror, pinned with a single thumbtack, one sketch had curled up around itself. She couldn't remember what the picture was, or when she had drawn it, or why she had not blu-tacked it out flat like the rest of the pictures. She had held it flat with the palm of her hand. Ink-and-wash. Yellowish skin, heavy lidded eyes, close-pressed little face: hers. It gave nothing away.

And now she lay awake, aware of the muddle of the room around her, listening to the sounds of her parents' evening ritual. The same ever since Dad came home. The TV was silenced, then she heard her mother's voice. Then the sound of opening and shutting doors, the toilet flush, a creak and sigh of bedsprings, and the house was silent.

She rolled over onto her belly, pressing herself down into the cool sheet, the solid yielding mattress. Her body remembered the weight and press of Paul's body, the smell of his skin, and the dark. She slipped her hand down, past the elastic waist of her pyjamas, underneath the smooth cotton of her pants. She slipped her fingertips into the wet.

From the moment she had woken, the sky had been thick with cloud, the skylight drumming with rain. Downstairs, the house was muggy and hot, the coal fire consuming, it seemed, more than its fair share of the front room's air. Claire, heaped in the armchair, half watching a mid-morning cookery programme, felt sluggish and achy, but knew she couldn't leave the room: to go upstairs would only elicit comment, would mean her mother could follow and corner her there. But she knew, nonetheless, that this could not be avoided forever. Her mother was populating the house with silences so pertinent and direct that sooner or later Claire would be obliged to fill one of them. She'd have to say something and "I don't want to talk" would never do. It wasn't allowed. But what could she say that her mother would actually hear? I cut myself. I keep on cutting myself. I fucked someone I shouldn't have. I came home because I thought it would help. I thought I might find something here, I don't know what, and now I can't help thinking I was wrong. Her mother wouldn't want to hear it, probably wouldn't even be able to hear it. Too much like I need help, and I need help wasn't allowed. So she'd have to put up with I don't want to talk. She'd have to lump it.

The fire spat as water dripped down the chimney. Claire reached over, lifted the newspaper from the coffee table, shook it flat, scanned the headlines. Arms extended to full stretch, she turned the page, folded it, shook it out again. Belfast was splattered all over the broadsheet. Features, analysis, comment. She turned the pages awkwardly, slowly, searched the print with a new eagerness. It would begin to cohere; it would be in there somewhere.

"Claire," her mother called from the hall door.

"Yes."

"Can you come and give me a hand?"

"Now?"

"Yes."

"I'm just in the middle—"

"It won't take a moment."

"I'll just finish—"

"It'll only take a minute."

"But—"

"Claire."

"Okay." She dropped the paper, gave her father a quick smile. "Coming." She followed her mother up the hallway. "What is it?"

Her mother was sitting on the edge of the bed, the old photograph album on her knees.

"I thought we would look at these. We never get a chance nowadays. Come and see."

She patted the bed beside her, sending ripples through the duvet. Claire sat down. There would be questions, sooner or later. She knew they were coming. This was just a tactic. They would look at the pictures and she would soothe Claire with the familiar rhythm of the stories and names, and then just when Claire felt safe she would slip in an apparently innocent enquiry and suddenly Claire would be spot-lit, paralysed, gaping.

Her mother spoke softly, turning the pages. The family stories twisted out like long pale roots growing into the dark. Claire sat, watching, listening, responding, filling in the gaps too quickly, leaving her mother no space to shift tack. She pointed to a photograph. Two little boys in football boots and shorts so big that they had to be held up with belts. The bigger one had his arm around the smaller boy's shoulders. Her mother said, "That's Ben and Sam, Aunty May's little boys."

But it was Great Uncle Sid and Granddad.

"Brought up Jewish, not like me."

That went with the picture of Aunty May. Not with the picture of the little boys. The boys were Granddad and Great Uncle Sid. Granddad and Great Uncle Sid played football. They had muddy knees. Great Uncle Sid had his arm round Granddad's shoulder. Granddad had a front tooth missing.

"They lived in Whitechapel round the time of the Fascist marches."

It was Great Uncle Sid and Granddad. Of course it was. It always had been.

"That's my Great Uncle Sid and Granddad," Claire said.

A pause.

"No, no," her mother said.

Another pause. She glanced at her mother's face. The older woman's head was bent, her hair falling around her face, but Claire could see her cheeks were flushed, her eyes deliberately intent upon the page.

"Oh," Claire said. "Right." She swallowed. "Must be my mistake."

They sat for a moment, saying nothing. Stories unravelled in Claire's head, silently: Great Uncle Sid, forty-two, muddy-knee'd and booted, studs slipping on a toppling chair and drifts of parlour curtains. And dot dot dot across the map from Godknowswhere to London, Great Granddad crosslegged on the back of a cart, a needle in his fist, a thread between his lips, his beard tucked into his collar. Two small boys squirming, crammed into the dark of a kitchen dresser, passed over.

And then it struck her. She felt a sudden sickening lurch.

"Who told you?" she asked.

"Sorry?"

It came out in a rush, uncensored.

"That it's Ben and Sam. Or Granddad and Great Uncle Sid for that matter. Who told you? You always said Granddad and Grandma died when you were little, so who told you the stories? Your foster-folks can't have known anything."

"I just remember," she said. "From when I was little."

"Ah," Claire said, her jaw tight, catching the flow of words back. "Right." She felt her heart beat thickly in her chest. Deliberately, she pressed her fingertip down on the paper beside the photograph.

"Go on," she said. "What happened next?"

Her mother breathed in shakily. "Nothing at all . . ." she began. She spoke quickly, leaving no space for Claire to comment, and did not look up. She turned the pages breathlessly. Claire sat in silence, watching the images as they flickered past. Names and faces shifted and slid and as her mother's stories twisted round her she thought she could detect other slips, other lapses, but couldn't be quite sure. The stories melted, the pictures bleached themselves with uncertainty. If they weren't who she said they were, who were these people? The photographs, with their shadows of Claire's face, were of strangers now, looking at her with familiar eyes.

Something else, however, had begun to make sense.

"Why can't Dad know we're doing this?" she asked.

Her mother hesitated a moment, did not look up.

"It upsets him," she said.

"Right," Claire said, and drew her lips back in a smile. She stood up, brushed her trousers down. "Well," she said. "I'll be off then."

The bed squeaked as she stood up. Her mother looked up at her, still flushed. Claire walked out, leaving the door open behind her.

"Claire—"

She unhooked her jacket from its peg by the back door. The latch grated noisily against the doorplate; her father called out something. She walked out into the rain. She would head up to the reservoir. It would be quiet there. Her feet slipped on the wet cobbles. The rain was cool on her face. She breathed.

SIX

※

Alan glanced at his watch for the fifth time in five minutes. The hands didn't seem to have moved. They were still standing resolutely at a quarter to eleven. He sighed, glanced up at the telescreen timetable. It still showed, beside the number of the bus, the increasingly irritating phrase "On time."

Alan did not like bus stations, particularly at night. He felt very uncomfortable. The bench was metal and cold; he could feel it through the seat of his trousers. The air was dirty with smoke and over-use. Three seats down from him a wino slept, wrapped in a dirty parka. The smell of sweated alcohol and old clothes made Alan's nostrils quiver. Alan stared anxiously at the shiny dirt of the sleeper's jeans, the battered trainers, the way he shivered in his sleep. At any moment he might wake up and start hassling him for money.

The coach was already fifteen minutes late and there had

been no announcements. He could well be stuck there all night. Part of him hoped that he would be; or at least for an hour or so, so that he would have a good reason to feel angry. He could not believe he had agreed to meet her there. What had possessed him? What was the point? There were plenty of taxis lined up on Glengall Street; he had passed them on the way in. It wasn't as if they were lurking there to take unsuspecting English girls hostage. She could have jumped in a cab, told them the address and she would have got to the flat in five minutes, ten minutes, tops. Right now, he would have been reclining comfortably on the sofa with a cup of tea and a Jaffa Cake watching *The Clive Anderson Show*. Instead, he had had to perch on this cold metal bench for a quarter of an hour, staring down the concourse of the stuffy, grimy bus station, expecting at any moment to be asked for ten pence for a cup of tea.

Headlights swept the dark tarmac. The coach rounded the corner, swung across the forecourt, and pulled up at Gate 17. The engine shut off with a rattle. Alan stood up reluctantly, not sure if he should feel relieved or even more annoyed. He walked slowly over towards the automatic doors, careful not to get close enough to make them slide open. It was cold outside. He didn't want to stand waiting in a draught. The coach door hissed open and the driver jumped down. He walked along the flank of the bus and swung open the boot. He began lobbing out bags and suitcases, tartan shopping-bags on wheels, rucksacks. Alan watched the passengers get off. A young couple with a baby, a dribble of elderly unsteady women, and some scruffy, denimed student-types. They all gathered round the side of the bus, picking through the baggage. Then, through the curved coach windscreen, he saw Claire coming down the steps. She walked out onto the tarmac. She seemed unsteady on her feet, she looked frail. He realised suddenly that he was surprised by her. She had managed, somehow, to seem unfamiliar. She was smaller than he had remembered. She was slender. Delicate even. He had never noticed before. If she wasn't his girlfriend already, he realised, he would have fancied her.

She stood at the back of the crowd, waiting for her bags. Alan watched her slim straight back for a minute, then glanced at his watch again. They would be there all night if she didn't push her way through. The young couple were already strapping their baby into its push-chair, the old ladies were navigating their way through the crowd, their bags bumping and knocking against shins, and a couple of the younger lot had hitched their rucksacks up onto their backs and were marching off down towards the taxi rank. The crush was clearing and still Claire stood there, waiting. Why didn't she shove past the others and grab her bags? There would be no taxis left at this rate. He drummed his fingers against his thighs, frowned, rocked back on his heels. Finally, she moved forward. He watched her thread her way between the remaining passengers, towards the driver. Alan didn't hear her speak, but she must have said something because the driver smiled at her. He was, Alan noticed, quite young. He lifted up a rucksack and held it out towards her. He spoke and she came closer and turned her back to him. He held the weight of the bag as she slipped the straps up over her arms. She said something over her shoulder to him and the man laughed. Alan took a step forward. The electric doors slid open with a blast of cold air. Claire glanced over. She saw him. She smiled. She bent and picked up two more bags from the tarmac and spoke again to the driver. This time Alan heard the words:

"Thank you. Goodnight."

And she turned, started to head for the doors.

As she came towards him, the last grains of his ambivalence crumbled away. He suddenly realised, for the first time, that she was, in fact, beautiful. The idea was startling, even terrifying. Even that evening nearly a year ago, when she had taken off her clothes for him to draw her, when she was utterly new and unknown to him, he hadn't really thought that she was *beautiful.* He had wanted her, right enough, but that was different. Perhaps, he thought, he'd been so focused on his thesis that he'd been unable to look past it, and see her properly. Perhaps her spell at home had refreshed and revitalised her, and she actually looked better than she used to. Perhaps she had lost weight. Alan couldn't be sure, but from the moment he knew that she was beautiful, he was filled with an unfamiliar and unpleasant sensation. A lurking, inexplicit terror. It made his teeth ache and his skin crawl. From that moment on, he was never quite rid of it. He never quite identified it. He never even really thought about it. It didn't occur to him that he might be jealous.

As she walked towards him, upright beneath the weight of her rucksack and bags, a small smile played on her lips, and Alan watched the way her hips swayed, and felt that it was intended for the bus driver's appreciation, and that her smile was just a little too self-satisfied. So she thought that he wouldn't notice. She thought that she could fool him. Anger suddenly bubbled up inside him like indigestion. How dare she, right in front of him, flirt with a *bus driver?* Had she no standards at all? And who else had she been flirting with while he was out of the way? His stomach lurched; he felt hot. What if it wasn't just flirting. What if she had *really* taken advantage of their time apart. What if she had been seeing someone else. What if she had *slept* with someone else. *What if she had been fucking all round her?* He felt his face burn. All the ignorant hamfaced yokels from the village. Shit on their shoes and accents like treacle. Hung like horses, too, probably. He gritted his teeth. His head began to throb. She wouldn't. She wouldn't.

She stopped in front of him. She dropped the bags down on the cigaretty floor. He kissed her angrily and quickly on the lips.

"Hi," she said.

"Hi." Her skin, he noticed, looked pale yellow in the artificial light. There were shadows underneath her eyes.

"Long journey," she said.

"Yeah." He glared at her, then looked angrily away. Even washed-out with travelling, she was beautiful. "Come on," he said. "There'll be no cabs left."

She picked up her bags and followed him down the concourse.

Mum and Dad had taken her to the Blackpool Illuminations. An autumn evening with a heaving dark sky. The gale had buffeted the little car. She had sat in the back gazing up at the coloured bulbs as they swung and rattled in the wind. She had felt safe and warm and proud of the brave, fragile lights that looked as if at any moment they might break themselves against each other, but always managed not to.

When they turned inland and the multi-coloured bulbs were replaced by orange streetlamps, white-lit windows, traffic-lights, Claire was melted by a vision of completion.

The world, containing her, her mother and father, their little metal car, the bright lights, the dark, the wind, and Blackpool there every day of the year, seemed suddenly whole and meaningful. She felt expansive and alive, as if she could wrap herself around everything. She felt suddenly happy, and at home.

The sensation had faded gradually as they left the bright town and suburbs behind them, and began the long drive in the dark. She had woken as the car turned into the driveway and stopped, a vague and anxious ache all that was left of her revelation.

The ache, but not the memory, returned as she sat in the back of the black taxi, looking out at the new city. After the rural dark of home, Belfast seemed brilliant with light. The cab sped them through pools of music, gusts of noise. A fluorescent strip spelt out the name *Dempseys*. Red dots formed the letters of a message and scrolled away before Claire could read it. A car passed them, windows down. Claire didn't hear the music but felt the visceral throb of the bassline. Along the pavements, underneath the brown-leafed trees, people were walking, talking, dressed as though this were Italy, and June. Ahead, high up, a giant telescreen flickered. They were past it before she could put the images together into sense.

Alan was staring out of the window. She could only see the back of his head, his pale neck as he leaned round, away from her. He hadn't spoken a word to her since they left the bus station. He would tell her, sooner or later, what she'd done. She didn't like the wait, but it was better than the row that would inevitably follow.

"How are you?" she asked tentatively.

"Fine."

So he wouldn't even speak to her. And she knew that if she

spoke she'd only wind him up even more. She leaned back in the seat, caught herself mid-sigh. The engine's rattle dropped as the driver slowed and shifted down a gear.

The road faded left, up a slight incline. As they passed, she glimpsed a Spar sign, a railway station, a Salsa club. There were trees. Some thick trunks, some slender, surrounded by a protective metal mesh. Lime trees, Claire guessed, by the shape of them. And more cafés, more bars. As the taxi slowed to turn she looked through the bright-lit window of a crowded restaurant and saw an elegant grey-haired woman sipping on a slender cigar. The woman glanced towards the window, smiled. For a moment Claire thought that she was smiling at her. She smiled back, then realised that the glass, lit brighter on the inside, would reflect. The woman was smiling to herself.

The taxi took the left-hand turn, then almost immediately turned right into a poorly lit side street. The trees here were bigger, heavier. There were cars parked nose-to-tail the length of the street. The taxi pulled over, engine rattling. In the dark, between parked cars and trees, Claire could see a flat-faced redbrick terrace.

"We're here," Alan said.

The bedroom smelt as if it were permanently dark. The bed was small, not quite a double. She lay awake beside Alan's heavy body, listening to the calls and laughter and shouted conversation on the street. She couldn't quite catch the words. Footsteps passed and repassed the window. Alan's breath became heavy and slow. She heard a distant car alarm, a door bang shut.

Cautiously, she turned on her side. She lay, eyes open, facing the wall.

She woke with the buzzing of the alarm clock and the lurch of the bed as Alan heaved himself out. She watched him walk away, down the room, scratching his hip. His blue-striped pyjamas were crumpled. She heard him lock himself into the bathroom.

She lay for a moment, becoming aware of her body. The blankets had got pulled up in the night, leaving just a sheet covering her feet. Her toes were cold. Her nose had an outdoors kind of chill. She stretched a hand over to Alan's side of the bed. It was warm, but faintly damp and uninviting. She crawled over the crumpled sheet and out of bed. Her bags were in a heap by the door. She padded over, dragged out a jumper and pulled it on over her pyjamas. She went through to the living room. Alan had already flicked on the electric fire. One bar glowed in the dim room. She walked down the corridor, past the bathroom, into the kitchen. Dark, dirty and cold. She heard the toilet flush, the burst of water as the shower was turned on. She set out things for breakfast on the kitchen table. Bowl, spoon, Weetabix, milk. The shower's hiss ceased. She heard the rattle and splash as he ran a basinful of water, then the tap of razor against ceramic. The cistern groaned and gurgled, refilling itself. She put the kettle on, heard the scrape of the bathroom door-lock, then Alan's footsteps as he walked back to the bedroom. She dropped teabags into the teapot. The kettle clicked off; she poured the water over the teabags. She watched the brown dye seeping out.

She heard his heavy tread as he walked back down the

corridor. He came into the kitchen. He was wearing a black
poloneck and trousers. She had never seen the clothes before.
His hair was scraped back, the tooth-marks of his comb still
visible; his scalp showed pinkly through the hair. He sat down
at the table. He peeled the plastic wrapping off the Weetabix,
dropped two biscuits into his bowl. He doused them with
milk.

"Sleep well?" she asked.

"Yes."

Alan leant low over his bowl, spooning Weetabix into his
mouth. She sipped her tea, watched the wallpaper-pattern
dance.

"I'm teaching at nine," he said. He glanced at his watch.

"Are you all sorted out for it?" she asked.

"Yes."

Claire nodded.

"I told you you've got to go down to Conroys sometime
today."

"Conroys?"

"I did tell you. I got you a job." Alan spooned up more of
the milky slush. Liquid dripped from the spoon back into his
bowl. He looked up at her coldly. Claire took another sip of
her tea.

"What kind of job?" she asked.

"I don't know. I left the address by the phone. Any time
after eleven, he said. You'll have plenty of time to find the
place."

"What kind of place is it?" she asked cautiously. "What
do they do?"

"It's a pub," Alan said. "They sell beer."

He had finished his breakfast. He stood up, scraping back

his chair. Claire put his bowl in the sink and stood there numbly, looking at the bowl, the tea-stained metal sink, her own cold hand. He walked out of the kitchen. She heard him moving around the flat. The wardrobe door opened with a squeak, was shut again. The bedroom door tapped shut. She looked up from the sink, up the hallway towards the living room. She couldn't see him, but could still hear him moving around. The creak of his jeans, a sharp exhalation as he bent down to pull on his shoes. He muttered a few words under his breath, reminding himself of something. She walked cautiously down the hall. He was pulling on a tweed jacket, tugging down the sleeves. It was neat, new. She had never seen it before. He picked up an armful of papers from the coffee table.

"I'll be back around six."

"Right."

"There's a spare set of keys in the kitchen drawer."

"Right."

He turned towards the door.

"See you," she said.

"Yeah. See you."

The flat door slammed behind him, then, a moment later, the door onto the street. She didn't move, didn't think. The cold made her gradually aware of herself. A shiver was gathering between her shoulder blades. Her toes were almost numb. The skin on her legs crawled. Her nose was icy. But the mug in her hand, she realised, was still hot. It was burning her skin. She looked round for somewhere to put it down.

The shelves were full. Alan's books. Hardback covers black like carapaces, paperback thrillers, broken and papery along the spines. The table was covered in computer; pale tangled wires and flexes trailed away from the machine like worms. The coffee table was cluttered with files and papers and polythene envelopes. On the narrow mantelpiece, above the boarded-up fireplace, was Alan's graduation photograph.

She walked through to the bedroom. Three paces. She set her mug down on the chest of drawers. Alan's comb, deodorant and aftershave were arranged on a cotton doily on the top. She sat down on the bed. Her feet looked pale and bluish. Beneath her feet, the carpet was dirty and patterned with obscure red whorls. She followed the pattern with her eyes across the room, towards the door. Her bags still piled up in a heap. Clothes, books, linen.

Any time after eleven, he had said.

She stood up slowly, walked across the room. She took her rucksack by the strap and, backing away, dragged it out to the middle of the floor. She knelt beside the bag and took the metal tab of the zip between her thumb and forefinger. She could hardly feel it. She dragged the zip across, pushed her hand down through the layers of fabric. She picked out her clothes one by one, laid them out on the carpet. Small piles formed around her. T-shirts, knickers, trousers, jumpers. Her other pair of shoes.

It seemed to take a long time. It seemed to be inordinately hard work. It took an incredible effort just to take hold of a corner of a cotton T-shirt and drag it out of the bag. Her feet and legs grew numb underneath her. The rucksack emptied. She saw sand-coloured canvas at the bottom. She reached in, felt around: there was nothing left. Around her the clothes had piled up like fortifications, walling her in. She wanted to stand, to step out over the ramparts, but when she heaved herself up she found that her legs had gone dead and there was nowhere to put her feet. She lurched, staggered, stumbled on her clothes, then subsided onto the bed. She sat looking vaguely at the emptied bag, the precarious piles of clothing, at her pale numb feet. Everything looked odd, like it wasn't hers, like it belonged to someone else. She became dimly aware of the blood beginning to prickle through her numb muscles. It was unstoppable; it would flush them pink and full. And that too felt somehow wrong, somehow distant. As if she were not feeling it herself. As if she were feeling it felt. And as the nerves in her toes and feet and calves came back to life, they registered an ache, they registered cold. And that, at last, seemed real.

She heaved herself up off the bed, bent down again, slid her hand under a heap of clothes and crushed them up against her chest. She walked stiffly over to the chest of drawers. She opened each drawer in turn, then closed each of them again. Every one of them was full. Slowly, she turned to the wardrobe, took the metal handle between her fingertips and pulled the door open. Jackets and trousers jammed up tightly together. No space. She looked back across the room at the dark open mouth of her rucksack, at the uneven stacks of clothes. She walked back over to the bag, dropped her armful back into it, then bent to shovel in the rest of the clothes. She pushed the rucksack back into the corner.

She picked up her mug and walked the three paces back through to the living room. Her tea had gone cold.

She went over to the window, drew back the curtains. Light came in slices through the treads of a metal fire-escape. Beyond, the algaed green of a damp back-yard wall. She felt unclean, as if covered by a thin grey film of dirt. Her hair, hanging round her face, felt heavy, greasy. She walked through to the bathroom. She felt as if she was watching herself walk through to the bathroom.

She turned on the shower. The room began to fill with steam. The shower was above the bath. The bath was pale yellow, greasy with dirt. There were two oily marks where Alan's feet went every morning. A bottle of medicated shampoo, its lid off, stood on the side of the bath. On the wash-hand basin, a bar of Shield lay in a clotted pool of blue slime. The taps were spotted with spat-out toothpaste. Sandy-ginger stubble stuck to the greasy ceramic. Lying on its side in a pool of gritty foam, was a silver-handled, fixed-head razor.

Beside it was a neat little plastic box. Claire watched her pale hand pick the box up. She watched her other hand move across to open it. The fingers pulled out a precise paper envelope, an inch long, and unfurled it. A clean cold razorblade. It was unfamiliar, odd-looking: the sharp edges looked innocent. It was the gap inside, the absence, that looked threatening, that looked like it might bite. Claire watched herself pick up the blade, fingertips pressing together through the space. She saw herself walk across the room and slide the bolt across the door. She sat down on the edge of the bath, but didn't feel the hard plastic through her thin pyjamas.

Slowly, almost thoughtfully, as if to see what would happen, Claire lifted her left leg, laid her ankle on her right thigh. Her pyjama leg fell back and revealed the smooth swelling of the calf muscle. Short, stubby hairs grew out of the skin, lay flat against it, where she had shaved herself, two days ago, in England, with a disposable blue razor. The anklebone seemed to press out against the membrane; the bone seemed almost visible. She cut a straight line across the thin skin.

She was surprised by the quantity of blood. It welled up

immediately, before she had even finished the cut. It ran down over the ankle, dripping onto the knee, splashing onto the dirty lino. For a moment she just sat and watched, fascinated and delighted by the brightness and the heat that was pulsing out of her. Then she began to giggle. Because it looked so dramatic. Because she had made such a mess. Because it was, in fact, so easy.

She glanced round the bathroom for something to sop up the blood. The toilet roll was sitting on top of the cistern. She hobbled over, wound tissue round her hand, held it against the cut. With her free hand she rummaged in the mirrored cabinet for plasters. She found one, lying flat on the shelf, probably left by the previous tenant. She opened it, stuck it on.

She glanced back across the room, saw a trail of blood, dot-and-carry-one, across the floor. Droplets of blood clung to the panel of the bath. There was a tiny red pool by the toilet, another one at her feet. There was blood on her pyjamas, blood on her hands. Next time, she thought, I'm going to have to be more careful. But looking at her bloody skin, feeling the cut glow with pain, she knew at last that she was alive, and real, and hurting.

Alan sat at his office desk and drank deeply from his cup of instant coffee. His throat was sore and his mouth was dry from the morning's work, but he was happy. The two-hour seminar had passed quickly. He had not stopped talking the entire time. And, as usual, it had gone right over their heads. He remembered the look of glazed incomprehension on his students' faces and smiled to himself. Philosophy was supposed to be difficult. It was supposed to be a rigorous, demanding, scholarly subject. He had sweated blood to get where he was. And he was buggered if he was going to make it any easier for anyone else.

He lifted his legs up, crossed them on the desk. He congratulated himself on arranging the job at Conroys for Claire. It amounted to foresight of prodigious proportions. Spooky almost, since he had done it before the meeting at the bus station. Or perhaps he had suspected her all along, subconsciously. Anyway, Gareth was an old friend. He wouldn't let her get away with anything. And he would probably notice what Claire was up to long before Alan would. Because, Alan had come to realise, he was not particularly observant. Gareth would be better at keeping an eye on her: he wouldn't suffer from abstraction in the way Alan did. And, perhaps most importantly, Alan realised with a shudder, Gareth wouldn't fancy Claire himself. He was, he thought, the ideal boss for his girlfriend. The pub situation was not perfect of course; lots of pissed men looking for an easy shag. But she would be busy, and she would be tired. She wouldn't have the time or energy to flaunt herself. Alan, if he hadn't been holding a cup of coffee in one of his hands, might have rubbed them together in satisfaction. Instead, he smiled grimly to himself, pulled open his desk drawer, and reached in for his packet of shortbread fingers.

Now, he thought, as he munched stickily on his biscuit, was the time to start calling people up. Now was the time to start socialising. Now she was here, he could display his happiness. He'd show them. Everyone who ever thought they were doing better than him. He listed his achievements in his head. Ph.D., job, girlfriend, flat. Claire was the only one that he could bring out for the evening to show people, unless of course he took his letter of appointment with him and wore his gown to the pub. And now, he thought, he had another reason to call people up and arrange a night out. He would show her how reasonable he was. How forgiving. And how popular.

He reached into his jacket pocket and pulled out a tiny plastic-covered address book with the university crest on the front. He licked his finger, leafed through the pages. He picked up the telephone, dialled a number.

"Hello. Can I speak to Paul Quinn please?"

Alan was aware of something different in the flat. He closed the door softly behind him, listening. He could hear voices— she must have the radio on—but that wasn't it. He could smell cooking—rich, warm scents—but that wasn't it either. His stomach grumbled. He was hungry. He went through to the bedroom, hung up his coat in the wardrobe, saw her heap of bags on the floor. She hadn't put anything away. Her stuff took up the entire corner. She was cluttering up the place. She was occupying too much space. That was what he had noticed. A psychic shift. He congratulated himself for once on the fineness of his senses, but decided that he would not take the issue up with her tonight. She could be as inconsiderate as she liked, but he was not going to allow himself to get angry about it. Tonight, he was going to be happy. He was going to be content. He was not going to let her spoil his evening. He closed the bedroom door behind him, walked through the living room and down the corridor to the kitchen.

She was standing at the cooker, her back to him. Her arm, shoulder, hip, moved slightly as she stirred something in a pan. Another pan, lidded, rattled gently on the back ring of the cooker.

She was dressed in dark trousers and a jumper. She looked neat and clean and soft. Her hair was caught up in a ponytail; he could see soft fine hair feathering the nape of her neck. He stepped towards her, put a hand on her hip, kissed the back of her neck.

She jumped. She dropped the spoon. It clattered against the side of the pan.

"Sorry," she said.

"Sorry," he said, irritated. He turned away from her, switched the radio off.

"I didn't hear you come in," she said.

"I noticed."

He sat down at the kitchen table. Her back was to him, so she couldn't see him, but he forced himself to smile anyway. He was determined he wasn't going to let her annoy him. He was going to be happy. He was going to be magnanimous. He was going to be the very model of patience. And he was going to show Paul and all the rest of them what true contentment really was. He smiled more broadly. It was beginning to make his face ache.

She fished the spoon out of the pan, began to stir again. Underneath the dark wool of her jumper her breast shook slightly with the motion of her arm.

"How was your day?" she asked. She did not look round.

"Fine," he said. "Busy."

"I'm making pasta. Is that okay?"

"Fine by me."

"It's just I didn't have much money."

"Right. How did it go at Conroys?"

"I start tomorrow."

Alan nodded. "Good. Just as well. I've arranged something for tonight."

"What's that?"

"We're heading out," he said grandly. "I'm meeting an old friend."

"Oh."

"Paul. Went to school with him. Then uni. He did architecture."

"Oh."

"He's got a girlfriend, apparently. When I told him about you he said he'd bring her along. We're going to Bar Twelve."

The stirring slowed. Her breast stopped shaking.

"Alan, I'm skint."

"Don't worry," Alan said generously. "My treat."

She lifted the other pan and held the lid on at an angle. She drained the starchy water off into the sink. A cloud of steam rose around her. She put the pan down, opened a cupboard, looking for plates.

"Down the bottom there, by your feet," Alan said. Her feet were bare, he noticed. They were stained grey with dirt.

She bent down, opened the cupboard, slid two plates off the pile. She dished out the pasta, poured sauce over each heap. She put a plate down in front of Alan, placed the other across the table from him. Alan waited while she fetched the cutlery.

"What does he look like, Paul?" she asked, handing Alan a fork.

Alan watched her seat herself, watched the blank expression on her face. His heart thumped loud and fast. He could feel it there, underneath his ribs, racing. He should have known this would happen. If he was honest, he thought, he *had* known this would happen. He felt fury rise inside him.

He couldn't look at her any longer. Couldn't stand looking at her beautiful, deceitful face. He leant down over his plate, began shovelling farfalle into his mouth.

"Does it matter?" he said.

"Not really."

Alan stabbed angrily at the pasta, stuffed another forkful into his mouth.

"Well then."

He chewed, scooped up more food onto his fork.

"I was just wondering."

"Right."

"I've never met him."

He glared at her, fork hovering above his plate.

"Of course not."

"So I won't know him when I see him."

Alan put down his fork.

"He's short," he said. "He's got dirty-fair hair. He wears glasses."

"Right."

"You've never met the girlfriend either and you didn't ask about her."

She glanced up at him, then back down at her plate.

"What does she do?" she asked, quietly.

"I don't know. Teacher, I think."

"What's she called?"

"Grainne, apparently." He stuffed the last forkful of food into his mouth. He was still hungry. He looked up.

"That's unusual," she said. She didn't look up from her plate. She didn't seem to have eaten anything.

"No it's not," he said, watching her push the pasta bows around in their pool of sauce. "It's quite common."

"Oh."

"It's an Irish name."

"Right." She put her fork down.

"Don't you want that?" he asked.

"Mn?" Her voice sounded thick.

"The pasta. Don't you want it?"

"Not really."

He reached over and took her plate.

"No point eating it if you're not hungry." He scraped the mess onto his own plate.

Alan didn't know quite what he was looking for. Some extra care, perhaps, in her choice of clothes, or an excessive precision in the painting of lipstick onto lips. He wasn't sure. He was sure, however, that he would know it when he saw it. There would be no fooling him. He sat waiting for her on the sofa, legs crossed, right foot bouncing in mid-air. He glanced every two minutes at the hands of his watch. When the hands had ticked round to eight o'clock, he sprang up and marched through to the bedroom, his knuckles whitening and his eyes narrowed. She had been ages.

"What's taking so long?"

She was just standing there in her knickers and bra, doing nothing. Not her best underwear: they were greyed, and elderly, and didn't match. He could see her ribs rippling the surface of her skin, the knots of her shoulders and the smooth ridge and dip of her collarbone. She had lost weight.

"You have beautiful bones," he said, startling himself, and reached out to touch her.

"Your hands are cold."

She ducked down quickly to hurry on her trousers. His chest tightened with annoyance.

"You're not wearing *them*?"

"I thought I would," she said, pulling a T-shirt over her head.

Alan sat on the edge of the bath. She stood staring at her face in the mirror as if she didn't know what to do with it. She must have done her make-up a million times and tonight, Alan thought, she didn't know where to start. He scowled.

"We'll be late," he said.

She picked up a powder puff and wiped it clumsily across her cheek.

He sat with his arm around her shoulders. He felt vividly conscious of every move and shift she made. She could not keep still. She rolled up till receipts, twisted her hair round her fingers, played with the cellophane off Paul's cigarette packet. And when she spoke, she blushed and stammered and looked down at her twisting, moving fingers.

Tonight, he told himself, he should have been relaxed, and happy, and proud. He should have been showing off his success, at last, to Paul. This was supposed to have been his moment. This should have been his finest hour. And she would not let him have even that. It was all so obvious, so graceless. She might as well have offered Paul a blowjob the moment they arrived. Alan bubbled with fury. And *Paul.* She would have to pick Paul. Paul with his A grades and his elegant girlfriends and his first class degree. Paul whose aura of self-contained contentment had dogged every step that Alan had taken, tainted every disappointing moment of Alan's success. Alan's only consolation was that he had sufficient grace not to let his anger show. And that Paul and Grainne seemed to have decided that they too would pretend nothing was happening.

He tightened his grip around Claire's shoulders. He felt her breathe, and was surprised to find his penis twitch and stir at the rise and fall of her narrow ribcage. This was, Alan felt, completely baffling, and a total pain in the hole. That he could feel so blindingly furious with her, and at the same time want to get her straight home and into bed. He pulled uncomfortably at his trouserleg.

"So where are you from, then?" Paul asked her. Alan felt her squirm, gritted his teeth.

"North of England," she said.

"You don't have much of an accent."

"I've lived in Oxford three years. And Mum and Dad aren't local." Alan watched in irritation the small hand that reached out and picked up a beermat. She began to pull it into shreds.

"Yous're blow-ins, then," Paul said.

"Blow-ins?"

"If you're not locals, you're blow-ins. Blown in on the wind," he explained.

Claire smiled.

"Offcomer. That's the word they use at home."

Alan snorted.

"That's the English," Paul asked, "for blow-in?"

"I think it's more of a local word," Claire said. "I've never heard it said anywhere else. Just at home."

"Where you're a blow-in," said Alan.

"An offcomer, you mean," said Grainne, smiling.

"Same as here," said Paul.

"Same as Oxford," said Alan.

"Yep," Claire said. She picked up her drink, brought it towards her lips. "That's about the size of it."

SEVEN

It must have been a Thursday because there was always double games on a Thursday and the whole memory was permeated by the sour odour of PE. And it must have been Third Year, because as she sat on the school bus next to Jennifer, they had both had their hockeysticks clamped between their knees and after Third Year, girls like Jennifer joined the school team, and girls like Claire were allowed to give up hockey altogether. And if they were playing hockey, it must have been the winter, so she wouldn't yet have had her fourteenth birthday. And Nick, Jen's brother, was sitting behind them on the bus. He left school after Fifth Year, so they must have been in Third, and Claire must have been thirteen when she had first told Jennifer.

"I didn't know you were Jewish," Jennifer had said.

"Not really Jewish. Mum wasn't brought up Jewish. Her foster family brought her up C. of E. And Dad's not Jewish, so I'm more of a mix, a mongrel. I'm Jewishish." And Nick had leaned over the chrome rail on the back of their seat and howled in Claire's ear.

Double History with Mr. Lownes. Room 21. That must have been Friday, then, or the following week. Jennifer had Miss Nelson for History. Her class was in room 19. They had thumped up the dirty stairs together, separated at the top.

The classroom was already full. It was dark outside. The big windows reflected back the room. She walked across to her desk, conscious of her movement, her reflection on the windowpane. She sat down. The seat next to hers was empty. It was still empty when Mr. Lownes arrived. It remained empty until the bell went. Sandra, who usually sat there, was sitting on the far side of the room, next to Sally Parry. She did not look up.

On the bus home, Nick started chanting. A stupid, moron chant, Claire told herself. It didn't matter, because he was a stupid moron and what could you expect. *"Little Jew Girl, Little Jew Girl,"* he sang, over and over again, leaning over the back of her seat and pulling at her hair and tugging on her brastrap and shouting it in her ear, and a couple of his mates started shouting too, and Jen turned round and screamed at him and everyone was staring and some of them were laughing and the big girls at the back were laughing. And she could feel her ears were burning and as they walked down the aisle he followed them, getting louder and louder and she didn't know where to look and there were games bags in the way and she stumbled and felt sticky and didn't know where to put her feet.

The bus lights swung away and left them standing at the lane end. Claire blinked, hitched up her hockeystick and turned towards the village. She heard Nick inhale open-mouthed, and, hot with misery, she turned back to snap at him, but before either of them could speak, Jennifer had leapt upon her brother. She grabbed handfuls of his hair and tore at it, screaming in his face, calling him a little shit and a dickhead and a stupid wanker. He gripped her fingers, trying to prize them off, his mouth now wide open, howling, eyes squeezed shut, kicking at her shins. She jabbed her knee neatly into his groin. He sank down onto the tarmac.

"Me goolies, me goolies," he wheezed, deflating.

"Mam says I'm not allowed to do that," Jen said, shouldering her games kit. "But sometimes you just have to."

Big purple bruises blossomed on Jennifer's shins, faded with the days to yellow flushed with pink. Claire swelled with pride every time she thought of them. Whatever anyone said, she wouldn't mind, now. She wouldn't mind anything. Jen had wanted to protect her. That, in itself, was wondrous. And anyway, Claire thought, she hadn't changed, so she couldn't change back. It was in her, in the spiralling strands in her blood and bone and marrow. It was there, always had been, always would.

So she was thirteen. She'd probably told Jennifer soon after she'd found out herself. So that left thirteen years to account for, thirteen years in which she had been unaware of Ben and Sam, crammed in between the pudding basins and the baking trays. Thirteen years before she'd heard about what had seemed, until this moment, to have been laid down in the deepest stratum of her knowledge.

The rain had stopped. Claire looked out across the flat surface of the reservoir, scuffed her hand in the grit. Her fingers found a pebble; she lifted it, lobbed it out across the water. Tiny ripples spread back towards her.

It could, easily, be just one of who knew how many fantasies, this Jewishness. For thirteen years, when Claire was a child, a baby, even before she was born, her mother might have been weaving away at any number of stories. Back before then, while she herself was still a child, standing out like a tasteless joke amongst the blond endomorphs of her foster family, her mother might have dreamed up a dozen different ways of explaining her own dark hair, dark eyes, pale olive skin. One year her forebears might have been Arab merchants, bringing silks and spices along the land route from Asia; the next year, she would have had an obscure Spanish ancestor, a sailor wrecked on English shores with the Armada. Another time, Romany. Cross her palm with silver, tell your fortune. And then time to up sticks again and move on. She would have found a dozen different reasons why her family would have had to change its name to something plain and English. But maybe even Taylor was a lie. Perhaps her maiden name had already changed a dozen times, and might change again. And Claire's father would have heard all these stories over the years, and knew that she was lying, and right now he would be bursting with frustration that he couldn't tell Claire.

The ripples faded, flattened. Above her, on the fell, a sheep called out baritone, was answered by a yearling's tenor.

Maybe not. Maybe for thirteen years there were no stories, just a hand-me-down knowledge that came from all the way back, through the fosterers and the children's homes, from the time before. Along with the album, a faint remnant thread of truth. Ben and Sam's story was just a way of telling, a parable in fact, made up to communicate something abstract and unfamiliar to a child. And it was a good story. It was believable. If more had happened in it, it would have seemed less real.

And the thirteen years, well, you had to wait, didn't you. You always do. People always save up this kind of information till you're old enough to understand, and still far too young to tell them to shut up, to ask them what the fuck they think they're doing telling you at all. And her mother, in particular, had had good reason to hesitate: this was, after all, no uncomplicated heritage, no restoration of tradition: this was, instead, an initiation in loss, a lesson in fracture. She had had to wait, because Claire had to be old enough, old enough to understand that loss.

The damp concrete beneath her was cold.

Claire scratched up a handful of gravel, scuffing her nails. She flung it out across the reservoir. The grit hit the surface like a squall of rain. She felt heavy, empty. She had, she realised, never grieved for them before. All those years she had looked at the pictures and heard the stories and known that these people were dead, and she had never felt bereaved. But now, suddenly, they were gone, and she missed them. She missed the pair of little boys who wriggled and complained in their hiding-place. She missed her schoolboy-Granddad's muddied knees, his gaptooth grin and Uncle Sid's arm around his shoulder. She missed Aunty May with her folded-in lips and folded-back arms. She missed the imagined dotted line on her mental map that had traced her great-grandfather's footsteps from Poland to South London. The stories had died. The people died with them.

The reservoir reflected back the grey sky and the deep perspective of the hills. Years ago, someone had handed her a new OS map, folded and refolded, still crisp along the seams. She couldn't remember the hand that passed it to her, or who had watched her face as she puzzled it out. Her father, it must have been. He was, after all, the teacher. Mum would just have told her, straight out, this is how it is.

"What can you see?"

She had looked at the map for a long moment, wondering if this was a trick, a game. Then, suddenly, the puzzle solved itself. The village she had grown up in was not marked. The reservoir was not there. Where it should have been, she saw a small reedy tarn, another village on its bank.

"But the reservoir's been there for ages."

"Yes?"

"I mean, the map's brand new, but it still shows the old village. If you didn't know the place—"

"—you'd get completely lost. You're right. You see, they just keep on printing the maps, just keep churning them out without checking, but all the time everything keeps changing."

Where was that, when? Were they out walking, catching their breath in the wind on Rise Hill? Were they emptying the clutter from the kitchen drawer and had just come across the map, amongst brown windowed envelopes, lighter flints and forgotten keys? It must have been him, before the illness, but she couldn't quite remember, couldn't catch the face that must have been looking down at her.

She threw another speck of gravel, heard the puck sound as it hit the surface. She heaved herself up. Her trousers were soaked through again; they stuck to her. Her hair was wet. Water trickled through to her scalp. She slid down off the dam. Heading downhill, she dug her heels into the wet earth, her eyes turned towards the mossy, slated roof of Jennifer's old house.

Hand on the gate, she looked up at the door. Its dimpled glass panels distorted the striped porch wallpaper inside. The glass always made it look as if Jennifer came to answer the door in a cloud of coloured blotches, which resolved themselves into Jen only when the door opened and she smiled out at you. You always felt like you'd conjured her up. But Jennifer wouldn't be there. If Claire walked up the path and rang the bell and waited, it would be Mrs. Rothwell who eventually peered out. Jen would be in New York or Stockholm or Bali or somewhere. Or Birmingham. She might even be in Birmingham. Wherever she was, she would be bright and breezy and buoyant, full of business, full of whatever it was she was up to. Stupid to imagine she might be there, waiting for Claire to call, that they could slip off up to the reservoir again and pull it all back together. That they could make it fit.

Through the distorting glass, Mrs. Rothwell was smeary fragments of pink and blue. She pulled the door open, stepped out, rummaging in her handbag. She turned, saw Claire, and her mouth fell open.

"Claire!"

"Hello, Mrs. Rothwell."

As Jennifer's mother came down the path towards her, Claire smelt the familiar scent of mince and fruit jelly. Mrs. Rothwell was a dinner lady at the primary school.

"Back from Ireland." She stopped at the gate, zipped up her anorak.

"Yes."

"I always knew it was a bad idea. I warned your mother. I told her it wasn't safe."

"I'm fine," Claire said.

"Well, it's just as well you came back when you did." She smiled sympathetically. There was pink lipstick on her flat front teeth. "I don't know why we don't just pull out. Anyone who isn't Irish has no real business being there, do they? They should all move back to Britain if they're so keen on being British. That's what I say."

"It's not quite like that, Mrs. Rothwell."

"Well, that's what I say, anyway." Mrs. Rothwell put her hand to the gatelatch. "Are you looking for Jennifer? She's not here."

"No, I know."

"I keep on telling her to get on the phone. It's such a pain not being able to call her. You may as well wander over though, she's probably in. It's a bit of a hike, but you know that anyway."

"Sorry?"

"You know where it is, don't you, Gorse Cottage?" Mrs. Rothwell continued. "Up that track on the right, just before Braithwaites' farm."

Mrs. Rothwell opened the gate. Claire stepped awkwardly aside to let her pass.

"Well, it's nice to see you," Mrs. Rothwell said. "I'm sure Jennifer will be delighted."

Claire nodded, lips folded in against her teeth. Mrs. Rothwell stood, smiling, waiting for her to go, and there was nothing for it but to turn and set off in the direction she had indicated.

❖

Claire followed the shore road. She walked warily, unsure of the ground beneath her. More than ever, the hills looked unconvincing, like they were painted onto canvas. The whole valley seemed to be made up of theatrical flats that could at any moment be lifted, shifted, whisked away. And the angle and camber of the road, the overhead segment of the sky all seemed to have, unnoticed, heaved a sigh and settled back ever so slightly different. She looked around her suspiciously. If it happened again, she wanted to catch it happening.

A drystone wall ran along the edge of the road, between her and the backdrop. As she walked, Claire ran a hand along the wall, brushing her fingertips over warm stone, cool moss, flaky lichen. The wall seemed real enough. It was warm; it felt almost alive. It seemed to swell with breath, to pulse. She twitched her hand away, stuffed it in her pocket. Everything was wrong; everything was strange. She resisted the urge to run.

She passed the head of the reservoir, followed the bend round into the dale. The road twisted out ahead of her, following the course of the beck. Half a mile ahead, it crossed the beck with a bump of a bridge, then hugged the far bank until it reached its terminus. A cluster of barns roofed with rusting corrugated iron, and the low, slated pitch of the farmhouse. Braithwaites'. By the bridge, a chalky track opened off to the right and crept up the steep hill. Gorse Cottage was at the end of the track. You couldn't see it from the road.

Claire hadn't been to the cottage for years. The last time was, perhaps, that party, when Tom had first moved in. And that was what, six, seven years ago now. Jennifer had done

Claire's make-up that night and lent her clothes, peeling them off the floor and handing them to her; she watched herself in the mirror as she changed. Walking up together with beer bottles clinking in their bags, Claire had felt a cloud of Jennifer's scent cling to her like a Ready-Brek glow. They had sat out in the garden as it grew dark and got dizzily drunk on Newcastle Brown, rolling their empty bottles away down the sloping grass. Later, Claire had thrown up in the bushes and fallen asleep on the sofa. She had long since stopped thinking about the uncomfortable, barely remembered loss of her virginity. It was just bumping into Nick that she didn't like.

The gravel rolled and skidded out from under her feet. The hill was steep. A sudden helix shift and it seemed as if she was crawling painfully down towards the sky. She became aware of a regular, echoing pulse. It was coming from up ahead, from the cottage. She could just see the wooden fence, silvered with age, and the end wall of the house. The noise grew louder. It sounded metallic, gritty. She rounded the last corner, came to the crest of the slope.

Tom Braithwaite was sitting on his doorstep, a block of pale limestone between his booted feet, a chisel in one hand, a mallet in the other. His arm rose and fell, beating out the chimes that Claire had heard. Tiny flakes of stone flew into the air, dust hung in a cloud around him. He seemed absorbed, content. She stood watching, trying to work out what he was making. He must have sensed her: he looked up. The mallet stopped, suspended above the haft of the chisel. He smiled.

"Well," he said. He put down his tools, ran his hand over the curve of the rock. Claire came up to the gate.

"Hi."

"Come in, come in." He stood up, rubbed a hand through

his dusty hair, then brushed off his dark jeans. "How are you? We weren't expecting you."

We?

"I'm fine," she said.

"You'll be after Jenny, then?"

Jenny?

"Yes."

He smiled again. His teeth, Claire noticed, were white and strong-looking. From breathing all that calcium dust, she thought.

"She's at work," he said.

"Ah," Claire said, and glanced down at her hands.

"At the pub," Tom explained. "You can catch her down there. She's not too busy, mornings."

This was all wrong.

"Or you could wait. She won't be too long. I'll put the kettle on. Come in."

"No, no. Thanks."

Claire turned to go.

"Well, you'll most likely meet her on the road."

"Right."

"She'll be glad to see you," Tom called after her. "She's been missing you."

This was all so wrong. Claire shivered.

Out of sight, she slithered down the gravel track at a half-run, reached the shore road. Setting off along it, she found herself breaking into an anxious, rib-clutching trot, her feet slapping down hard on the tarmac, her chest raw. Jen was here, she was definitely here somewhere, and everything was out of kilter. At the dam, the road dipped down into the valley and as she ran she could see again the mossy pitch of Jen's house; nearer, the pub's slated roof glistened wetly. The cloud was breaking up, the rain had ceased. Striding stiff-legged and breathless down the last slope, her arm wrapped around her stitch, she felt an ache in her bones and a tightness in her throat and lungs. She hadn't had a cigarette, she realised, since she last saw Jen, but for some reason she was desperate for one now. She stopped at the corner, leant against the wall. She coughed, spat, waited as the cramp in her chest eased. Association, she thought. I associate associating with Jen with smoking cigarettes.

The front door was open. She slipped through.

It was dark inside. Even after the dubious light of the summer afternoon, she had to stop and wait for a moment while her pupils readjusted. A slim figure, back towards her, was bending over a low table. An aerosol can was shaken, polish sprayed and wiped across the surface with a duster. Dark jeans, dark top. Hair caught up in a bun on the back of her head.

"Jen?" Claire said, uncertain.

The young woman straightened, turned.

"Bloody hell," she said. A half-second's hesitation, then she came up to Claire, wrapped her arms around her and squeezed, almost lifting her off her feet, duster and spraycan still clutched in her hands. "Bloody Hell!"

Claire's arms were crushed to her sides, her cheek was pressed against still-damp hair. She closed her eyes, breathed in the clean smells of shampoo and furniture-polish and washing-powder. Her throat tightened.

"Fuck, you've got thin," Jennifer said, loosening her grip. She looked Claire gravely in the face. "You're skin and bones." She let her go, set her duster and polish down on the table.

"Nah," Claire grinned back at her, happy with relief. "Same as ever." This was Jen. No question about it. Whatever Tom said, this was still Jen.

"How long you back for?"

"I don't know yet."

"Where's Alan?"

Claire shrugged. "There's no Alan anymore."

"Well thank fuck for that. Did you take him out yourself or did you get someone else to do it? Should've asked me. I'd've done it for free. I'd've paid *you*." Jennifer, grinning, put a hand on the round of Claire's shoulder, shook her gently. Claire's nose prickled. A moment's silence, then Jen laughed.

"How the fuck are you?" she asked, with another shake.

"I'm okay."

"And how's The Emerald Isle?"

"It's grey."

"We should come over and see you sometime." Jennifer released her, moved across the room towards the bar.

"You should. Of course. You should."

Jen lifted a hatch in the counter, slid through. She walked back down the bar's length to face Claire. She smiled.

"It's good to see you."

"It's good to see you."

"Is it weird, being back?"

"Yeah. It's weird."

Jennifer nodded towards the taps. "What are you having?"

"It's a bit early, isn't it?"

"It's early-ish, I s'pose."

"Are you having one?"

"You bet ya. This is a celebration, you know: it's not every day I have you back." She rested her hands on the counter, businesslike. "What'll it be? Kamikaze, Newky Brown? No Mitchells anymore. They went bust. I *could* make you a cup of coffee, of course, but I don't think I will. I do do a nice pint of Guinness, though."

"I doubt it."

"I pour a great pint! I can even do the shamrock thing." Jennifer pulled a face. "So, what'll it be?"

Glancing up, Jen plucked a pint glass from an overhead shelf. Tom, Claire thought, didn't know what he was talking about. Jen was Jen and hadn't changed, and wasn't, it could be safely said, *Jenny*. Maybe Jen was pleased to see her, but she hadn't actually been missing her. Jen was always far too busy, far too happy to *miss* her.

"So you're working here now?" Claire asked.

"I'm just about finished. You can see we're not rushed off our feet this time of day." Jen held the glass up. "You still haven't told me what you're having."

"Och, I'll have whatever you're having."

"'Och?'" Jennifer, angling the glass under the Kamikaze pump, raised an eyebrow at Claire. "When did you start saying 'Och'?"

"Must have picked it up in Belfast."

"Och's not Irish. It's Scottish."

Claire shrugged. Jennifer handed her the beer, rummaged underneath the counter and fished out a packet of crisps. "Seabrook's finest. Prawn Cocktail Crinkle Cut. Bet you can't get those in Belfast." She slid the packet across the bar. "Eat them. Put some weight on for fuck's sake. You're making me feel really lardy."

"Don't be daft."

"No arguments. Jen knows best. You just take a seat over

there near the fire, and I'll be with you in a minute. Kick old Bonzo out of the way."

Claire, drink in one hand, crisps in the other, stepped over the sleeping lurcher and slid onto the fireside bench. So Jen was back here for a while at least, since she was working in the pub. That was clear enough. And whatever Jen did it was always the best possible thing to do. That had always been clear. Claire sucked the beer-foam through her teeth, eased open the crisp packet, caught a whiff of saccharine and salt. The facts jostled for position. She couldn't quite make them settle.

Jennifer came round from behind the bar, put down her pint, pulled back a stool and sat down. She placed her tobacco pouch on the table and began to roll a cigarette. Claire watched her face. There was something different about her. Her skin was clear, clean, tanned. There were the first hints of lines at the corners of her eyes. She blinked and Claire saw the crust of mascara on her eyelashes, and realised what had changed. Jennifer, who had worn foundation, concealer, powder, blusher, lipstick, eyeliner, eyeshadow, mascara, the lot, every day since she was fifteen, was now making do with what looked like a scraping of mascara and a smear of lipsalve.

"You're looking well," Claire said doubtfully.

Jennifer glanced up from her hands, smiled. "Thanks a lot. You look like shit. Are you going to tell me what's up, or aren't you?"

"I'm tired?"

"Bollocks. Tired doesn't make you thin. Not eating makes you thin. Why aren't you eating? If you're worrying about the Alan thing, don't. You did the right thing."

"I didn't," Claire said. "He dumped me."

Jennifer half laughed, shaking her head. "Fucking hell, Claire."

"Or at least, that's what it felt like. I'm not really sure what happened."

"Someone else involved?"

"No. Not really."

"Well, there should have been. You could do with some fun, fuck's sake." Jen lifted the half-made cigarette to her lips, licked along the paper's edge. She gave it a final twist, tucked the cigarette between her lips, lit it.

"What about you and Tom?" Claire said. "Last I heard of it, it was just a fling."

"Oh, it was. Still is. Hope we'll be flinging till we're old and wrinkly and smell of wee. Best fun I've ever had." A pause. She grinned at Claire. "No offence."

"None took." Claire looked into her open packet, picked out a crisp, put it into her mouth. It stuck to her tongue and gave off a faintly suspect flavour. She swallowed. "I was up at the cottage," she said thickly. "I saw him."

"He's working on his carving. He's gone part-time with Halls."

"Uh huh."

"We do okay. Just sold one of his sculptures. Rates needed paying." Jennifer spoke quickly, over a held-back lungful of smoke.

"Oh."

She exhaled. "His stuff's beautiful. He doesn't talk about it much, but when he does, you can't help believing him. He knows what he's doing and he knows why he's doing it."

"Oh. Right." Claire hesitated. "That's great."

So that was it. Jen had fallen in love. She had fallen in love with Tom, and had decided to stay. Tom was an artist. He made her happy. It was unexpected turn of events, but not impossible: it kind of made sense. Claire picked up her glass, took another mouthful of beer, swallowed. The liquid seemed to go solid in her throat.

"So you didn't go to Birmingham, then?" she asked. "Didn't fancy it after all?"

"Oh no, I went."

"Oh," Claire said. "Right." She paused, reconsidered, shuffling her thoughts around again. "You've got some time off then? Up to see Tom, just helping out around the place here?"

"Nope. Packed it in. Never going back."

Claire looked at her pint glass, reached out to set it more centrally on the beermat. Soon as it seemed like she'd got a grip, everything shifted sideways.

"You'll be off travelling before long, then?" she tried, after a moment. "Going together? You always fancied heading off into the wide blue yonder . . ."

"No. We're staying here. At least for the foreseeable." Jennifer pressed her cigarette down into the ashtray's notch, pushed her tobacco pouch across to Claire. "Sorry. D'you want one?"

"Aye," Claire said, reaching out for it. "Why not."

"'Aye'?" Jennifer said. "I've never heard you say 'Aye' before."

"I must have picked it up in Belfast." Claire tugged a paper out of its cardboard envelope, began teasing out tobacco along its length.

"Bollocks. That's local. You know that's local."

"It's Belfast."

"It's from round here. You're just being contrary. Learning to speak Lancashire when you're blatantly living in Ireland."

"You're no better. Ever since you went off to college. Your

accent's all over the place." Claire lifted the paper, began rolling it between her fingers.

"That time in Birmingham didn't help," Jennifer said, and sucked carefully on her cigarette. She paused to pick a shred of tobacco off the tip of her tongue. "When I started in November, just in time for the Christmas rush, I was sharing a flat with four Londoners. What with that and the customers all speaking Brummie, I kind of lost it. The accent, I mean."

"You must have been having a great time," Claire said.

Jennifer pouted, gave a half-shrug. "It was hard work. The place stayed open till three, then we had to tidy up afterwards. Stack all the chairs and tables so the cleaners could do the floors when they came in first thing. It'd be going four before we finished. Then we'd have a few beers, smoke a joint. Head home around six. Go to bed, sleep all day, get up in time to go to work. I didn't see daylight for three months."

Claire felt her smile go fixed and twitchy. She glanced down at her hands, watched her fingertips as they rolled the cigarette. "But you had a laugh," she said, lifting the narrow cylinder to her mouth to moisten the glue. "You had loads of friends. You enjoyed yourself. You had a great time."

"I couldn't settle. I felt lost."

Claire's smile stiffened. Her jaw clenched. Her hand, as it reached out for Jen's lighter, looked odd and unfamiliar.

"Birmingham's a big place," she suggested.

"And ugly as fuck. Not that I ever saw it. Not by daylight." Jennifer paused, took a deep drink. "I did have friends."

Claire scraped a flame from the lighter, drew on the cigarette. Tobacco tendrils glowed, shrivelled in the flame. The smoke hit her lungs. She shivered.

"Because the club was new, we all started work there

around the same time. So we were all kind of in the same boat. Most of us new in town, just out of university. And I was sharing the flat with work people, so we got to know each other quite quickly. But it was still kind of lonely. Everyone had their own thing going on. Everyone was kind of fighting their own corner, somehow. Nothing seemed reliable, or permanent. Well, it wasn't, was it? I'm back here now."

"You needed a break. You missed Tom," Claire said.

Jennifer settled back, narrowed her eyes at the ceiling.

She hadn't missed him at first, she said. She was so busy, and for a while, there was someone else, one of the bouncers at the club. But it didn't last, and when they broke up, it was pretty difficult. They still had to work together, and she had to try very hard not to notice when he picked up girls at the club.

She hurt her back, lifting a stack of chairs. It got so bad that for a while she could hardly sleep. And she had stopped eating. At first, it was just there was no time to cook, no time to eat. Then she started throwing up anything she did manage to get down her. Which was mostly toast. Worst thing, she said, in the world, throwing up toast. Revolting. She didn't think she could ever eat toast again.

With her back gone, she was useless at work, so she took a week off sick, and came home, and slept for two days solid. The third day, when she got up, her back was a little less sore, a little looser. But she didn't know what to do with herself. She felt twitchy, nervy; she couldn't settle. She decided to go and see Tom. Up at the cottage he invited her in, made her a cup of coffee and they sat in front of his fire. They got on really well. Much better than over the summer. She had, she said, been a bit of an arsehole over the summer. All that crap about freedom and independence and her big plans. She spent the rest of the week with him. Did a lot of walking, as much as she could with her bad back. In the evening she'd lie on his hearth-rug with her back to the fire. The warmth seemed to help. At the end of the week she had to go back down to Birmingham. It was horrible. She was no sooner back than she started being sick again.

They'd arranged that he would come down to visit sometime the following month. It was rough, she said, thinking she wouldn't see him for so long. Turned out he couldn't handle it either. She got home from work early that Saturday morning and he was there, asleep on the sofa. One of the girls had let him in, he'd dropped off waiting up for her. It was like an extra Christmas, she said. She just leapt on him. She couldn't help herself.

They hardly slept that night. Talking, mostly. Her back was too sore to do much else. The next day she was exhausted and her back was killing her. She was almost ready to cry. She couldn't face getting up, couldn't take any more painkillers. Couldn't really do anything much but lie in bed, trying not to whimper. Then Tom said he was just going out for a bit. She assumed he was going for cigarettes, or a paper, or maybe just to get a break from her. She lay there, thinking how pissed off he must be, coming all the way down to see her and all she could do was lie in bed and moan. I'm crap, she thought, I'm no fun at all. If I were him, I'd be bored too. If I were him, I'd dump me.

"He came back about ten minutes later. He stood there in the doorway, with a hot water bottle in his hand. He'd gone out and bought it. He'd filled it for me. He was looking round for something to wrap it in. You know, so it wouldn't scald me. All my towels were wet, my clothes were all in a heap on the floor, all damp and smelly. You know what I'm like. So he took off his shirt. He took off his shirt and he wrapped it round the hot water bottle and held it against my back. He stroked my hair. And then, when the heat had taken the stiffness out a bit, he pulled my T-shirt up and began, ever so gently, to stroke my back. He sat like that for an hour. Gently massaging my back. I handed my notice in that night. I came back up here soon as I could."

"But you're not staying," Claire said, urgently. "You've got plans. You'll be off to London, or travelling, or something."

"I don't think I could leave now, even if I wanted to," Jennifer said. "I've only just got myself back together. Things had got pretty bad, down in Birmingham. I don't want to risk losing it like that again. I'd started breaking glasses at work. Deliberately. Started cutting myself with the glass." Jennifer held out her hand. Across the ball of her left thumb was a series of parallel pale lines. "I always said it was an accident," she added. "No one seemed to notice I always cut myself in the same place. I guess they were all too busy with their own stuff."

Claire, looking down at the brown hand, at the pale scars, felt the floor lurch under her feet, felt the ancient wall behind her buckle and sway. She put her hands down flat on the table, either side of her pint. She closed her eyes.

This is wrong, she thought. This is immeasurably, irredeemably wrong.

She breathed deeply, opened her eyes. Jennifer was still looking down at the ball of her thumb.

"Stupid, really, but I felt guilty as well," she was saying. "Really angry with myself. For being so self-indulgent. When you come down to it, it's really just attention-seeking. I was lonely. I wanted someone to notice. If I'm honest, that's what it was. Nothing more."

Claire looked at Jennifer's bent face, the open pores on her nose, the faint lines traced from nostrils to lips, the faint lines radiating from the crooks of her eyes across her temples. Suddenly, she was flooded with relief.

She had been wrong, she realised. She had made a mistake. This was not Jen. She did not sound like Jen, she did not even, when it came down to it, look like Jen. Jen's skin was peach-smooth, perfect. Jen was confident, unassailable. So this was definitely, she thought, not Jen. This was, in fact, nothing like her.

"Listen," Claire said. "I'll have to head on."

Jennifer looked up.

"Where you going?"

Claire slid out from between the table and the settle.

"I don't know."

"Stay, then."

"No. I can't. I have to go."

"Are you okay?"

"Yes. Yes, I'm fine."

"I'm glad you're back. I've been missing you."

Claire shivered.

"Yeah well," she said. "I'm not staying."

EIGHT

Claire worked most nights. She collected glasses, emptied ashtrays, and on Friday nights she served the food. Her feet hurt
her and sometimes she burnt herself on the serving-dishes and
usually a cut wept discreetly on her ankle. Mostly it was end-
of-the-evening work, so she was there until after the bar had
closed. Afterwards, she would walk back up to the flat. There
were always taxis available for the staff, but she rarely took
one; she was never in any rush to get back. There was often an
invitation to come back to someone's house for a drink, but
she never went. She couldn't help suspecting that even though
Alan was always asleep when she got in, he would somehow
know if she came home any later than usual. She couldn't face
the explanations, the argument, the silence that would neces-
sarily follow. And anyway, if she did go, what would she say.
She had got out of the habit of conversation. On the whole,

it seemed easiest just to go back to the flat. So she would walk alone up the Dublin Road, up Botanic Avenue, and then down Wolseley Street to their front door. It was a cold walk. The streets were always almost empty. She never felt scared. She would get back around two-thirty, three. The flat was always cold when she got in. She would pull off her shoes at the door, fill the kettle, then switch on the electric fire. With a cup of black tea cooling in her hand she would curl up on the sofa, trying to gather her nerve. Three paces through to the dark bedroom, climb over Alan's sleeping body and into bed. Sleep. She rarely managed it. Usually she was woken when Alan flicked the light on and the fire off in the morning. The room would be parched and airless. It was like burning money, he said, leaving the fire on all night like that. So the first word she said every morning was, "Sorry."

Once he had showered, breakfasted and gone to work, she would haul a blanket out of the airing cupboard and curl up again on the sofa. She didn't like to go through to the bedroom. The bed would be crumpled, cool and damp. There would be pale curling hairs on the sheets.

She would sleep until lunchtime. When she woke, stiff and cold, she would change into yesterday's clothes, pull on her thickest jumper, then head out. She would walk into every second-hand shop on Botanic Avenue, leafing through every close-packed rail of old-smelling clothes. She had left her coat behind in England. She had to replace it, but couldn't find one she could really afford. They all seemed to be very expensive. Ten pounds, more or less, and she never had that much cash to spare. Her money never seemed even to last the week. There were always bills, there was always food to buy. And Alan was strictly fair in the division of costs. They split everything fifty-fifty, even though, as he pointed out, she used the electric more than he did. Eventually she would give up looking and go to the Spar instead to buy something for their tea. She was never entirely disappointed that she hadn't found a coat. If she had managed to buy one, she would, she realised, then have to find something else to do with her afternoons.

By half-four, as she returned to the cold flat with her green-white-and-red plastic carrier bag, the afternoon would be fading into grey, tainted by the foreshadow of Alan coming home. There was only an hour between his arrival back at the flat and her departure for work, and he hated that hour. Claire knew he hated it. His irritation showed in every inch of his body. Every night as she served his dinner, he sat at the kitchen table rubbing his eyes wearily, his shoulders knotted with irritation. The meal finished, he would walk through to the living room and switch on the TV. While she showered, washed her hair and put on make-up in the bathroom, he watched *News Line.* He would call through to her, from where he sat. Every evening the same thing.

"I don't know why you have to make such an effort. It's only work."

And then silence. Not a word out of him as she walked past him in her bathtowel, as she dressed in the bedroom. As she stood, half an eye on the telly, pulling on her jumper and smoothing out her hair again. Not a word from him until she said, "See you."

And after a moment's pause, to prove that he was engrossed in the current local-interest story, and that she was disturbing him, he would reply, "Yeah. See you."

And she would close the door behind her, slip out through the front door of the house, and onto the cold leaf-littered street.

She had tried talking to him about work. She had tried

telling him about the hordes of customers, about how when Paul and Grainne came in to the bar, they always spotted her and called her over to talk. About Dermot who had asked her name then teased her. "Claih?" he had said, exaggerating Claire's accent. " *'Claih?'* You mean *Clurr.* That's how you say it. *Clurr.* " About Gareth who shared the tips with her even though she never got any herself, and had asked her how she was settling in, and when Alan would be down. But Alan had not wanted to hear. As she had spoken a frown had gathered on his forehead, his jaw had set as he gritted his teeth. They knew where he was, he told her. If they were so bloody interested, they could call him. They could just ring him up and ask him down for a drink. So she had stopped talking. She apologised. She had not spoken about it since.

By mid-November she had realised that she couldn't earn enough money before Christmas to pay the forty pounds for a coach ticket home, let alone the hundred and fifty for the air fare. Alan might have lent her the money, but the weeks went by and she still couldn't bring herself to ask. She could barely bring herself to open her mouth and speak, let alone ask for money. And when it came to it, she realised that she couldn't go home. She wouldn't be able to pretend to be at ease, not for any length of time. She could deal with a phone call, but she didn't really believe that she could lie convincingly, for days or a week, to her mother's face. And the idea of seeing Jen, of dealing with Jen's confident, delighted energy made Claire feel tired and defeated. It was bad enough after Oxford, but now . . . If she could just curl up beside her father, his heavy hand on her shoulder, and lean against his warmth, speechlessly. But it wouldn't be allowed. It was never allowed.

Around teatime on the last Sunday in November she

phoned her mum. She told her she had to work over Christmas. She was sorry, but there it was, unavoidable. It was that or lose her job. And not to worry, she would have a great time. It was always good craic, the other staff had told her, working over Christmas and New Year. And Alan sent his love. And she promised she would visit as soon as possible. She hung up, biting her lip, then she keyed in Gareth's number. She asked him if there were any extra hours going over Christmas, if she could work Christmas Day. "I'm skint," she said, which wasn't a lie. "I don't mind. I'll do Christmas Eve as well, if you want."

Twentieth of December and Alan came home pissed. An after-work end-of-term afternoon drink at Dukes had turned into three or four or five. Claire was on her way out of the door. He held his arm out, half-embrace, half-barrier. She stopped, standing on the doorstep. She looked at the olive wool of his turtleneck sweater. He asked her when she was stopping work for Christmas.

"I'm working every day," she said.

"But we'd agreed we'd go to my ma's."

"I'm sorry. Gareth's really stuck. And it's that kind of job. Busiest time of the year."

"You let him take advantage of you."

"I know. But I need the money."

"He doesn't pay you enough."

"I know."

"I can't believe you let him treat you like this."

"I'm sorry."

"You shouldn't be such a pushover."

"I'm sorry."

"So what am I supposed to do?"

"You go. Have a great time."

At about half-two on Christmas Eve Alan set off down town to catch the bus to Glengormley. He took a stack of books with him. He would not be back till the day after Boxing Day. Claire wrapped herself up in her yellow waffled blanket, hunched on the sofa, and watched *It's a Wonderful Life* on TV. She had to switch the TV off three-quarters of the way through the film. She would be late for work.

A fresh post-Christmas paypacket in her bag, she sat in the back of a black-and-white tiled hairdressers and watched the silent young woman slice off tranches of her hair. She watched as the scissors began to cut close against her head, the clippings falling like pine needles onto her lap. The style did not, she thought, particularly suit her: it left her looking boyish and exposed. She turned her head, watching her reflection. She felt jittery, satisfied.

"It got in the way at work," she told Alan, who had blanched.

"It was beautiful," he said, an ache in his voice.

"It was a pain, though."

"It was beautiful," he said again, his tone shifting. "You did it to annoy me."

"No," she said, and rubbed the soft short fuzz with a hand.

A door slam.

"Claire?"

He was back from work. Unexpected. A little earlier than usual. The new semester had left him more irritable, more unpredictable than ever. He had started calling her at work, he had started popping home at lunchtimes. And now, it seemed, he had started coming home early.

There was something about the way he spoke her name, proprietorial, belligerent, sexual, that made her flinch, shoulders hunching up, eyes closing, as the hot water poured down over her. She knew he knew she was in the shower. In the small flat, the sound of running water and the groaning of the hot tank were audible in every room.

"I'm in the shower." She said it anyway, because it was easier. She soaped her underarms. She shaved. She listened as he moved about the flat.

She heard his bag hit the floor with a thump. Heavy. Lots of marking. That meant he would be irritable. His feet were heavy on the old boards. Putting his books on shelves, setting out his work on the table, hanging up his jacket in the wardrobe. He trudged noisily down the hallway. She put her razor down on the side of the bath. He was going to try the bathroom door. She had locked it, but the lock was unreliable; the bolt would shift out of the socket with a gentle tug or push at the door. She waited, frozen, listening. He walked past the bathroom, went through to the kitchen. He ran the cold tap, the water rattled against the metal base of the kettle, and the shower ran for a moment blisteringly hot. Claire shrank back against the icy tiles, out of the spray. She heard him turn the tap off, flick the kettle on. She stepped back into the cooling water, heard him walk past the door again, walk through to the bedroom. She ducked her head under the shower. She reached down for her shampoo bottle.

Hot water streaming down her face, eyes closed, she squeezed a slug of shampoo into one hand, put the bottle back down on the side of the bath. She rubbed the shampoo into her cropped hair. It thickened and foamed, dripped down her arms. She kept her eyes shut, enjoying the warmth and the silkiness of the foam, hearing nothing but the gushing water and the mulchy sound of her hair as she rubbed.

The doorhandle creaked. A draught of cold air hit her skin. He was in the room. She turned and saw a strip of pale naked back as he passed. Then she heard the chink of plastic against ceramic as the toilet seat was raised. Through the steam and the citrus scent of the shampoo came the rank musty smell of piss. Then she heard the toilet's rattling, gurgling flush.

A cold hand on her hip. She jumped.

"What's the matter?" Alan climbed into the bath beside her.

"Nothing."

He stood, his skin pimpling in the steam. He had the beginnings of an erection; his penis was becoming stocky and pugnacious. "Let me get warm," he said.

He moved round her to stand under the water, letting it run over him. His skin blotched pink. The fair hair on his chest, belly and legs darkened. He lifted up his head and wiped back his hair, let the spray wash over his face. His eyes were closed.

"You've a while yet before work," he said.

"Yes." Claire leant against the cold tiles. Shampoo dripped from her hair, trickled slippily down her skin. It felt greasy. She was vividly conscious of her nakedness; her breasts felt tender, vulnerable; the sudden dark scribble of her pubic hair seemed ridiculous. The cut on her leg throbbed, as if trying to draw attention to itself. She smiled at him unevenly. "But I still have to get ready," she said.

He smiled. It wasn't a natural smile, Claire realised. Because he wasn't a natural smiler. "Plenty of time," he said.

He put his hands on her waist, pulled her towards him, back under the shower. The water ran over her head and down across her body, rinsing the shampoo out of her hair. It got into her eyes, her mouth. His penis pressed against her belly, hardening. She reached up to rub her eyes, to wipe away the soap, but he took her hands and held them, pulled them down to touch his penis. He kissed her on the mouth. His spit was sticky. Eyes tight shut and stinging, she took him in her fist and rubbed.

He came quickly, shuddering, one hand to the tiled wall for support. Pale translucent semen spurted onto her belly, cooled, began to drip down her. He groaned thickly and leaned back against the wall, eyes closed, as the water washed over him and the last drops of semen were rinsed off his cock and down into the drain. He sighed. He opened his eyes, looked around him. He picked up the soap, began to wash. He washed himself thoroughly: armpits, ears, crotch, feet. Then he got out of the shower and wrapped himself in Claire's towel.

"Love you," he said.

Claire's eyes were still smarting with shampoo. Her hair was slick with it. She leaned against the cold tiles, rubbing her eyes, trying not to gag, listening to his wet feet slap against the lino as he headed for the door. She stepped back into the water, rinsed her hair, rubbed her eyes. She took mouthfuls of hot water and spat, rinsing away the taste of soap and spit. Then she reached out for the shower-control and turned it up as hot as it would go. She would wash herself clean. She would wash away every scrap of the stuff that was trickling down her, creeping down towards her public hair. She would not let it get inside her. She would flush it down the drain, be rid of it. She turned in the stream of scalding water, arching herself forward so that the water washed over her belly. She wouldn't even have to touch it: it would rinse away, then she would pick up the soap and scrub herself all over, wash herself cleaner than clean. She glanced down at her belly, expecting to see it smooth and flat and clear. But his semen was still there. It had coagulated in the hot water, curdled into strands and soft translucent crumbs. It was sticking to her skin. It looked like scrambled eggs. She gagged, tasted stomach acid in her mouth.

She picked up the nailbrush, scrubbed at the clinging threads, tried to scrape them away. Her skin came up red, hatched and cross-hatched by the bristles.

"What are you doing?"

She had thought he had gone. She froze.

"Claire?"

What had he seen?

"Claire?"

Had the shower curtain covered her, or had he seen her gag, seen her scrubbing him away?

"Just washing," she said.

She heard his feet again on the wet lino. He tugged the shower curtain back. She saw him look her over. The hot water now stung her skin, dilating capillaries, dragging blood to the surface. She had scraped bright pink weals across her stomach. She had scrubbed herself raw, and yet there were still crumbs of his come stuck to her. She could not cover herself. She couldn't speak. There was nothing she could do.

"You've hurt yourself," he said.

She looked down at his bare feet on the dirty white lino, the fake tiles marked across the bathroom floor.

"I'm sorry," she said.

"Why did you hurt yourself?"

"It's nothing."

"You've all but scrubbed your skin off. You must have felt pretty dirty to scrub yourself that hard."

"I'm sorry."

He looked her up and down again, his face red and puckered. He too seemed unable to speak, unable to find adequate words. She could almost see, in the workings of his face, his desperate rummage for the right vocabulary. He gave up. He reached forward, almost slowly, and placed a hand on her chest, between her breasts. For a moment, she thought it was a caress, and was about to reach for him, when he pushed her.

He didn't push her hard; he pushed her hardly at all, in fact. It certainly wasn't anything as dramatic and final as a punch, or even a slap. It wasn't something you could really hold against him, when it came down to it. If Claire hadn't been scrubbing herself so vigorously and made the bath slippery with soap, she would probably not have fallen. And her razors had retractable blades. If she had remembered to click them back after she had shaved herself, she wouldn't have got cut. As it was, he pushed her slightly and she lost her footing and slipped, cracking her head against the wall, putting a hand out to save herself and putting it straight down on top of her razor. Slicing herself on its twin blades.

There was a lot of blood. More than when she cut herself deliberately. Claire was aware of the blood, and a throb in her head which crystallised immediately into pain, and a vague smarting from her hand. And feeling suddenly, utterly bewildered. And lying in the bath, water running over her, and being all angles and joints, one hand held in the air, red streaming brightly down her arm, and slipping and slithering as she tried to dislodge herself, to get herself upright, and feeling as if she never would, and, absurdly, giggling.

And Alan standing back from her, looking down at her as she floundered in the empty bath like a beached starfish. Blank and pale. Tears pouring down his face.

"I'm sorry," he said.

He reached out a hand towards her, grabbed her wrist. It anchored her. He helped her sit up, then stand. He held her arm as she stepped out of the bath. He steered her over to the basin and turned the cold tap on. He held her hand under the cold water. The cut stung. Claire pulled away, but he held on. The water ran clear. He dried her hand then wrapped it up in toilet roll. There were tears on his face. He sniffed back the gathering mucus. He took off his towel and wrapped it round her. Naked, he put an arm around her and guided her through to the bedroom. He sat her down on the bed, pulled the blanket round her shoulders.

"Warm enough?"

"Yes."

He pulled on his underpants, stepped into his trousers. He paused, holding them up by the waistband.

"I didn't know," he said.

Claire looked up at him.

"I didn't know that you felt like that."

She drew her lips back in against her teeth.

"You could have told me," he said. "You *should* have told me." He zipped up his fly.

"I'm sorry."

"How long have you felt like that?"

She screwed her eyes shut.

"Have you always felt like that?"

She swallowed.

"You should have told me. Why didn't you tell me? I'm not a complete bastard."

"I—"

"Didn't want to hurt me? How do you think I feel now?"

She opened her eyes, but couldn't look up at him. The bathtowel was in a heap on the floor. It was green. It needed washing. She opened her mouth.

"I—"

He stood in silence a moment, waiting for her to finish. She folded her lips back in, unable to.

"You think I'm a complete bastard. You must," he said. "Do you really think I'd've done that if I'd known how you felt? I wouldn't have touched you. I wouldn't have gone near you. How could you let me do that?"

"I'm sorry."

She glanced up at him. He looked at her for a long moment, then bent to pull on his shoes.

"I'll go get some plasters."

She watched him tie his shoe laces. He stood up, pulled a jumper over his head.

"What should I do?" she asked.

"Hold that hand up above your head. It'll slow down the bleeding."

"I mean—"

He was gone. She heard the door fall shut behind him, then, a moment later, the street door. She sat on the edge of the bed. Her skin goosepimpled in the cold. He was gone and it was over. Her throat ached, swelled, and she began quietly to cry.

Slowly, one-handed, she dragged her bags out of the corner of the room, unzipped the largest. She pulled out her black trousers, her white shirt, pants and bra. Slowly, she dressed, then slowly tied on her shoes. She unzipped the smallest of her bags, and emptied it, piling the books it had contained on the floor around her. The blood had begun to seep through the tissue; she held her arm above her head and used her left hand to pull a few clothes out of the largest bag and stuff them into the smallest. She took two changes of clothes, some underwear, socks, make-up, a couple of books. Not much, just what she could carry, just what she could leave in the staff room at work without it being noticeable. She zipped up the other bags, pushed them back into the corner. Out of Alan's way. She went through to the bathroom, unwound the tissue, flushed it away. She took another wad of paper, held it against the cut. She blew her nose, wiped her eyes, looked at herself in the mirror. Mess. Complete fucking mess.

She placed her keys on the kitchen table, hefted her bag onto her shoulder, cast around her. Nothing else she should do before she left. Nothing else she could think of, anyway. Outside the door the streets branched and forked and crossed and merged and tangled, and along each street were houses, shops, bars, cafés and offices. Moving through the streets were people who knew where they were going and who would be waiting for them when they got there and what they would say and how they would feel and she didn't fit into any of that. Didn't have as much as a toehold in anyone else's life. There wasn't even a crack between the pavingstones that she could slip down. There was no one to go to. There was nowhere to go. Apart from to work, of course. She had to go to work. Because of course they couldn't manage without her. The whole place would grind to a halt if she stopped emptying ashtrays. She stepped out of the flat, into the communal hallway. Daylight falling through the dusty fanlight. Fliers and junkmail scattered on the carpet. She stepped over the litter, reached out a hand towards the street door. She turned the lock, the handle, and dragged it open.

"Oh." Alan was standing on the doorstep, key in hand. "You're leaving."

"I . . . Yes."

"I got you the plasters."

"Right."

He reached into his pocket and pulled out a cardboard wallet. He opened it clumsily, hastily. He pulled out a plaster. Claire lifted off the wad of tissue and held out her hand. The cut was red, welling up. He peeled off the paper backing, stuck the plaster down on her cut. Gently. He looked at her.

"That won't last long. Take the rest of them." He handed her the box.

"Thanks."

"Where will you go?"

"Work."

"After that?"

"I don't know."

"Right."

"I'd better go. I'll be late."

"What about your stuff? Won't you be needing it?"

"I'll come back for it. Sometime."

"Right."

She hitched her bag up her shoulder, looked down at the plaster. Blood had already begun to seep through, turning the fabric brown. She looked up at him. His face was pale, his eyes red and wet-looking.

"I'm sorry," she said.

"Yes," he said. "Me too."

"Yes. Well. See you."

"See you."

And she slipped past him, turned down Wolseley Street. She didn't hear the door close. He must have still been standing there, watching her walk away, as she turned the corner onto Cromwell Road. Out of sight, she hugged her arms around her. She felt her face glow. February air; cold and dry, and the city emptying around her.

Claire didn't see Grainne and Paul come in. She was in a daze, threading her way through the crowds, collecting empty glasses, when there was suddenly a hand on her arm. She swung round, heart pounding, but it was Grainne. Grainne smiled, stepped forward, and hugged her. Claire clutched her glasses awkwardly to her chest, staring up over Grainne's neat black shoulder.

"I heard," Grainne said, stepping away, looking Claire seriously in the eyes.

"Ah."

"I just wanted to say, if you need anything. Anything at all."

"Right. Thanks."

"There's a spare room at my place. You can stay with me. Long as you want."

NINE

∞

A cold white room. Rising steam, grey-blue greasy hot water. A blue-painted wooden lid propped back against the wall. She leant over the edge of the copper, holding onto the smooth wood of the paddle handle.

You could hide a child in there, someone said. *You could boil a child alive.*

And that was it. After that, cold, echoing voices, and the guilty sense of something left carelessly behind. A long white room. The girl in the next bed had plaits and smelt warm and musty. She cried all night. Snuffling and yelping and hiccuping: Anne heard her as she lay awake. Anne was a good girl, and did not cry. Because no one wanted little girls who cried.

And then Ray and Fran's house, with the white-flowered tree, and no other little girls at all. Because she had been a good girl, and never cried. And she couldn't help but wonder about the girl in the next bed and if they cured her of crying, and although the sense of something missing never left her, she didn't try to remember what she had lost. Because, as Fran said, that was gone now, and best forgotten.

Beside her, propped up on pillows, Joseph lay sleeping. His face was smooth, his breath came evenly. While Anne slept his breathing permeated her dreams. When she woke, it was the first thing she became aware of; before the light, before the buzzing of the alarm clock, before the winter-morning cold. His breath was as necessary and insistent as the ticking of a clock.

In the hospital she had often fallen asleep by his bed, her forehead flat on the cool thick sheets, lullabied by the familiar soothing sound of his breath. It was not him breathing, they had told her, but she had always known that they were wrong. There could be no question about it. This was the gentle, ceaseless sigh that had drifted through her dreams for the past fourteen years. It was his strong lungs that made the sheet rise and fall. He *sucked* the air out of the ventilator.

And now, when she lay awake at night, she still listened to his breath. It never faltered, never hesitated, but she listened always and intently for the slightest indication of a change. She had been adamant with the doctors, she had been stubborn with the nurses. She had determinedly refused to listen, but they had nonetheless planted the seed of a doubt. She had to keep on checking, she had to keep on assuring herself that it was him, and that he was breathing.

As she lay awake listening, Anne watched the tree-shadows, the branches jostling and shifting across the ceiling. A windy night, she thought, and so a brighter day tomorrow. And a bright moon, though cut across by clouds. Clouds scudding across the sky, driven by the wind. A wild night, and so a brighter day tomorrow.

She knew Claire was awake. She had heard the scrape of the latch as she opened the door. She had listened to the water rattle through the pipes, the footsteps climbing up the stairs. Her bed had creaked as she sat down, the floorboards had shifted and moaned as she walked around her room. She heard her cross the landing, come back down the stairs again. Heard the tangle of voices when the television was switched on, then silence as it was switched off again, or the volume was turned down. Doors opened and closed as she moved around the house. Then footsteps back up the stairs, movement above. Overhead, the bed creaked again.

Anne couldn't let her go. In her mind she followed her daughter's every step. She saw the worn patch on the carpet she was walking over, the way the shadows fell behind the furniture. As she heard the click of each light switch, she could almost feel the smooth plastic underneath her daughter's fingertips.

It was worse when Claire was in Belfast. Attenuated by distance, her mind strained towards her daughter across the dark. As if she could find her and wrap her up in her awareness, as if she could make her safe. Eyes open, she tried to thread her way around the unknown city, to follow her daughter through the crowded bars, to see her safely home through dark and risky streets, to watch her fall asleep beside that lumpen boy. While Claire was home, it was easier to chart her movements, to see what she was seeing. What she could not follow were her thoughts.

She had told Claire: "There's nothing round here for you." She had told her it again and again that summer after Claire had finished her degree. Like an English-speaker abroad, Anne had kept on saying it, louder and louder, as if repetition and amplification could make the meaning clear. It had taken Claire leaving to make Anne understand what she was saying, what Claire had heard. "There's nothing round here for you," meant to Claire, "We don't want you anymore." It didn't mean half the things Anne had wanted it to mean. And now it seemed too late to go back and explain. It seemed graceless to peel away that much misunderstanding. So Anne lay awake listening, stretching herself out through the house, waiting.

Because something would have to be done soon. Something graceless and muddled. Now that Claire knew, or was beginning to know, Anne had started to scrape away the layers and look back beyond her stories. She had to find something to tell her daughter, something that would hold her. A new straight clean line that she could pull out from the knotty mess of ideas. And all that she could find was a memory of steam, a cold room, and dirty water, and a voice that said *You could hide a child in there; you could boil a child alive.* And that wasn't enough. And with every passing second, the risk of her child slinging her bag on her shoulder and walking away again grew, swelling in Anne's brain like an aneurysm. She wanted to climb out of bed, to push her way through the silences, through to her daughter, to cram her to her chest and claim her.

She had sat over her husband's smoothed-out sheets, dry-eyed. Smiling for her daughter, rational and resolute with the staff. In childbirth she had been quiet, apologetic for the noise and mess. When they had buried Moss underneath the willow tree, she had held Joseph's head in her hands as he shook with tears. It was years since she had cremated her adoptive parents' bodies and buried the ashes, but she still had not cried for them. Years before that, a silent, dry-eyed child had been handed over to them. A silent child had lain awake in the long white dormitory, listening to the nightsounds. A silent child had peered nervously into the copper and heard those words: *You could hide a child in there; you could boil a child alive.* Grown, the silence had grown with her, suffocating. She wanted to rage, to shout, to howl apart the darkness. She missed them. She missed them and they didn't know. She wanted to scream it out so loud that they could not help but hear. Joseph. Her baby. Ray and Fran. Those unknown familiar people whose images filled her photograph album. And the young woman who sat in the dark in another room, who was always moving further and further away.

Claire had walked. All day, all evening, she had walked. She walked along the riverbank, sat on the damp earth a while and watched the water purl over the stones, then got up and walked on. She had climbed up to the limestone pavements on the top of Rise Hill and looked down at the flat surface of the reservoir, then followed the same path back down the fell again. She was exhausted, couldn't stay in one place, couldn't decide where to go. She kept on tracing the old paths that looped out from the village then swung back in again. The drink had gradually cleared from her head. It left behind a sedimental ache and a bitter taste in her mouth. The path brought her eventually back home. As she climbed the field-wall, picking her way carefully down the grannies' teeth steps onto the road, she could hardly see her feet in the dusk. She looked up towards the house. The windowpanes reflected back the night. Her parents were in bed.

She pushed open the gate and followed the stippled concrete path around the side of the house. Damp tips of ferns and iris blades brushed against her legs. She opened the back door and, as always, the latch scraped noisily against the metal plate. The sound was ugly and comforting. She pulled off her muddy shoes and left them by the door. She ran a glass of water from the tap. A faint scent of geraniums and grass. Peat water. It had seeped through the ground that she had walked that day. It had welled darkly into a pool, spilled into a beck, tumbled brown and frothing down the hill. It was, for Claire, the taste of earth and home. She drank again, inverted the empty glass on the draining board, walked slowly upstairs in her damp socks.

Still she couldn't settle. Calves aching, toes burning with blisters, she moved quietly around the room, opening cupboards, pulling out drawers, lifting books off the shelves, putting them back. Then down the stairs again, knowing which treads would creak, placing her feet on the outmost edges of the boards. She didn't want to be heard and she wanted to be heard. When her father had fallen ill and the house and the night and the world had for the first time seemed empty, she had cried insistently and quietly every night for hours, alone in her room. Quietly, so that she could be heard only if someone really wanted to hear. And her mother, eyes open staring at the ceiling, had been so muffled up in her own misery that she had never heard a sound. Now Claire paced damp-footed through the house, through the living room, the dining room, the kitchen, back again, past the dark open doorway of her parents' room, hoping they were asleep, waiting to be noticed.

Her mother had never noticed, Claire thought, because from the moment of her father's illness, she had refused to recognise any weakness. Claire had to be strong, they had to stick together. They had to do it for him. There was not, really, any choice. Well, Claire thought, she had been strong, she had stuck together. And she had done it for them. She had done it because she had thought she and her mother were a partnership, that they were in it together, and that they were equal. And all the time her mother had been lying to her.

And what was most infuriating was that she knew what would happen. She knew that nothing would be explained, that when it came down to it, nothing would be resolved. Claire would be obliged to be understanding, and to be strong, and not to make a fuss. For his sake. She would be obliged to forgive her mother, even though rage and grief would still be eating away at the lining of her gut. And nothing more would be said. They would pretend it had never happened. So when would she get the chance, Claire wondered. When would she get her chance to be weak, to let them down, to be unreasonable, to be a teenager, to scream and shout and tear the house down?

She squatted down in front of the TV, switched it on. Flickering blue light and adverts for chatlines and catalogues and cheap holidays. Blue seas and white teeth and long slender legs. She turned down the sound, stood up, walked to the window. She stared out at the trees. A wind had gathered. Leaves and moonshadows fluttered. She looked down at her hands, arched on the cracked and bubbled windowsill. Thin skin, piano-wire tendons and bluish veins. She thought of Jen and the glasses and the pale lines across the ball of her thumb, and underneath the damp cotton of her trousers, her own tracery of scars seemed to sing at her through closed lips. She cocked her head to listen to the silence of the house. She heard the soft creak of timbers cooling; outside, branches grated against each other in the wind. Apart from that, nothing. No animal sounds. It was an empty night; uninhabited. But even so, she could not cut, not here. It would go wrong. The bathroom was carpeted; there would be bloodstains. At any moment her mother might stir, wake, and come padding down the corridor and knock on the bathroom door. But wasn't that, after all, Claire thought, what she wanted? Wasn't that what she was listening for every time she brought the blade to her skin and began to carve? The footfall in the hallway, the soft tap on the door, a gently insistent voice demanding to be let in. Wasn't that what she was waiting for? Wasn't that why she did it?

She paced back across the room, climbed the stairs. They creaked underneath her. She switched on her bedroom light and sat down on the edge of her bed. She looked blankly at the white formica wardrobe door. Then she was on her feet again, pacing across the landing, back down the stairs again, each tread creaking underneath her. She walked through the dark rooms, through the flickering light of the silent TV set, through the moving shadow-branches on the carpet. She found herself come to a halt outside her parents' open bedroom door. She listened to the frightening ebb and flow of her father's breath.

"Claire?"

She was propped up on an elbow.

"Mum."

"Can't sleep?"

Claire looked at her a moment, but couldn't think what to say. She turned and walked away, back through the dining room, back into the kitchen. She heard the bedclothes rustling back, heard her mother's feet on the floor. Heard her urgent whisper: "Claire—" but just kept on walking.

"Claire—"

She came up to the kitchen door. The door was still unlocked, the key still slotted into the keyhole. Through the glass panel she could see across the valley. Brilliant moonlight picked out, briefly, the tracery of lines and mounds and hollows. Cloud shadows scudded across the silvered grass.

"Claire—"

She reached out for the doorhandle.

"Claire!"

Her mother's hand was on her hand. There was broderie anglaise on the cuff of her nightdress.

"What?" Claire said.

"Where are you going?"

Claire couldn't turn round to look at her. She felt her sleep-soured breath on her neck. They stood in silence, too close.

"Are you going?" her mother asked.

Claire just stared at the old hand on hers, the dark softened skin.

"Claire."

Claire pulled her hand away.

"Love—"

"What?"

"Talk to me."

"About what?"

"I'm worried."

"Really."

"Claire."

"Well, what do you want me to say?"

The old hand was lifted away from the doorhandle, but she

was still there, close, fervent, just behind her. Claire slid away, walked across the kitchen, putting the table between them.

"I want us to talk," her mother said.

"So you said."

"What's the matter, love?"

"What do you mean, what's the matter?"

"I mean, since I have to spell it out, what was it that made you think it would be okay to stay out all day and half of the night without telling us where you were going. You worried your father and me half to death."

"Oh, so it's all my fault now?"

"Claire, love—"

"Don't."

"Don't what?"

"Don't make this my fault. You lied to me," Claire said. There it was. Out. She could almost see the words, scrawled in sparkler-writing across the air between them.

"Claire."

Claire raised her eyebrows, wouldn't speak. Her heart seemed to have swollen up; it was choking her.

"Claire, you've got to try and understand . . ."

"No. Bollocks. I don't have to try and understand. I'm sick to death of understanding. I've had enough. You lied to me. You lied to me and you couldn't remember what you'd said. You slipped up, I caught you. No one would forget the truth like that. One way or another, you *lied,* and you kept on lying until I found you out. That's it. That's all there is to it. There's nothing else to say."

"Claire, listen, please."

"Why? Why should I?"

"I want to explain. I want you to try and understand."

"Why the fuck should I?"

"Darling, your father—"

Claire clenched her fist on the tabletop, her nails digging into her palm. Already she was in the wrong. Already this was about her behaviour and not about her mother's. Her eyes narrowed. She dropped her voice to a whisper. She wouldn't wake him. Of course she wouldn't wake him.

"You've been lying to me for years," Claire said. "How can you stand there and expect me to swallow any more? You have no fucking clue who those people are, do you? You made the whole thing up."

"It's not like that."

"What is it like, then?"

Her mother's dark eyes were luminous. The creases round her eyes and the lines on her forehead were clear. Her throat looked pouchy and soft, marsupial. Claire realised suddenly that she had never seen her mother cry. She wanted to pull her close, to dig her nails into her, to shake her.

"Well?"

Her mother drew a chair back from the kitchen table. She sat down, facing Claire across the formica tabletop. "They're mine," she said. "The photographs. They're mine."

"Right."

"I inherited them. When Ray and Fran died."

"So it's still all bullshit you've been telling me. All fucking bullshit. They're Ray and Fran's photos. They're your adoptive family."

"No. They're mine. Don't look a bit like Ray and Fran's lot."

"Why should I believe you? You lied to me before."

"You were just a baby. I wanted the best for you."

"You made the stories up. Every last one of them. You had no idea who those people were."

"No. They *are* mine. I know they're mine. But that's all I

know for certain. They didn't believe in keeping things, back then—they didn't believe in remembering—" She folded her hands on her lap, she looked down at them, watched as she twisted them together. "Best forgotten, that's what they said—maybe they were right—trying to hold onto it—" she hesitated a moment, swallowed. "Anyway," she continued, "I was luckier than most. Some things had come with me; from the children's home, from before the children's home. A few clothes, and the album."

She looked up at Claire. Claire gritted her teeth. Her mother went on.

"I found them all together. In an old trunk. We were clearing the house after Fran died. I was so angry. I can't tell you how angry I was. You think you're angry with me, but can you imagine—" She looked down at her hands again, shook her head. "Ray and Fran had been all the family I'd ever had. And, you know, even then I'd never felt like I belonged. I'd always looked different. And then I saw these photographs. People who looked like me. Who looked *at* me, it felt like. Ray and Fran, they'd kept the photos from me. They'd kept my family from me. And now they were gone, too. I couldn't even tell them how angry I was. And, you see, they must have known something, how else would they have got hold of the album. Someone must have passed it on to them, told them something. Someone must have wanted me to have it. But by then it was too late to ask. I felt as if I'd lost everyone. Forever." She stopped wringing her hands. She looked up at Claire.

"Babies are born with blue eyes. Kind of misty blue. But even when you were very little, almost from the day you were born, you had my eyes. Even through the misty blue I could see you had the same eyes as all the people in the photographs. You belonged. You were suddenly, really family. I realised that I hadn't lost everyone. Not forever. There was you, and you were one of us, and we were a family. So I told you the stories. I wanted you to *know* that you belonged. I wanted you to have what I could never have."

Claire felt her skin bristle. She wouldn't be persuaded. She wouldn't understand. And she wouldn't be blamed for it.

"That's bullshit. You weren't doing it for me. You did it for yourself."

Her mother hugged her arms around herself, thought for a moment.

"Maybe," she said.

"You told me they were Jewish. You made that up. Admit it. You can't have known that. And Sam and Ben and Granddad and Great Uncle Sid and Aunty May: you made them up, too. You made me believe in them and they never even existed."

Claire felt her eyes fill again. They had been snatched away from her. They had been wiped out. It was her mother's fault. She had done it.

"They are real. Somehow, I'm sure that they're real. I must have had a family."

"But you made them up." Claire's voice was rising. She knew it was, but couldn't stop it. "Those people, those stories, they were never real. That's all there is to it."

"Claire—"

"You lied to yourself to make yourself feel better. And then you lied to me."

"You have to try and understand, Claire—"

"Ah, but that's just it," Claire said. "In fact, I don't."

Claire moved around the side of the kitchen table, towards the door. She reached out for the handle, turned it.

"Love, please, don't—"

"Why not?" said Claire. She found that she was crying. She wiped the back of her hand angrily across her eyes, sniffed noisily. She pulled the door open, the latch grating against the metal plate. "Why shouldn't I?"

"Because I miss you."

"Bullshit."

"It's true. I miss you. And I worry."

Her voice sounded strange, thick. Claire glanced back at her. She could only see the back of her head, the grey hair silvery in the moonlight. She was leaning over the table, looking down at the scuffed surface. She was tracing a scar across the tabletop with her forefinger. Then she looked round at Claire. Her eyes were swollen. Her face was crumpled, sore-looking. It was wet. She sniffed, wiped the back of a hand across her eyes, and looked suddenly, incredibly young. And something in Claire expanded, gave.

"It didn't help, you know," she said, reluctantly. "Those stories. That identity. Didn't help at all."

As she watched, the creases on the older woman's face deepened. She shook her head slightly. Claire dropped her hand from the doorhandle, came over to the table, sat down. She reached out a hand across the formica, halfway.

"There must be something," she said. "There must be some records left, still. You could try and find out."

Her mother rubbed at her eyes, kept her hands over them, nodded.

"I could help you."

Claire scraped back her chair, slipped round the table, and

let her hand rest, gently, on her mother's shoulder. Then she crossed the room, lifted the kettle, filled it at the tap. Setting down mugs, turning to fetch milk from the fridge, and standing for a moment, just looking at the brushed steel of the kettle, she couldn't help but wonder if the truth would be any better, any more help than her mother's stories, just because it was the truth.

TEN

✃

Mechanical cranes hung over the city streets like mothers over children, carefully putting things in order, setting things to rights. The Seacat, sliding into its berth, drew past the ends of canyon-streets, past office windows, past shopfronts and car-parks. It seemed to be sailing straight into the city. It seemed to be sailing up a street. Claire saw the gasometer-barrel of the Waterfront, the squat green dome of the City Hall, the distant glow of the Europa's neon sign. Unexpected perspectives, new distances and juxtapositions. She realised for the first time how close everything was, how close it was to everything else. She hadn't noticed until that moment the straight, obvious lines that linked each of her landmarks, that laced them all together. And now, at the end of almost every street, a crane stooped, Meccano-frail, transparent against the sky. Putting things together, setting things to rights.

As the Seacat slid past the quayside buildings, Claire glimpsed pale expensive offices, suited workers. People who tapped on keyboards, poured coffee from filter-jugs, leant against desks to flirt. On the pavement below, a woman in a red-white-and-blue Kangol jacket was pushing a buggy with one hand, trailing a toddler from the other. Traffic streamed around a bend. The lights changed, the traffic lined patiently up, bunching together, and a new flow of cars swept past, dispersing, spilling out across the lanes. She saw the flashing lights of an ambulance, heard the wailing siren, and watched as the cars slid in towards the kerb, stopped, and the ambulance slipped past them and away. It looked natural, it looked balletic; it was almost beautiful. And she wondered, for the first time, who all these people were, and what they did, and where they were coming from, and where they were going to.

"Excuse me—"

A uniformed woman stood near her, holding open a grey plastic binliner. She nodded to the empty cellophane wrappers, the dry plastic coffee cup on the tray-table. Bright hazel eyes, kohl-lined. Claire recognised her. She had worked on the trip over. She was the one Claire had spoken to, before running off to throw up. Claire smiled up at her, knowing she would not be remembered.

"Have you finished?"

"Yes. Thank you." Claire swept the debris into the binliner.

They had gone to Helen's Bay. They had taken the train. It was three carriages long. The seats were bright blue. The track ran between houses, hedges, then alongside the smooth blue lough. Grainne, released from school for Easter, was like a little girl, all smiles, head turning to look out of the windows on either side of the carriage. She leaned forward every few minutes to offer Claire her open packet of Milky Way Stars. Grainne's mum and dad ran a newsagent's in Armagh. She always had a packet of sweeties on the go. When she yawned you could see her fillings.

"This is us," and Grainne was on her feet, at the doors, stuffing her sweet packet into her coat pocket, hand on the "open" button before the train had even stopped.

It was a brilliant, blustery April Sunday. Low sun, the wind chasing clouds across the sky, wringing out sudden spatterings of rain. The sand was perfect, rich, marked only by a few booted prints, dogtracks and the delicate patterning of birds' feet. The water's surface was mottled with cloud-shadows and sun. Ahead, it frothed against sharp black rocks. The sand was strewn with blue and silver mussel shells, kelp, and limpet husks worn away to pale translucent quoits.

"When I get round to decorating the bathroom," Grainne said, "I'm going to paint it these colours."

"The water's beautiful. We should have brought our swimming stuff," Claire said.

Grainne crouched to pick up a pebble. She skimmed it out across the water. It sliced into the surface, sank.

"It wouldn't feel beautiful," she said. "You'd be foundered. It's very deep. And not very clean."

"It doesn't look polluted."

"No, right enough, it looks fairly clean." She scuffed her toe around, looking for further skimmers. "Sometimes you see the odd seal. So I s'pose it can't be that bad."

Claire strained her eyes after cormorants, ducks, buoys, as

they bobbed and turned just nearly out of sight, hoping that what she could barely see was the blunt-nosed turning head of a seal. But it never was. A cormorant flapped its wings, a duck took off, a buoy bobbed too long in the one place.

On the far side of the lough, there were smokestacks, low industrial buildings, a lighthouse. White-sailed yachts scudded out towards the sea; bits and scraps of rainbows opened out like fans, folded away again. And, slowly, like a scene-change, the Stena HSS slid by, vast, incongruous, much too close.

"This place is incredible. You can't quite believe it," Claire said.

"It's nice this time of year. Nice and quiet."

"So many rainbows," Claire said. "I've never seen so many rainbows."

Grainne smiled.

"You get this much rain, you're bound to get the odd rainbow."

Which didn't solve anything, Claire thought, stabbing at the pedestrian-crossing button with a forefinger. Which did not, in fact, help at all. The temple-square Customs House was behind her; she crossed the road towards McHughes's. She would, she realised, be passing within whispering distance of Conroys. She felt herself bunch up inside, like a finger-touched snail. She wouldn't be calling in. She couldn't, yet.

A pink folded towel on the end of a neatly made bed, a warm dim room, pale curtains drawn against the streetlamps.

"I'm just glad the room's ready. I'm only after decorating."

"Right."

"D'you like it? What do you think of the colours?"

Claire looked round at the pale walls, up at the dark reddish ceiling. "Yes. It's nice."

"Only, if you don't like it, we can always change it—"

"No, no, it's fine. It's lovely. Cosy, you know." Claire dropped her bag down on the floor. She smiled round at the curtains, the wardrobe, the chest of drawers. She felt again that sudden sad suspicion that she and Grainne would never quite be friends.

Which didn't help either. Which only, in fact, made things worse. The sun was warm, almost directly overhead. St. George's Market was scaffolded and rigged up with tarpaulins. The sheets snapped in the wind. A grey car passed, then a white van. She stood waiting unnecessarily on the kerb, looking out across the slate-blue tarmac. The lights changed and she crossed the empty road. The urgent bleep of the crossing insinuated itself into her stride, making her walk faster. No rush, no rush, she told herself, and dragged her feet back to slow. Get there soon enough. Get there far too soon. She stuffed her hands in her pockets, tugged her jacket tight around her. Not even her jacket, really, she thought, remembering Grainne chucking it at her as she had hesitated at the front door one evening. It had been raining, and she was coatless. Hang on to it, Grainne had said, for as long as you need it. I've got plenty. Claire watched as the breeze rolled decaying cigarette filters around in the gutter. Tiny whorls and plumes of dust were lifted, settled, lifted again.

Ormeau Avenue opened out to the right. Halfway down, concrete pillars and steel girders rose out of the ground, nursed by two tall mechanical cranes. It had been a carpark, not so long ago, Claire remembered. There had been cars pulled up snugly beside each other, an automatic barrier and a man who sat in a yellow fibreglass box and took money and handed over tickets. A fleece zipped up to his chin. It must have got so cold in the winter. Just him in his little pod and a hand stretched through the slot, chapped by the wind, soaked when it rained, always colder than the rest of him. Now there was a hoarding, a picture in elegant muted shades. A substantial, confident structure in red brick and glass. Claire peered at the lettering. A hotel and leisure complex. The artist had even sketched in the clientele and passers-by. Elegant, slim, busy people who nonetheless had the time to pause and chat to one another after work, on their way to drinks in the hotel bar or callisthenics class in the hotel gym. They didn't seem real, these people. They must exist, or why build the hotel, but Claire couldn't quite believe in them, or in their lives.

She passed the entrance to the old gasworks, glanced up at the high spiked railings, the chained and padlocked gates. Through the fence she could see sculptures: stone obelisks and bronze astrolabes on smooth, new-laid lawns. New offices and apartment blocks rising out of the old brown earth. Traffic lights, not yet hooked-up, not yet synchronised into the city's choreography, stood blind, waiting for the gates to open, waiting for the streams of cars and vans and lorries and slim-legged boys on bikes with dispatch-bags over their shoulders. The buildings were unfinished, unfurnished, and, the billboard said, already sold. Who on earth bought these things, Claire wondered. Who purchased hectares of earth and metres of air and storeys of brick and glass and steel? Who earned enough to buy a *place*? Whoever it was, Claire thought, they wouldn't be stopping to chat outside the new hotel-leisure-complex. They would be far too busy. They would be rushed off their feet.

She crossed the Ormeau Road slowly and inattentively, at an angle. She turned the corner into University Street. The breeze tugged at her hair, blew grit into her eyes, made her jacket billow and bulge. Ahead, visible between the bosomy Victorian terraces, was the dark gothic spire of Fitzroy Presbyterian Church. A corner of a flying buttress, a sliver of algaed tiles. Opposite the end of Wolseley Street. She would be passing right by. She wavered in mid-stride. Alan still lived there. He could be on his way back from the newsagent or from lunch at Maggie May's or dragging the washing back from the laundrette. There were any number of reasons he would be walking down the street towards her now, just around the corner, just a step away. And her bags were still there. Her stuff still heaped up in the corner of the bedroom. Clothes that she couldn't quite remember anymore. Odds and ends of winter-coloured make-up. A book or two. Her old ink pen. Unless he had thrown it all away.

Which he might have. She wouldn't blame him if he had. He wouldn't want her stuff lying in the corner of his bedroom, first thing he saw when he woke, last thing he saw when he went to bed. All this time. Claire could almost see him, the evening that she left, lugging her bags down the street, his breath misty in the lamplight. He would have heaved them off his shoulder, into a waiting skip. He would have turned away and rubbed his hands together as he walked back towards the flat. He would, perhaps, have smiled to himself.

She kept her eyes unfocused, looking vaguely down at the paving-slabs. If he was there, if he was nearby, if he was walking right at her shoulder, she wouldn't see him; she was determined she wouldn't see him. Because if she saw him, he would catch her eye and open his lips, and speak, and she would have to stop and stand there watching the spit sticking to his lips, or look down at his hands, flat against his thighs, and the words would loop around her again, drawing her back in, describing her, delineating her, marking her out.

The lights changed; she crossed.

She chewed the cuticle on her thumb, pressing her fingers down onto her cheekbone as she counted out the months. March April May June and now into July. Four and a bit. Four and a bit months. She should have taken a taxi and fetched her bags that first night. She should have got Grainne to drive her round that weekend. It could've been dealt with at that stage, if she'd only dealt with it at that stage. Because now it was too late, it had swelled and grown and been ignored, like a headache you keep telling yourself is just a headache, but doesn't go away.

She passed through the park gates. A custard-coloured cat sat in a patch of sun. The tarmac path wandered between lawns and shrubbery, meandering up towards the far gates. Grainne's house. Just out of those gates and round the corner. A cramp in her ribcage made her flinch, curl up on herself. There should be a blade to draw across her arm. Lightly, sinking in a little like an inkpen into thick paper, and the skin beading with blood and the blood curling round the curve of her arm and dripping down to her wrist and trickling through her fingers to the ground, and the pain gathering itself together so she would clap her hand down over the cut and hold it there as it stung and smarted with the salt from her palm. It had all seemed to simple at home, when she was drinking tea with her mother in the half-light of the kitchen. She knew she had to get back and sort things out. She had to, somehow, deal with it. Quite how she would do this she had not considered, but she had nonetheless felt a kind of vague confidence that she would know, when the time came. But the time had come, and she did not know.

She tugged at a cuticle with her teeth, tore off a strip of skin. The flesh stung, but did not bleed. She turned the scrap of skin around with her tongue, bit through it again. Her shoes were wearing out. She could feel the sharp grit through her soles.

A tennis ball was thrown across the balding grass, bounced. A dog ran, low and fast, caught it on the rebound. A collie. Liver and white. It hared back towards its owner, a young woman in a green summer dress. The dog bounced up at her, ball between its teeth. The woman took it gingerly, grimacing, and Claire remembered the warm softness of a dog-spittled tennis ball, the rainbow in the shower of spit as Dad whacked the ball for six, and Moss speeding off up the village street after it. The young woman threw again. They had the park to themselves, today. They had the run of the place.

Claire climbed the sloping path out of the park, through the narrow arched gateway, onto Colenso Parade.

Everything would be blown sky-high. Everything would shatter. She would have to pick up all the sharp little bits and try and piece them back together again. She would have to find a new place to live. She would have to find a new job. Gareth would sack her. Of course he would sack her. If she told Grainne, that was it. It would be public knowledge. She would be on her own.

She turned the corner.

If she told Grainne it would hurt her, that was obvious. It would hurt Grainne and it would solve nothing except for the aching muddle in Claire's mind. And it wasn't worth it. When it came down to it, she could live with the ache. It would be better, it would be more responsible, really, to live with it: confession would only pass the pain along, increase it.

She climbed the concrete steps to the front door, rummaged in her pocket for her key. She hesitated.

What day was it? Monday? Grainne would be at work. If it wasn't July. The school holidays must have started. Claire stood, hand in pocket, listening. Nothing. No TV, no radio, no music playing. Maybe she was round at Paul's. Maybe she was out shopping. Maybe she was curled up on the sofa with her *Elle Decoration* and a cup of tea. From where she stood, Claire couldn't see past the dusty slats of the venetian blinds, but she wouldn't move any closer to the window. Grainne might be in there, looking out. Claire glanced down at the tiny front garden. At her feet the silver-grey sage bush was wilting, the leaves curling up, going powdery. Unwatered. So perhaps she was away. Perhaps she had gone on holiday. Perhaps she had gone off travelling for a month or two. Or perhaps she had just forgotten to water it. She did sometimes.

It was never meant to be a permanent thing, her living at Grainne's house. It was only supposed to be until she got herself sorted out, until she got herself settled. So the obvious thing was to sort herself out. If she got a new job, if she started looking for a room, it wouldn't be long before she could move. Simple as that. No big deal, no questions asked. Just gone.

And if she bumped into Grainne in the street afterwards, they would be all hi and hugs and how are you, and Claire would apologise for not calling, and they'd talk for a while, and agree they should go out for a drink sometime, and Claire would promise to phone. But she would, somehow, never get round to it. It would slip her mind: she would lose the number, or always manage to phone while Grainne was out. And after a while, it wouldn't take too long, Grainne would stop telling herself she must get in touch, stop expecting to hear from Claire altogether, stop thinking about her entirely. No big deal. That kind of thing happened all the time. People lost touch. They drifted apart.

Claire exhaled, felt her shoulders loosen. It was the best thing to do, she was sure of it. It was the best thing for everybody. After a while, no one would really notice she was gone. It wouldn't be fun, but it would be okay. It would be better than anything else she could think of.

She reached up, slipped her key into the lock, prepared a smile. It would be okay. It would be okay. It would take a couple of weeks to get things sorted out, then she would be out of there. For good. She could handle that. Just a couple of weeks. No need for explanations, no need for arguments, no more harm done. It was for the best. Eventually, it would all work out right. She turned the key.

It didn't move.

Puzzled, she twisted it the other way. It still wouldn't budge. She pulled it out, stood looking at it. Chrome-plated, copied from Grainne's original. It couldn't be the wrong key. It was, in fact, the only key she possessed. And it was smooth, straight, undamaged.

She glanced back up at the door. Number 12 in dull brass italic numerals, blue paint, stained glass. A brass handle and a Yale lock. It was the right door. But, she realised, it was the wrong lock. The keyplate was bright, undulled by weather. Grainne had changed the lock.

She knew.

And she might, at any moment, come back from wherever she'd been. Her car might pull round the corner, slide up to the door, and she would slip out, come slinking up towards her—or she still might be sitting quietly inside, waiting, waiting for the sound of the wrong key in the lock, waiting to—

—to what?

Claire was halfway across the park, still going fast, when the thought occurred to her. Exactly what did she expect Grainne to do?

Hit her? *Kill* her?

There were girls at school who, when they got their shoes dirty or tore their skirts, would say, my mum'll kill me, but they were always back at school the next day, alive and well, with freshly shined shoes and sewn-up tears.

She slowed down, dug her nails into her arm. She had come back to sort it all out, and there she was, running away again. And running out of places to run to.

Glossy leaves reflected back the sun. Bushes heavy with blossom. A solitary magpie stalking across the grass. The park was silent, deserted. The woman and her dog had gone. Claire rubbed a hand through her hair, walked slowly on. If Grainne knew, who else knew? Desperately, Claire tried to trace the pattern of infection, to work out who might still be ignorant.

The cat was still sitting in the sun, paws tucked up, eyes squeezed shut. Claire walked out through the wrought-iron gates, past the graffiti-scribbled walls, back down Botanic Avenue. Her bag bumped against her back, dragging on her shoulder as she walked, the rhythm of its movement beginning to subdue her skitterish thoughts. Toothbrush, pyjamas, make-up, clothes. Toothbrush, pyjamas, make-up, clothes. Things. Her things. Her things in her backpack. All that she had got left, thumping against her as she walked. Toothbrush, pyjamas, make-up, clothes. She'd abandoned everything else, leaving it behind her, deposited in different places. Little pockets of possessions. Pinned to her old bedroom wall. Pushed into the corner of Alan's bedroom. Piled around the edges of Grainne's spare room. Books and clothes and just the one photograph. Mum and Dad on the doorstep, she pregnant and miniskirted, Dad with a cheroot clamped between his teeth, reaching out to grab the dog, to turn its attention to the camera. Faded to a pinky-orange now, the glass dusty and fingerprinted. On the dresser in Grainne's spare room. And now, now that probably everybody knew, there wasn't anywhere left in the city, there wasn't anywhere to go. Just the loops and tangles of streets, endless, knotted, twisting back on themselves.

They locked the park gates at night, but she could climb them. There would be darkness underneath the rhododendrons. She could crawl under the branches, lie down on the damp earth, on the dead leaves, her eyes open in the dark. Distant voices getting closer, a movement that might be the cat, a sigh that might be a breeze or might be breath. City dark was not like dark at home. City dark was inhabited.

But it was still day, and the city seemed strangely empty. She saw one car, a little red car, briskly turn the corner onto Botanic Avenue, and accelerate away. Rushing home. She realised she had seen hardly anyone since she left the Seacat terminal. Just that woman in the park with her dog, and that was it. Where were they all, the passers-by, the danderers?

Worse than the crowded city dark, this empty daylit city. Unnatural. She looked around her, unsure of what she was looking for, unsure of where she should be going.

She was past the door before she noticed that Vincent's was open. Windows gaped onto the dark and smoky interior. A handful of customers lingered in the dim room. People, at last. She found herself melting with relief. She turned on her heel and went back. She pushed in through the door. She found herself smiling. She would sit for a while. She would drink a cup of coffee. She would let the cigarette smoke and coffee fumes and voices wash over her. Human scents, human sounds. She would let herself be enveloped. Just for a while. Then, later, she would work out what to do.

There was an empty table near the counter. As she walked over towards it, Claire picked through a handful of change, counting. One pound fifty. Should be enough for a coffee. She sat down.

"Would you like to order?" The waitress's voice was careful, heavily accented: French. She didn't smile.

"Just a coffee, please," Claire said.

"A coffee."

As she watched the young woman walk away, she wondered briefly if she could ask if she knew why the streets were so empty, then, if there was any work going. The sentence formed in her head, but she abandoned it unfinished. Vincent's was too close for her to work there. It was too close to Alan's, too close to Grainne's. Grainne was in there all the time.

What if she walked in now?

The waitress put a cup of coffee down in front of her. Claire smiled uneasily, watched the waitress walk away. She turned the cup round and round on the saucer, waiting as the coffee cooled. The surface of the coffee was iridescent, glazed with oil. She gazed down at it, mesmerised.

"Well, what if I did?"

Grainne. Poised, cool, and completely imaginary. Claire could almost see her scrape back a chair and sit down. Behind her would stand a shady, inexplicit version of Paul. He would lean against the counter. Claire couldn't work out what his expression would be. She had, she realised, no idea what he would be thinking.

"Well?" she could almost hear Grainne saying. "What if I did walk in now? What would you say?"

Claire shook her head slowly.

"I don't know." She spoke quietly, under her breath.

"That's pretty fucking feeble."

"Yeah but—"

"I thought you'd come up with something more impressive than that. I thought you'd at least have *some* kind of excuse worked out. You with all your GCSEs and your A levels and your fancy Oxbridge degree and everything."

"I'm sorry."

"Sorry! Sorry? That's supposed to do the trick, is it? Jesus, Claire you're really not getting this, are you? We're not messing around here. This is serious stuff. This isn't your run-of-the-mill let down or disappointment. This is full-scale full-on betrayal we're talking here."

"I know—"

"When I took you in you were completely fucked. You really were. You had nowhere to go, nowhere to live, you had no one. And I gave you a roof over your head. A really nice roof at that. And I took care of you. I thought we were friends."

"I know."

"And what did you do? After all I did for you? You fucked my boyfriend. You fucked my boyfriend and all you can say is, I don't know, I'm sorry? That's bollocks, Claire. Bullshit. And you know it. You betrayed me. Big time."

Claire hunched over her cup.

"Did you think I'd forgive you?"

"I—"

"You didn't even think about it, did you? It didn't even occur to you, how I'd feel. You just carry on in your own sweet way, doing exactly what you want, and never once thinking how it affects other people. You just expect to get away with it. And then when you don't, when suddenly it all blows up in your face, you just run away. And you leave the rest of us to pick up the pieces. You're just completely selfish. When are you going to fucking *grow up*, Claire?"

Paul's face seemed to be getting clearer. He would be frowning slightly, nodding, agreeing with Grainne. That made sense. Of course he would.

"Yeah, well," Claire hissed silently. "It was you who changed the locks. That's not exactly adult is it?"

"What did you expect? A welcoming party? A ticker-tape parade? *Ferrero Rochers?*"

"No, but, I did pay the rent. It's not unreasonable to expect—"

"Would you listen to her! This is the next of it—"

"No, but, I'm just saying. It suited you well enough, didn't it, a great wodge of cash off me every month and don't tell the tax man. You don't mention that now, do you? But you were happy enough taking the money off me. You're no fucking saint yourself, Grainne."

"Oh, so *I'm* the bad guy now. Well thank you very much."

"That's not what I'm saying—"

"So now it's all *my* fault you fucked my boyfriend. Jesus Christ you're some woman."

"I—"

"And now you're going to tell me what a tough time you have, aren't you. With Daddy disabled, and you cutting yourself up, bleeding all over my nice clean bathroom, never had a decent shag in your life—until Paul, of course—"

Claire dug her nails into the tabletop.

"Just shut up. Just shut your mouth. I don't have to take this from you. You know nothing about me. You have no fucking idea what it's like being me."

"I know plenty."

"I never told you about Dad. I never told you about the cutting. I didn't tell you anything. You never gave me the chance."

Grainne would shrug, perhaps.

"But you wanted me to know, didn't you. You wanted *everyone* to know. You still do. You know you do. Anyway, doesn't matter. Doesn't make any difference. You'll just carry on in your own sweet way and don't mind me. Or Jen. Or your mum or dad."

"Why don't you give me a hard time about Alan while you're at it?"

"Alan? No. No point. He's better off without you. He's happier without you."

"And what about Paul? Why'd you think he wanted to be with me?"

"*Be* with you?" Claire could almost hear the laughter. "*Be* with you? He didn't want to *be* with you, love, he just wanted to fuck you."

Claire flinched, squeezed her cup tight between her palms.

"How did you find out, anyway?" she wondered. "Who told you?"

"Who do you think?" Fading, translucent, she tilted her head back. "He did. At least he had the balls to."

Claire brought a hand to her face, wiped her tired skin.

"You're on your own now, honey."

Claire glanced up, around. Dark figures hunched over tables. Cigarette smoke, coffee scent, voices. No one seemed to be looking at her. If she had spoken out loud, they had chosen to ignore it. She was on her own. She picked up her coffee cup and drained it. She counted out her coins.

ELEVEN

꤮

Because it was early, the light seemed strange in Conroys. It filtered in at odd angles, bathed the scuffed boards golden, made the inverted bottles on the optics glitter. Claire walked through dust-constellations, setting her feet softly on the percussive floor. Nonetheless, her footsteps resounded, loud and confident, unsettling her. The place looked empty, but she knew it couldn't be. There would be staff and customers, somewhere. Leaning over the payphone, lifting a glass of Guinness, wiping a tabletop. Someone would, inevitably, hear her coming and think she knew what she was doing there.

One hand flat on the counter, steadying, anchoring him as he crouched. That was all she could see, just the one hand. He must be counting out bottles underneath the counter. Shunting last night's remainder to one side, lifting new bottles from a plastic crate, stacking them up on the shelf. And all the bottles whitened, frosted with reuse. Close now, she watched the knuckles pale and the tendons roll and shift as the hand pressed down, heaving the body upright, joints creaking in relief, cheeks flushed, face to face.

"Gareth."

He still held a bottle of Club Lemon in his hand.

"Well bugger me." He put the bottle down on the counter. "You're back."

Claire tugged on her bagstrap, grimaced.

"Yeah."

And unexpectedly, incredibly, Gareth opened his mouth, and laughed.

"Just after you left. That same night. We were back at my place. We were just having a drink. You haven't been back to ours for a drink yet have you?"

"No—sorry—"

The sunlight teased out tobacco and spilt-beer smells from the upholstery. Gareth set out brightly coloured cups and saucers, a milk jug and a sugar bowl. He put a cafetiere down in the centre of the table. He drew out a chair and sat down.

"You must come sometime. Anyway, that night they'd been on the beer since seven, eight o'clock. By the time we got back to our house they were pissed, the three of them. Completely fucking blocked. And not in a nice way, not happy-drunk. Pissed-off pissed: you could tell something had gone wrong. Paul wasn't saying much, he was doing his strong but silent act, and Grainne had a scowl on her like you wouldn't believe—"

"What about Alan?"

"Man on a mission, he really was. There was no stopping him. But he wasn't having a good time, not as far as I could see. Tell you the truth, I don't know why he'd come out with them. I don't think he really likes them. Him and Paul always rub each other up the wrong way."

Gareth leaned over, pressing down on the cafetiere's plunger. They watched the coffee well and bubble through the metal mesh.

"Anything in particular, d'you think?"

"No, I don't think so. Not at that stage, anyway." Gareth lifted the coffee pot, filled Claire's cup, then his own. He grinned. "Anyway. So. We were back at our place and they were hammering into the beers. I'd just sat down, first time I'd got off my feet all night. I'd just opened my first beer, and was ready to neck it, playing catch-up, you know, and let's face it I had a fair fucking way to go. But I hadn't even had one mouthful when I went and opened my big gob." He picked out two sugarlumps from the bowl, dropped them into his cup, stirred. "You see, the pub had been bunged all night. I'd been so busy I hadn't had the chance to talk to anyone, not since I'd seen you, not privately. And it dawned on me as I was sitting there with my beer in my hand and my big fat feet up on the table, that the last I'd seen of you, you were sitting in the dark in our store cupboard with your head between your knees. And it bothered me. Correct me if I'm wrong, but it looked like a sign that something was up."

Claire drew her lips in against her teeth, nodded. Gareth grinned more widely, shook his head.

"So I opened my mouth and put my foot straight in it. I asked did anyone know what was up with you. I'd barely got the words out of my mouth when Grainne butted in. Really sharp, like, and asked why I was asking. Which should have been a clue, but thicko here didn't notice. You know yourself she can be a bit harsh, and I just put it down to that. So I just fired on: I told her I'd seen you, and that you'd seemed really upset. I told her you said that you were going home, back to England." Gareth picked up his coffee cup, paused with it halfway to his mouth.

"You could almost watch the penny drop."

He took a mouthful, rested a finger momentarily along the line of his lips, then lifted it away, coffee-damp.

"She looked round at Paul. Slow-motion, it seemed like. She looked round and stared at him. He was sitting back, leaning right back in the sofa. He had his eyes half shut. Playing it cool, playing it hyper-cool. He couldn't pull it off though." Gareth smirked. "He'd taken a beamer."

Claire smiled uncertainly.

"Beamer?"

"He'd gone bright red: he was blushing."

"Fuck."

"Fuck is right. They sat there for what seemed like ages, saying nothing. Her staring at him, him looking at nothing, with this strange little half-smile on his face. Alan's eyes were swivelling round like Eagle-Eye Action Man's, looking at the both of them. You'd think there was someone flicking a lever on the back of his head. Like I said, that went on for ages. Then—" Gareth spluttered, "all of a sudden, Paul jumped up, and ran out."

"He didn't—"

"He most certainly did."

Claire brought her hand to her mouth. She shouldn't smile.

"Grainne and Alan were just left there, sitting there.

Grainne staring out after Paul, Alan's eyes still flicking like mad from her to the empty place where Paul had been. Then, ever so calm, too calm really, Grainne got up, and went out. I don't know if she went looking for him or what. Maybe she just went home."

"And Alan?"

"Alan?"

"Was he alright? Was he upset?"

Gareth snorted.

"You wouldn't believe how long it took him to work it out. Though I can't say I helped much. Didn't think it was fair to give him any more clues. I really didn't think it was any of his business. *He* did, though. Thought it was his own personal tragedy. Should've seen him, fucking Hamlet and Othello all rolled into one. Oh my prophetic soul, et cetera. Seemed to think the pair of you had been planning it since word go, that yous'd got together just to piss him off. He drank all the drink in the house, even finished my bottle of Laphroiag. I was gutted, I can tell you; I'd've liked a wee whiskey after all that excitement." Gareth glanced over at the bar, then back at Claire, smiled. "How's about we have one now?"

"Have you seen him since, though—is he okay?"

"Don't you worry about Alan. Alan'll take care of himself. In fact, that's pretty much all he's good for. You'd think with all that thinking he does he'd be all sensitive, you know, considerate, but I'm telling you, in the end it all comes back down to him. What Alan wants, what Alan thinks, what's best for Alan. He doesn't really give a shit about anyone else. I'd put it down to too much German philosophy at an impressionable age, if I didn't know that Alan's always been a selfish wee cunt. We could never understand why you went out with him."

Claire hesitated, caught. She turned her cup round on its saucer. They had been thinking about her, talking.

"I think I made him go out with me," she said.

"Poor soul."

"He's not all bad."

"No. Of course not. At least he sorted you somewhere to stay that time."

"Sorry?"

"Sorting out that room for you. At Grainne's. Typical really. Why let someone do something their own way when you can make them do it yours. Even when he's being nice Alan still somehow manages to be a dick."

She brought the cup to her lips, sipped. The coffee was warm, soft in her mouth, and the taste reminded her faintly of acorns.

"I didn't know."

"Grainne never said?"

"No."

"Typical. Typical her and typical Alan."

"I thought you lot were all good friends."

"Aye well I don't know. Sometimes I think old friends are a bit like tattoos. When you're a kid and you know no better they seem like a great idea, and then you're stuck with them for the rest of your life. Can't get rid of them, not without surgery."

Claire fitted her cup carefully into the centre of the saucer.

"Do you know what happened afterwards?"

"With Paul and Grainne? Shit must have hit the fan. But I don't know exactly. Grainne's not been in, and you know what Paul's like."

"No," Claire said. "Not really."

"No. I know what you mean." Gareth lifted the cafetiere. "More coffee?"

Claire watched him fill her cup, watched the soft fine hairs on his wrist catch the light, turn golden.

"Paul—" she said, but couldn't finish the sentence.

"What about him?" Gareth filled his own cup. He held a lump of sugar by one corner, watched as the coffee soaked up through it. He dropped it in, picked up another cube.

"What he did."

"Yes—"

"Running away. That's what I did."

Gareth considered this a moment; they both watched the sugarlump as it browned.

"Yeah. Well. No one laughed at you."

"But it was as much my fault—"

"Maybe. But Paul knew what he was at, Paul always knows what he's at; it was good to see him lose it, just the once. And anyway, you were in bits. You were having a really hard time. Anyone could see that. It was obvious."

"And Grainne—"

"This kind of thing never happens for no reason. Paul can't have cared enough about her or he wouldn't have done it, and she's better knowing that sooner than later. Which is not to say she won't be hurt, but, if they were married—if there were kids—" Gareth paused, dropped the sugarlump and picked up his spoon. "That's a different story. So as it goes, it's better that she finds that out now, not later. When it would be a real problem." He lifted his cup. "She might not thank me for saying so, but she will get over it."

"She's changed the locks."

"Has she? Wonder was that meant for you or for Paul?"

"Or the both of us."

Gareth winced. "Och, you're not thinking—"

"No," said Claire. "I didn't mean it like that."

"Good," Gareth said. "Steer well clear there. Paul's alright, you know, for having a drink with, but I wouldn't trust him." Gareth pushed back his chair. "Come on through to the office," he said. "We're shut over the Twelfth, but we'll see what hours we can give you up till then."

Claire straightened, looked up at him. "I didn't get the sack?"

"Because you copped off with a customer? Don't be daft. I'd have no staff left. I'd have to sack myself."

"But—"

"Unless you don't want to—"

"No, no, I do, really. I need the money. It's just won't it be awkward, with Paul coming in."

"He's hardly been here. And you can brazen it out, can't you? Tough little cookie like you?"

Claire watched Gareth stand up, begin gathering the coffee things onto a tray. There were creases in his shirt, a thin scab on his upper lip where he had cut himself shaving. She felt a sudden, almost overwhelming warmth for him. He thought she was a tough little cookie. There must be something she could say.

"C'mon then," he said.

She scraped back her chair and stood up, followed him. He set the tray on the counter and they walked down the length of the room. Out of step, their footfalls syncopated through the empty building. Gareth pushed through the double doors and Claire followed, letting them fall shut behind her. She fell into step beside him, watching their feet.

"Why's the town so quiet?" she asked.

"Coming up on the Twelfth," he said. "It's always like that."

"Course," Claire said, with no real sense of what this meant. They stopped at the office door. Gareth rifled through his keys.

"If she changed the locks," he said, "you'll be needing somewhere to stay."

A glass-and-brick church on the corner. On its gable wall, a clock, ten to three, and, in bold white script, *Time is short.* The car slowed. Gareth shifted down a gear.

"Paisley's place—go check out the windows sometime. Himself at the stations of the cross, almost."

They turned the corner. A broad street, front lawns, three-storey shabby-grand redbrick semis. Gareth stopped the car.

"This is us."

He got out, slammed the door behind him. Claire shuffled her bag out of the seat well, fumbled for the doorhandle. Outside, on the pavement, Gareth pulled the door open for her and held it as she struggled out. He shut it neatly behind her.

"This is yours?" Claire asked.

"This is mine," Gareth said. He turned to go up the path, tossed his keys up in the air, caught them. "Well, I share it with Dermie, and the building society owns most of it. But it's home."

The hallway was dim and cool. Claire stood blinking. A hall table with a telephone. A silky wooden floor. Darkly carpeted stairs, soft light from the landing window silvering each tread. Gareth pushed open a panelled white door.

"Front room," he said, then stepped aside to let her peer

in. The curtains were drawn: she got an impression of quiet uncluttered space. "Dining room." She turned back into the hall, towards Gareth. "And there's a loo under the stairs. Come on up."

He set off up the stairs, two treads at a time. Claire followed.

"Bathroom—" She glanced in, and he was off again, up a brief flight towards the front of the house. "That one's my room—I'm using this one as an office at the moment but I can clear it out no bother if you'd like it. Or further up—"

He turned and set off again, thumping up the narrowing staircase. He paused on the half-landing. A skylight looked out into clear blue.

"You okay? You'll soon get used to it."

Breathless, she followed him to the top.

"The back room's probably quieter, but the front one's bigger."

He pushed the door open and they stepped inside. The room was empty. Bare boards, white walls, the whole room full of diffuse, moving light. The window looked out into the green stirring branches of a tree. Claire breathed.

"Thought you might like it. We'll bring you up a bed later on. Or a mattress. That'd be less hassle on the stairs. You'd be okay with just a mattress, wouldn't you?"

"That'd be great."

"Me and Dermie are just below, so you'll have to behave yourself."

"I will. How much—?"

"Ah, don't be worrying about that, now. We'll worry about that as and when."

"I'm not sure I can afford—"

"Och, wise up, will you. That's what I'm telling you. Nothing. No rent. Gratis. Free. On the house. See if you like it, see how we get on, see how it goes. Then we'll see about rent."

"No. Are you sure? No, really. I can't."

"Now don't try changing my mind. It won't work."

She grinned at him, let the bag slide off her shoulder, down her arm. It hit the floor with a sigh.

"Thank you."

"No bother. But I'd best be off now. If they notice they can run the place without me, I'm done for." He tossed his keys into the air. "There should be hot water if you fancy a bath. And help yourself to whatever's in the fridge. I'll see you later. It's half-seven you're due in, did we say? Can you find your way back from here?"

"I think so. Thank you."

"No bother." He turned to go.

"Gareth."

"Yep." He looked back at her, hand on the banister.

"I was going to sleep in the park."

He snorted. "Yeah, right," he said. "And you're supposed to be the clever one."

She unlocked the back door, pushed it open. A shaft of light slipped into the dark indoors. She saw a strip of algaed concrete, an overgrown, grass-tangled lawn, and beyond it a fence, and the back of another house.

As she filled the kettle at the tap, she could see her face, stretched out and liquid, in the rounded metal surface. She glanced into cupboards, found teabags, mugs, pyrex dishes, an empty biscuit barrel, tins of tomatoes, corn and beans, a jar of peanut butter and a half-finished loaf of Ormo bread, its wrapper twisted tight. She made toast, spread it thick with peanut butter. She licked her finger and picked up crumbs from the counter.

Sitting in the sunlit doorway, half indoors, half out, she tugged up her trouserlegs and sleeves to let the sun warm her skin. Claggy peanut butter stuck to the roof of her mouth; she teased it off with her tongue. Crumbs rolled down her shirt, down her chest, lodged in her bra. The hot tea seemed to go solid in her mouth. She swallowed it in lumps.

The concrete gave off a tangy, green smell, like the river. She felt her cheeks burn. She felt the grit pressing into the heels of her hands, felt the lino gently give under her weight. She felt the arch of her shoulders, the locked joints of her elbows. She flexed her toes, spread them out like a fan, watched them as they moved. She laid her feet flat on the concrete. It felt warm and damp, like river rocks, like the reservoir overflow when the water's low. She stood up and walked, feeling the soft growth of the algae, the sharp stipple underneath. She stepped off the concrete onto the grass. Her feet found the dark places between the growth. She felt the soft damp earth, the tangled grass like hair knotting round her toes, the flick and shiver of tiny life.

Claire slept that night, and did not dream. Her muscles grew heavy and soft, her mind dark and smooth as cat fur. Pressed down onto the mattress, tugged in tight towards the centre of the earth, her legs and arms flung wide, her head thrown back, as if to stop herself from sinking. A blanket lay across her body, smoothing over escarpments, hollows, scars. Her lips had fallen open. The rise and fall of her breath barely, slightly, folded and refolded the blanket's shadows.

A pint glass of water, two-thirds full, smeared with finger-prints, stood beside the mattress. Her bag slouched, crumpled on the floor. Shoes, dark and empty, worn to the shape of her naked, vulnerable feet, lay askew, laces trailing, underneath the window. The windowpane refracted sodium-orange light. Pocked and wrinkled, soft; like water. And outside the window, in the streetlamp's glow, the leaves rippled and stirred, they whispered.

Beneath, in thickly curtained darkness, Gareth and Dermot lay sleeping, Dermot's hand resting lightly on Gareth's hip. A thick duvet covered them, making them a little too hot, making them dream. Discarded clothes, reeking of cigarette smoke, lay in two heaps on the bare wooden floor.

In the bathroom, a droplet gathered on the faucet, fell. Shadows sliced, dipped down the smooth stairs. The living room was full of orange glow and silence. Green lights flickered on the video recorder, indicating the decibels of unheard speech and music. In the kitchen, the fridge clicked into gear, it hummed.

Lined up along the street, underneath the moving, rustling trees, were beetle-sheened cars, cool to the touch. Somebody's black-and-white cat was folded into an under-car shadow. A car skimmed past the end of the street, a blur. Going fast to catch the early-morning ferry. The driver, tired and head-achy, considered for a moment the way the sky was growing pale towards the east, the way the profile of the hills was cut against the sky, and remembered the flatness of the landlocked town that he was heading for, its emptiness. His headlights slid across the park, raked through the arched cave of a rhododendron's branches, where a young man shivered in his sleep, curled himself up tighter, smaller, amongst the leathery fallen leaves. He muttered words from his dream. A truck passed, a snarling dog in the dark inside his mind, a bread van, the back stacked with fluffy, plastic-wrapped loaves, driven by Rosie, whose back was killing her, and whose period would, she hoped, be starting soon. Indicator ticking quietly, the van filtered onto the motorway, slipped in to join the increasing, thickening flow of traffic, heading south.

Above, a seagull drifted across the paling sky. The streetlamps dimmed, blinked out.

TWELVE

The traffic lights changed. Gareth released the handbrake, revved high against the pull of the hill. He swung the car right, across two lanes, into a wide suburban street.

"When I first got the car, three–four years ago, I brought Dermie up here," he said.

They passed pebble-dashed semis, parked cars, garden walls. The car slowed, climbing, engine labouring.

"Thing was, I hadn't driven in years."

He changed down a gear. They passed the last of the houses. The road narrowed, growing steeper. Claire watched the blur of thick hawthorn, saw foxgloves and a clump of dog daisies. Long grass and gauzy cow-parsley brushed the side of the car.

"But I'd promised Dermie I'd take him up to the Rocky Road. So we drove up here and the car was getting slower and slower and slower as the hill got steeper. And instead of changing down like any sensible person would, I kept on changing up. The engine was revving to high heaven and the car was slowing down and all I could do was shout the car's broken, the car's broken, like a total eejit. Had my foot to the floor and still it kept slowing down until we got to about *here,*" he said, changing down again, "when we started rolling backwards."

Claire turned, smiled at his profile.

"What happened?"

"I remembered the handbrake. Thanks be to God."

The road levelled out ahead of them. They passed a fieldgate. Claire glimpsed a stretch of grass, a stationary head-bent cow.

"Can't believe you've never been up here, you know."

"Bit much on the bike."

They turned right onto a two-lane road, passed a solitary villa, then turned right again, indicator ticking. And by association, as the indicator ticked, Claire found herself imagining a line dot dot dotting itself out across a map, her route from here to there and back again. And intersecting this, and paralleling it, and diverging, other lines. Her mother's. The people in those fading photographs. Alan, Gareth, Margaret. Each line intricately connected. It was not, it could never be, fixed and finished.

"Sometimes I forget you're not from here," Gareth said.

She hugged her legs up towards her, tucked her feet onto the seat and felt the sun on her bare shins.

"Just a little bit further," he said, "then you'll see."

They rumbled over rippled, pale concrete, towards empty sky.

"There."

Gareth stopped the car, hitched up the handbrake. They had come to a halt on the cusp of the hill, high above the city. Nothing but air between them and the far hills. Below, buildings encrusted the valley like salt in a drying rockpool. The lough was brilliant blue, the sky was clear. Claire watched a seagull dip, lift, turn on an updraft.

"What a great place," Claire said, "to build a city."

They sat in silence, looking.

"What's that?" Gareth said.

"What?" Claire watched the tiny cars moving through the city streets. Pushing and jostling like corpuscles.

"That."

She glanced back at him, face soft with a smile. He was staring down at her exposed leg, his face compressed.

"What have you done," he said.

Her chest cramped. She glanced at her naked ankle, the still obvious marks of her cutting. She reached down to tug at the hem of her trousers.

"Shit," she said.

He took her hand, held it.

"What have you done to yourself?"

She straightened her legs quickly, lowering her feet down into the seat well.

"It's nothing," she said, gently tugging Gareth's hand, smiling uneasily, but he would not let go.

"Jesus Christ, Claire," he said.

The tone of his voice was unsettling. Claire drew her lips in against her teeth, shrugged slightly, couldn't think what to say.

"Jesus, Claire, what made you go and do that?"

She felt a slow blush creep across her face.

"I'm sorry."

"Why sorry? It's not a question of sorry," he said. He sounded angry, but when he leant over and took hold of her lower leg, brought her foot back up to rest on the seat, he was gentle. She watched as he drew up her trouserleg, ran his fingertips cautiously over the scars.

"Why on under God would you go and do a thing like that?" he said. He looked up at her, continued looking steadily at her face. He was waiting for an answer. She still couldn't think what to say.

"I—" Claire hesitated. "I haven't done it for a while now."

Cautiously, she met his eyes. They were, she noticed, grey. He shook his head slowly.

"Why would you go and be so completely cruel to yourself?"

He waited a moment, but she couldn't answer. "You wouldn't even for a moment consider being anything like that cruel to someone else . . . In fact, don't think I've even ever heard a harsh word out of you."

"I'm full of harsh words," she said.

"I don't believe you."

"You should hear me when I get going."

He shook his head again.

"You mustn't do that again. You have to promise me you won't."

She couldn't answer.

"If you ever feel like you have to, just you come and be nasty to me instead."

He tapped her shin gently, almost playfully. "No knives now, no razors, you understand. I'm a big wuss really, under this tough exterior . . ." She found herself beginning to smile.

His tone shifted, becoming grave again. "But any harsh words, you come to me. I don't want to find you've been up to this again."

"Okay," she said, slowly.

"Just remember, for harsh words, I'm your man. Just you get them off your chest."

She looked down at his hand, and at the contours of her skin and bone and muscle. The most recent cuts were already old; they were pink, puckered, healing. And the earlier ones, fading, had become a fine tracery of lines and loops and spirals, had begun to have the intricate allusiveness of a map. They were, she realised, beginning to be beautiful.

Claire eased the lever forward, angled the glass under the flow. She watched the liquid stream into the glass. Straighten gradually. Fill only two-thirds full. Concentrating, eyes half shut, she straightened the pint glass, set it down on the drip tray. She turned to Gareth, raised her eyebrows. He half nodded, half smiled, encouraging.

"That'll be two pounds please," she said.

Tommy counted out the coins from a dry, creased palm. He placed them in her hand. His fingernails were ridged and hard and yellow. She turned to the till, slowly, listening to the list in her head. Guinness, total, cash. Guinness total cash. Press the keys in that order and the till'll do the rest. And receipt. Hand over the receipt. However drunk they are, they can't argue with a receipt. Not that Tommy was drunk. It was only his second pint. She scanned the touch-pad, pressed the keys in turn. The cash drawer sprang open: Claire jumped. She glanced round at Gareth. He was creasing up, grinning.

"I'll never get used to it," she said.

"You're doing grand. You've only just started."

Claire turned back to the bar, lifted the glass, pulled on the lever again. She watched the liquid swirl and boil. It looked like floodwater. Peaty floodwater straight off the moors. She placed the full glass down in front of Tommy. Carefully, dead-centre of the barmat. They watched his pint settle. The foam gathered, rose, did not overflow. She smiled. He reached out a papery hand, lifted the glass. He held it to his lips, drank.

"Not bad," he said. He sucked the foam from his upper lip. "Not a bad pint."

She grinned.

"Thanks."

"You're doing grand."

"Thanks."

"You've been away," he said.

"That's right."

"But you're back now." His eyes were watery, blue. The pink bits at the corners looked sore.

"Yes."

"And everything's all right?"

"Yes," she said. "Yes, I think so."

"Good." He settled back on his barstool, settled down to his pint.

The door opened. She glanced up. Paul walked in. He wouldn't have seen her yet. That change from daylight to bar-light blinded everyone for a moment. She watched him walk towards her, pressed her palms down on the counter, hoisted herself onto her toes. Smiled.

He saw her. She saw the moment that he saw her. She saw

him register her, hesitate, then decide to carry on. Just the slightest flicker in his stride. She watched him come towards her, scanning the bar, head turning, looking everywhere but at her, as if he was expecting to see someone he knew, even though it was perfectly obvious that the place was dead. Making out he hadn't seen her, that as far as he was concerned, she wasn't even there. He reached inside his jacket and pulled out his cigarettes. He came to a halt at the counter, flicked the packet open.

"Hi," she said.

He tucked a cigarette between his lips, glanced up at her.

"Oh hi," he said. "I didn't see you there."

He pulled a matchbox from a trouser pocket, shook it, pushed it open.

"You back then?" he said.

He watched himself pick out a matchstick, pinching it between his flat thumbnail and his index finger.

"Yes," she said.

He struck the match, lit his cigarette.

"Right."

He dropped the match into a clean ashtray.

"You on the bar now?" he said.

"Yes."

He nodded slowly, slid a hand into his trouser pocket.

"I'll have a pint of Stella then," he said.

She reached down a glass, flicked the tap. She watched the beer flow into the glass, watched him without looking up. He stared out across the bar, towards the wrought-iron rails and the stone-clad wall.

"Two-fifty," she said, placing the drink down in front of him.

He handed over the money, picked up his glass, and walked away.

Tommy's pint was two-thirds gone. His glass was ringed with stout-suds. Claire shifted her weight onto the sides of her feet, leant back against the counter, easing her insteps. Paul sat at the corner of the bar. Dermot had arrived in, sat down, was talking to him. Claire, listening to the looping, dandering tracks of Dermot's speech, wondered suddenly if he fancied Paul. And if he did, did Paul know, and did Gareth suspect. Dermot eagerly waved his cigarette in circles, talking. Paul nodded slightly, looking off across the room. He didn't seem to be listening at all. Gareth rattled the change in his pockets. She glanced round at him, grimaced. Between them, the till sat silent, almost empty.

"Quiet night," she said.

"Dead," he said. "Shouldn't have bothered. The whole fucking town's deserted."

"It'll pick up."

"Not till August. Might as well shut up shop now."

"What d'you think's going to happen?"

"What do you mean?"

"Here. D'you think it's going to be okay?"

"Jesus. Now you're asking."

"It's just I don't know anything at all about this stuff."

"Who does."

"What do you think, though?"

"It'll be okay. It has to be."

"Right."

"But don't you quote me on that."

"Right."

"And having said that, I'm not sticking round for the fun and games. We're off to Lanzarote for the duration. Got one of those last-minute deals."

"That's nice."

"What about yourself? You going to head off somewhere?"

"I think," she said, "I'll stay here. I think I might do some drawing."

THIRTEEN

"I didn't think you'd come."

"No."

"You're here for your stuff."

"Yes."

"You'd better come in."

Claire could still hear her moving around downstairs. Doors opening, footsteps, floorboards creaking, the oiled tick of Claire's bike. Grainne was wheeling it out through the house. Claire heard it bump down the front steps, a moment's pause as it was leant against the wall. Then the gritty sound of Grainne's feet on the steps, then the scrape of the latch as she came back in and shut the door behind her.

Then silence. Grainne standing still, leaning back against

the closed door, breathing. Upstairs, Claire pushed the drawer shut, pulled open the one beneath it. She began lifting out her T-shirts.

A creak. Footsteps muffled by the carpet, then loud on kitchen lino, and the floorboards still protesting. She must be pacing out the length of the house. Hallway, dining room, kitchen; kitchen, dining room, hallway, living room. Stopping dead at the window and staring straight out across the street. Gnawing at a thumbnail. Digging her nails deep into her forearms, bringing up the skin with little red crescent moons.

Claire picked the photograph up off the top of the chest of drawers. She wiped the dust off with a sleeve. The footsteps started up again: across the living room, down the hall, through the dining room, back into the kitchen. Hands on the worktop, looking out across the narrow yard at the brick wall opposite. The wall was painted white. Grainne had bought pots and plants and a trellis. Tried to grow things. Would the clematis be in flower, or was it too shady back there? Claire dropped the picture into her bag, drew the drawstring tight. She hefted the bag up onto her back. Heavier than it had been for a long time. She glanced round the room.

The bed was rumpled, untouched since she'd heaved herself out of it last. Whenever that was. Years ago, or days. Hairs still clung to the pillow, the duvet was still moulded to the shape of her leaving. She couldn't abandon it, leave it for Grainne to deal with. She dropped her bag down onto the floor, crossed over to the bed. She stripped away the sheet, pulled off the pillowcases, peeled the duvet from its cover. She carried the heap of linen to the bathroom, stuffed it into the laundry basket. She folded the duvet on the end of the bed, piled the pillows up on top. She heaved up the window-sash, letting air and sunlight in, and looked around the room again. The circles in the dust were where her things had stood. The smear of foundation on the chest of drawers carried her fingerprint. Her hair was tangled into the carpet. The whole place must smell of her. She heaved the window higher, picked up her bag. She closed the door behind her.

The stairs were dirty again. Dust and fluff and grit had already crescented the corner of each tread. Green blue red light filtered through the stained-glass door, stretched out along the hall carpet like spilt inks. She reached out a hand towards the bright new latch, turned it, pulled the door open.

"Claire—"

Her fingers were already hooked around the lip of the door. Her bagstrap was dragging at her shoulder. A pool of green light bathed her eyes. She turned. The backpack brushed against the wall, made her stumble forward slightly. She saw Grainne standing in the dining-room doorway. She looked bent, thin, slightly crumpled.

"Grainne—I'm sorry—" Claire heard her voice crack.

"I just want to know. Are you two—"

"I can't tell you how sorry I am—"

"I just want to know—"

"I'm really sorry. I've—"

"Are you two together?"

"What?"

"Are you going out with him?"

"No."

Grainne exhaled, leaned against the doorjamb, her head falling forward a little. As if her strings had been cut, Claire thought. Claire took half a step towards her, stopped. Grainne lifted her head, but didn't look at Claire. She stared at the wall in front of her, seemed to be studying a join in the paper.

"Have you seen him?" she asked.

"Who?"

"Who do you think?"

Claire hesitated.

"Yes," she said.

Grainne seemed to absorb this slowly, thinking.

"Will you be seeing him again?" she said.

"He's been in. At Conroys. He's in most nights now. I'm still working at Conroys."

Grainne nodded, swallowed.

"I'm really sorry," Claire said. "I'm really sorry."

Grainne nodded again, slowly. She turned to look directly at Claire.

"Don't come back here again," she said.

Claire caught her breath.

"Right."

Grainne looked at her, blinked. She turned and walked back into the dining room. Claire reached out to touch the sunlit wall with a fingertip. The useless phrase "I'm sorry" came back up to her lips again, but she didn't speak. Her hand fell back to her side. *I'm sorry.* Slowly, she turned, walked back through the translucent colours, through the open door.

The pieces shifted, grated, would not slide into place. Like some massive 3-D jigsaw, like a Star Trek board-game going on inside his head. And he just couldn't get the pieces into a new pattern. He couldn't get so much as a toothpick into their surfaces. He understood the argument. Of course he understood it. He just couldn't make it different. He couldn't make it his.

He hadn't touched a key for ten minutes. After three minutes his screensaver had blinked into life. Multi-coloured Spirograph and Etch-a-Sketch lines spiralled and squared and formed solids and suddenly folded away on themselves into dark. He had chosen the screensaver himself when he bought the computer. It was, he had come to realise, the most infuriating screensaver he had ever come across.

He cupped a hand round his neck, leaned his head over, easing out the muscles. Stiff and sore and tired and bored and ever so slightly panicky. A bad day, he told himself. Just a bad day. Nothing to worry about. Everyone had bad days. He had been working too hard, he had lost focus: what he needed was a break. A breath of fresh air, a leaf through *Camera-Europe* in Easons, a packet of Mintola to eat on the way home and he would be fine. He would, in fact, be refreshed and revitalised. Ready to tackle the problem, to write the article, to get his argument straight. And he had to get it straight. It had to be good. It had, in fact, to be perfect. Because people were so unkind. There was no generosity in academia. If anyone found the slightest hole in his argument, they would, he knew, tear it to shreds, just to get another article out of it in the process. The principle was ruthless, Alan had realised; it was Darwinian. The academic journals arranged the regular cull of the weak, and they hosted the feast that followed. It was kill or be killed. And you couldn't hide in the long grass: you had to get out there and show yourself. Even if you knew you were a bit feeble; even if you were, like Alan, having a bad day. If you didn't publish, you lost your job. This was, as far as Alan was concerned, a no-win situation. He was beginning to feel there was a case to be made for conservation, because everyone, sooner or later, had bad days.

He stood up from the computer, stretched. One of his vertebrae clicked. He was getting old. Arthritic. Or was it rheumatic. Definitely one or the other. These things crept up on you, joint by joint, and before you knew it you were in a terrible way. His knuckles would swell up, his knees would creak, his hipbones would grind in their sockets. This was what he had to look forward to. It was, he realised, downhill from here. Aching bones and excruciating academic articles and everyone already busy whenever he suggested going for a drink. He hitched up his trousers, cracked his knuckles, and the doorbell rang.

Which wasn't usual. Not at half-past three on a Friday afternoon. At half-past three on a Friday afternoon the doorbell was uniformly silent. In fact, during the vacation, he could spend the entirety of Friday afternoon lying on the sofa with a volume of *The American Journal of Philosophical Studies* splayed open on his chest, meditating on the articles he had just read, safe in the knowledge that he would not be disturbed by the doorbell. Even during term time he could be pretty sure he would not be interrupted. He would be halfway through first-year Ethics, a faint whiff of alcohol coming off the students, their heads heavy, their eyelids drooping. Locked into his snug little office, windows pulled tight against draughts, he could be quite confident that—short of the genuine urgency of a fire drill—there would be no sudden noises to shatter his concentration.

There it went again. Harsh, confident, demanding. And incredibly annoying. What on earth could they want at half-past three on a Friday afternoon? He hadn't rung for pizza. He looked round the room. The slithering heaps of *TV Times,* the unwashed cups caked with cup-a-soup and the smeared plates pushed halfway under the sofa gave nothing away. He rubbed his hands down over his jumper, brushing at biscuit-crumbs, at the streels of coffee and yoghurt on his grey cableknit.

"Coming—" he muttered to himself.

His socks had got twisted round. The place where his heel was meant to go was now on top. It was saggy, like a drained blister. And the toe of the other sock hung loose: flipper-like, it flapped as he walked. But he wasn't, he thought, going to stop and pull his socks up. Whoever it was, calling round at half-past three on a Friday afternoon, they could take him as they found him.

"Coming," he said again, and turned the doorlatch.

It was so bright outside. The trees were so green and the sky was so blue that they stung his eyes. And warm. Much warmer than the flat. He blinked, dragged his glasses off his nose, pulled a corner of his T-shirt out from underneath his jumper and wiped the lenses. The air smelt clean and dry. He pushed his specs back up onto the bridge of his nose. He blinked.

Claire. She'd cut her hair again, or grown it, or lost weight or done something to herself, he wasn't sure what. He didn't know what to say.

She laughed; a startling, unfamiliar sound, almost as bad as the doorbell, and Alan, quite understandably, jumped.

"How are you, Alan?" she said, and smiled.

Why was she here, and smiling at him, when last thing was she'd hated him and he'd hurt her. He winced. The memory of blood and goosepimples and her floundering hopelessly in the bath came back to him, and tacked onto it the unex-

pected image of a spindly, longlegged crab he'd seen in the
Ulster Museum when he was little, that couldn't move without water to hold it up. Why was she here? Was she going
to insist on *them* again, ask him "what about me" again, slip
past him into the flat and then be there, just *be* there, all the
time? When he went to bed at night, when he got up in the
morning. While he fried his eggs in lard, while he cut his toe-
nails in the living room. The thought made him shiver with
guilt. He reached out across the doorway, placed his hand flat
against the doorjamb, arm barring the way. She wouldn't get
past him easily. He would put up a fight this time.

"I just called round," she was saying, "to collect my stuff."

"Oh." Alan straightened. "Is that all?"

She smiled at him. Broadly, sunnily. What was it? Was
that a new top? Had she got a tan? Had she grown? She was
too old to grow, of course. How old was she? He couldn't
remember. As he looked down at her, Alan realised he should
be feeling something else. Different emotions jostled inside
him uncomfortably. A sense of satisfaction glowing underneath the unmistakable burn of indignation and the creeping
nauseous consciousness of loss. He was left feeling slightly
sweaty. He had been right about her: that should make him
happy. She had slept with Paul: that was the unpleasant cor-
ollary of being right. He realised he might rather have been
wrong. He found that uniquely upsetting.

"Yes," she was saying, almost laughing again, and he found
himself lowering his arm. She stepped past him, into the hall.

She laughed because she was nervous. She could hear it in
her laugh. It sounded thin, tinny, like a bad recording. And

Alan must be able to hear it too. And if he had noticed, was that better than if he thought that she was laughing at him? It kind of depended on how he felt already. Whether he was angry and wanted to be more angry, or whether he was hurt and didn't want to be hurt any more. She felt her face freeze over as she looked up at him. Her grimace was beginning to make her cheeks ache. He wasn't just hurt or angry: he was right. That night, when she had sat and rolled till receipts up like cigarettes, had twisted her hair into knots, had turned the rings round and round on her fingers, she had wanted to lean across the table and say to Paul, *this is not me.* And that, in itself, was bad enough.

"Oh," Alan said. "Is that all?"

"Yes," and she didn't know why she almost laughed again.

His arm sank to his side and she slipped past him, into the communal hallway. Dark, musty and familiar. She stepped over the scattering of flyers and junkmail, almost shivered. Quick as possible, she told herself. Grab the bags and go. Don't talk. Don't get tangled up in anything. Get back out into the sunshine. March up to Gareth's and don't look round. She put a hand against the door to the flat, pushed through.

That slight sour smell of old onions. She remembered the weight of Alan's body, his damp skin. She mustn't wince. He mustn't see her wince.

She came to a halt in the middle of the bedroom, trying not to see the crumpled bedlinen, the soiled heaps of clothing. She couldn't see her bags. They weren't there. He'd dumped them in the skip. His breath frosting the early spring air. Rubbing his hands together as he walked back towards the flat. Job well done.

"They're in the wardrobe," Alan said. He was behind her;

he had followed her in. He stood between her and the wardrobe. She couldn't turn and go past him. She couldn't stay where she was. One way or another he would trip her, tangle her up. He would talk.

"Right."

She walked pointlessly over to the dresser, put a hand down on the surface, stood there.

"I'm surprised you came," he said.

Beside Alan's black and bitty comb was the plastic cap of his deodorant, the aerosol elsewhere. She flicked it; it spun around in a circle. Don't answer, she thought. Don't say a word. Grab the bags and run. Fuck the bags. Just go. Don't get sucked in. Don't start *discussing*.

"I mean," he said, voice heavy, slowish, thinking as he spoke. "I'd begun to think you wouldn't ever bother." He came across the room, passed her, sat down on the edge of the bed. The springs creaked. She turned her head a little to look at him. He smiled. "You've managed all this time without them," he said. "So it's a bit of a surprise that you should decide you need them now."

She stared at him a moment in silence, watching his smile falter, his lips begin to twitch and quiver. Go, she thought. It's not too late. Walk out through the door and into the sunshine and keep on going. You don't have to explain yourself.

She turned towards the wardrobe and tugged on the door. Her bags were on the floor, underneath fallen ties, winter boots, and greying trainers. She grabbed the straps, heaved them out in a muddle of laces, belts and ties. She turned to go. Alan was still perched on the unmade bed, still smiling, and the smile was still unsteady, flickering. He blinked.

"I think at least you owe me an explanation," he began. His voice sounded unnaturally deep and dusty.

Claire hesitated, looking at him. His lips were, she realised, actually beginning to tremble, his eyes were wet.

"I think it's probably best if we just leave it."

He stood up. "This isn't like you," he said.

She hefted one bag onto her shoulder, gripped the straps of the other. She watched his fingers flutter slowly at his sides, like butterflies, watched his eyelids bat gently till they became still. She shifted the weight in her hand but didn't put the bag down.

He had made sure there was somewhere for her when she'd left. Made sure she wasn't completely lost. And she remembered also, *I think I made him go out with me* and Gareth's *Poor soul,* and the cold, outside emptiness of Oxford, and the fog, and how she'd stumbled upon him, and clung to him. It wasn't, she knew, his fault. Certainly no more than it was hers.

"Yes," she said, and blushing, she tried to find something that might do, might move some way towards him.

"How are you?" she said eventually. "How's work?"

Which was, Alan thought, a final kick in the head. How the fuck did she think work was? How could it be? With already too many students to teach, and hassle from faculty that there weren't enough students applying, with the tidal floods of marking, the endless admin, and the increasing, ear-popping pressure to publish. And the conferences. He shivered, pressed his hands against his thighs. The conferences. Why did he always let himself down in a crisis? When that wee git from Trinity had suggested that Alan's paper said nothing that had not been said twenty years ago and better, Alan should have—he should've told him—he should've told him to— Alan still wasn't quite sure what he should have said, but it

definitely wasn't "Where?" because that had just meant the
wee git from Trinity could reel off a list of sources and preen
himself and look smug.

"Fine," he squinted at her. "What about you?"

"Few days off," she said, still weighted with her bags.
"Getting myself sorted out. I got promoted."

Ah. Alan almost said it out loud. So that was it. She'd
come round here to brag. To show off about her crappy little
promotion in her crappy little job.

"What to?" he said, his smile reinstating itself. For once
he wasn't lost for a witticism. "Bouncer?"

She smiled.

"Barperson. Pulled my first pint of Guinness the other day.
Perfect, it was."

"Whoopee doo," Alan said, and felt unexpectedly foolish.
He blushed, looked down at her feet. Her shoes looked worn
and old.

"I'm thinking about going back to college," she said
brightly. "Art College, this time."

He found himself bristling, but wasn't sure why.

"You can't draw. You always said you were crap."

She shrugged. "I know." She shifted the bagstrap, settling
it more comfortably on her shoulder. "Listen," she said. "I just
wanted to say thank you."

Alan looked up, opened his mouth, but couldn't work out
what to say.

"No worries," he said.

"I only just found out," she said.

"Ah."

"Grainne never told me."

"Oh."

"That's why I never said before. I would've." She looked, he realised, a little uncomfortable. She looked slightly tearful. Grateful, even. Actually grateful. He felt himself expand. It was familiar, he could remember it from somewhere, this sense of warmth now spreading out across his chest. It was a long time since he'd felt like that.

"Right," he said, and rolled back on his heels, enjoying the sensation diffusing through his body. "Well. Don't mention it." He stuffed his hands into his pockets, smiled proudly. "Think nothing of it." Whatever it was.

It was only after she had left, and he had returned to his computer, and shuffled the mouse around to get rid of the screensaver, and reread his final paragraph, that it occurred to him he should have offered to help her with her bags.

Through the open sash of her window, Claire could hear the music of the pipe bands. They had been marching past the end of the street for half an hour now, one after the other, but she hadn't recognised a single tune. Until this one. Played by boys in blue braided uniforms and peaked caps. It seemed to want to be the theme from *Some Mothers Do 'Ave 'Em,* but it couldn't be, surely. The tune had, in any case, brought to mind a memory of childhood evenings, of soft cotton pyjamas and the smell of soap, and the drowsy warmth of her father's encircling arm, the awareness of him there, watching TV over her head.

The house still smelt faintly of smoke and alcohol. Two days ago now, after shutting up Conroys for the Twelfth, they had come back there, the whole staff. Cracked into the beer, passed round a couple of spliffs. Later on, slumped into the sofa beside her, whiskey glass in one hand, cigarette in the other, feet on the coffee table, Gareth had asked blurredly:

"You going to be okay all on your own here?"

Claire, caught with a mouthful of beer, had not been able to answer.

"I don't just mean the marching, now, you know."

She swallowed.

"I'll be fine."

He had looked at her a moment longer, then nodded.

"That's all I wanted to hear."

Blinking, he had dragged on his cigarette, blown the smoke away, smiled. "If you get bored while we're away, you know, feel free to get on with landscaping the garden." He grinned at her. "I think there's a trowel out there somewhere, rusting away on the back lawn."

The next day, he and Dermot had driven off to the airport together, looking pale and sickly, Gareth's hands shaking slightly on the steering wheel.

Claire shifted, felt the sun warm on the back of her neck. They would be on the beach. Baking under the dark sky. Baring their pale bellies to the sun. Blistering slightly, pinking; rubbing in lotion and wincing. Or, shirts flapping open, they would be wandering along the promenade, glancing into souvenir shops, on the unacknowledged sniff for English-language newspapers. Silently eyeing the turned-down TV in the corner of a cool dim bar, sipping cold beer as they waited for the sight of dark familiar streets, fire, and the metal hulk of armoured vehicles. Along with everyone else. The whole vast migratory crowd. Crowding around hotel lounge TVs, passing round a copy of yesterday's useless *Mail,* dismissing gossip but passing it on anyway. And in Malone mansions and riverside apartments and damp flats and back-to-backs the stayers-on held their breath and waited. Because no one, really, knew what was going to happen. No more than she did.

Claire shifted again. The cushion wasn't really comfortable and the windowsill was digging into her back, but from where she sat she could see all the way up the street, all the way down. The warmth of the sun was pleasant, the breeze was stirring her hair. She took a swig of coffee. It was cold. She spat it back. She glanced into the half-full cup, wondered how many times she had done that already this morning. She pushed the cup away, picked up the A3 sheet again. Unpacking, she had found it zipped up in the side pocket of her rucksack. It had been sitting there, unnoticed, since Oxford; she had been carrying it around all this time.

Folded into halves, quarters, eighths, it was frail along its creases. The image was dirty, smudged and unclear. The whole thing looked much older than she knew it could be; it seemed, despite everything, to have no connection with her at all. The perspective was terrible. No one's legs could lie like that, unbroken. The black scrawl in the centre of the belly looked more like a gunshot wound than a navel. And those were not her breasts. Not remotely. Hers weren't nearly that big. And hard or soft, no nipples could have looked like those nipples. Not without needing medical attention. And the arms were different lengths, they buckled at the elbow, tapered into spikes instead of hands. And the face, roughly ovoid, blank, featureless, didn't stare back at her: it couldn't.

She folded the picture up along its creases, weighed it in her hand, then skimmed the fattish square out across the floor. It landed near the wastepaper basket. Alan had tried. He had really tried. He had sat and scraped away at his A3 sheet with energy and determination. It was just a shame he couldn't draw. The picture was terrible, empty. It said nothing.

There was a large rectangular mirror on the landing wall, she knew, just one flight down. And Gareth had told her to help herself to anything, to make herself at home. She heaved herself up from the floor, headed for the door. Passing the wastepaper basket, she paused to pick up the folded paper, and dropped it in.

The mirror was heavy, thickly framed in wood. She took its weight carefully in her arms, lifted it from the wall. As she turned to carry it back up to her room, she found herself imagining that her father was there, climbing the stairs beside her. He would have put a hand to the burden; he would have steadied her.

"I'd do that for you," she could almost hear him say.

"That's okay," she thought. "I'll manage."

"You be careful. Don't hurt yourself."

"I won't."

She set the mirror down on the floor, angled it against the end of the mattress, then squatted back down on her cushion. She felt as though he was settling down near her, perching on the windowsill, looking at their twin reflections. She picked up her new-bought sketchpad, her old ink pen. She unscrewed the cap. She could almost feel the brush of his faded cords against her shoulder, his breathing in the concentrating silence.

"I haven't done this in ages."

He would have smiled at her.

"I know."

She smoothed out the paper with a hand.

"D'you remember?"

"Of course. I always hoped you'd get started again. You get it from your mother, you know."

"No . . ."

"You got the pen from her, didn't you?"

She lifted the pen to look at it, then squinted at the nib. She picked off a strand of fluff, staining her thumbnail black with ink.

"Yeah, but . . ."

"All that stuff. You get it all from her." His fingers moving, a ripple in the air.

"Like what?"

"Finding the right lines, putting the patterns together. Linking things. It's like her mapmaking, back at college. It is a cartography pen, after all."

Claire saw seamonsters and spouting whales blossom in the margins of her blank page, *here be dragons* calligraph itself neatly across the bottom. She paused, smiling, looking down, pen against her lips.

"And one more thing: once you've finished, send it to your mother. Show her what you're up to."

"I don't know . . ." Claire said.

"It matters to her. She needs to know that you're okay."

"I am okay."

"And Jen. Give Jen a call."

"Yes."

She looked up at her reflection. The sketchpad protruded above her knees. The mirror caught its edge, the narrow black pen in her right hand, the upturned palm and curling fingers of her left. It caught the soft pink bunch of her toes, spreading slightly on the carpet, the smooth slope of her shins and the curve of her knees. It showed the rounds of her shoulders, the dips and hollows of her collarbone and the way the light seemed to curl around her throat. There wasn't a black line limiting her, marking out the space she took up in the world, telling her where she stopped and everything else began. There couldn't be. Her body curved away beyond its horizon.

Her hand descended, rested on the paper. She began again to draw.